# *Adoring*
# ABIGAIL

OTHER BOOKS AND AUDIOBOOKS

BY CHALON LINTON:

*An Inconvenient Romance*

"Christmas Grace" in *Christmas Grace*

*A Tangled Inheritance*

"A Christmas Courting" in *A Christmas Courting*

*Escape to Everly Manor*

# Adoring ABIGAIL

a regency romance

## CHALON LINTON

Covenant Communications, Inc.

*With love to my ever-charitable aunt, Lady Marion Brown*

# ACKNOWLEDGMENTS

THIS WONDERFUL ADVENTURE IS ONLY able to continue because of the constant support of so many.

My husband and children endure my seclusion, become my live thesauruses, and cheer for my success. My life is complete because the five of you are in it. The Lord has blessed us in so many ways, and the chance to spend eternity with you is my greatest blessing.

The Covenant Communications team excels in all they do; from Kami, with her amazing patience, advice, and editing skills, to Kimberly Kay, for creating a gorgeous cover, to Amy Parker, for promoting my novel to the masses, to Paige Sorensen, for helping me dress for success.

Kodie, Melissa, Laura, and Andrea, many thanks for joining me in this amazing journey as my beta readers and, most importantly, my friends. Your honesty and love of the written word propels me to put forth my best effort in every sentence I write.

And to my readers—none of this would be possible without you. Thank you.

# Chapter One

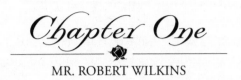

## MR. ROBERT WILKINS

*Herefordshire, England, July 1818*

MY GREAT-AUNT, LADY MARION BROWN, had visited my parents' home in Lincolnshire for a single night of which I have no recollection, for I was still in leading strings. I'd never considered that the blabbering of a babe could win a woman over, but I must have made quite an impression, because she'd bequeathed her grand, prosperous estate to my care. Mother had mentioned Lady Marion's generosity on occasion, a generosity by which I was both overwhelmed and humbled. Wills were funny like that, springing surprise, hurt, or envy upon those they affected. My great-aunt had accomplished all three.

The walls of the grand edifice seemed to grapple with the sky for dominance. Their construction of warm tan stone that matched the coat of my mare, Barkley, made the giant structure somehow welcoming. Mother had been to Cattersley once as a young child. She had told me it easily housed twenty bedchambers, an exceedingly grand ballroom, and five different receiving rooms. My assumption that her youthful imagination had aggrandized the estate was glaringly wrong.

I clicked my tongue, and Barkley moved forward. Her hooves crunched along the neat gravel path. The drive circled trimmed hedges and a marble statue of Zeus. The second I stopped my horse, the grand double doors opened. A man emerged and stood with his shoulders taut, reminding me of a soldier at attention: his suit pressed, his hair immaculate, and his gaze narrowed. He wriggled his shoulders a bit, as if trying to accommodate for his short stature, for he was decidedly . . . short, although his lack in stature did not diminish his reproving glare.

I was the rightful owner of Cattersley and a seasoned military captain, but my tongue felt thick in my mouth. I dismounted, stared up the three wide steps at the man I assumed to be the butler, and swallowed. My hand fisted around Barkley's reins, and the butler raised a single eyebrow in question.

"Good afternoon," I said. "I'm Mr. Robert Wilkins."

The man's second eyebrow met the first, and he turned his gaze down the lane, perhaps searching for an entourage.

I waited, and when nothing more was said, I tried anew. "Is there perhaps a lad who could tend to my horse?"

The man seemed to remember himself. "Yes, sir." He cleared his throat and quickly bowed. "I'm Mr. Manning. At your service, of course." When he raised his head, he turned toward the house and snapped off directions to someone I could not see.

Several awkward minutes passed. The butler looked me over, from my worn hat to my dusty boots. My stance did not falter. Serving in His Majesty's army meant I had mastered holding my bearing, despite my rapidly beating heart.

A young man came running around the far side of the house. He arrived with half of his shirttails untucked and sucked in a ragged breath. "Pardon me, sir. We was told you weren't arriving 'til next week, Captain." He attempted the same stiff shoulders as Manning, but his posture was so rigid I thought he might fall over backward.

Suppressing a smile, I handed Barkley over to his care. "And might I know your name?"

"Yes, sir. I'm Pratt, sir. Lucas Pratt. Mr. Kane is the stablemaster, but he's gone to Town on some business. Left me in charge." The lad reminded me of the eager new military recruits, although their excitement vanished after their first taste of battle.

"Very well, Lucas. This is Barkley. She's easy enough to manage; just don't attempt to brush or saddle her while she's eating." I rubbed my hand along Barkley's neck. "We've had a long ride today. Please ensure she gets an extra helping of oats."

"I'll do it, sir. Not a problem. Not at all, Captain." Lucas practically bent in half while bowing with Barkley's reins in hand.

My recent association with the title *Captain* had been inherent with my rank as an officer in His Majesty's army. I'd been content in my service to the people of England, but I was grateful Napoleon's defeat had allowed me to return home. War had left ugly scars upon both the people and the land. The title had become synonymous with battle and only reminded me of those scars.

Manning cleared his throat. Pratt glanced at the butler, bobbed his head, and led Barkley in the same direction from which he had appeared. I hadn't yet spied the stableyard and had half an inclination to follow Pratt rather than face the butler.

With a sigh, I turned back to Manning. His face was unreadable as he stepped aside, and I walked through the massive doors. I'd known the interior of Cattersley would match the grand impression of the structure. And while the furnishings and decor bore obvious signs of wealth, the air of the place retained the same welcome as the outside stone. Bountiful windows filtered natural light through the foyer; not a single candle need be lit. Various portraits and tapestries were tastefully hung on the high walls, enough to decorate the space and make one feel welcome.

"Oh, goodness. Forgive me, Mr. Wilkins." An older woman with strands of white hair peeking out beneath her mobcap came bustling from the corridor on the right. "I was not aware you would be arriving today. Mr. Manning and I would have assembled the staff, but not to worry; Monsieur Gastineau will be able to whip up a proper dinner." She stopped in front of me. Her wide eyes searched my face, waiting for a reaction.

I offered a smile, albeit a small one. My journey to Cattersley had taken its toll. "You're the housekeeper, I presume? Mrs. Sommers?"

"Oh." She shook her head, and a flush spread across her full cheeks. "Where are my manners?" She offered a shallow tilt of her head. "Mrs. Sommers, sir, at your service. We're not usually addle-brained. Mr. Manning and I have been working together for a long time. I pray you will not perceive our lack of preparation as anything other than that we were caught unawares."

I liked Mrs. Sommers and her forthright manners. "Not at all. I apologize for my early arrival. My mother and sister are due in two weeks, as originally planned. I simply wanted to become somewhat familiar with the estate before their arrival." Manning remained stoic; I doubted he'd even blinked since Mrs. Sommers's arrival. I swallowed my exhaustion. "There is no need for a formal dinner tonight, nor until my mother and sister arrive. However, I am quite hungry. Perhaps I could take a tray with some simple sandwiches in one of the sitting rooms."

"Of course, Mr. Wilkins. I'll have it sent to . . ." Here she turned to Mr. Manning. He stood with his hands clasped, staring like a statue. I looked between the two servants, and finally Mrs. Sommers scoffed and smacked Manning's arm.

Manning's eyes shot wide before he glowered at the housekeeper. "The west library," he replied.

"Yes, the west library," Mrs. Sommers repeated, not looking the least bit bothered. She tilted her head in another small bow and scurried back the way she had come.

Manning cleared his throat and resumed his statuesque posture. "Right this way, sir."

I extended my stride to walk beside Manning, rather than behind. My new role would include countless duties, many of which would require the help of the butler. Gaining his favor was vital. "The west library? Does it stand to reason there is an east library as well?" I asked.

"Yes, sir. However, the west library is brighter, as the sun warms that side of the property in the afternoon. Also, the east library is the late Lady Marion's collection. Those books are . . . less factual."

"Are you saying my great-aunt was a fan of novels?"

"Quite."

An interesting habit of my gracious benefactor. At last, I had some tangible insight about her. I wondered how vast her collection could be. Surely not large enough to fill an entire room with fanciful stories.

"Have you read any of my late aunt's books?"

Manning came to an abrupt halt and turned his nose up a quarter of an inch. "Definitely not."

"So you found her reading interests to be imprudent?" I asked.

Manning straightened himself, his lips pressed into a tight line as he slowly worded his answer. "I would never use such a descriptor for Lady Marion. She was kind and fair, and heaven is lucky to have her home."

His balled fists led me to believe he would fight to the death if I contradicted his glowing praise. I redirected the conversation. "You prefer more factually based texts?"

A single huff marked his response. He turned on his heel and marched for what seemed to be another ten minutes before turning left into a darkened room. Manning disappeared into the shadows, and a moment later blinding light streamed into the space. Dark wood paneling lined the walls. Green, the shade of faded moss, accented the room, from the tall, thick curtains to the couch. An artistic oriental vase in the same sullen shade of green sat on a table in the corner. The shelves of books stretched to the ceiling, lining the two walls that were not covered in windows.

"And the books in this room—where were they procured?" I asked.

"The late Lord Brown's collection, sir." Manning snapped out the appellation. "His years may have been limited upon the earth, but he loved the written word."

Mother had told me the sad tale of my late uncle. He had been but five and thirty years old when he was in a fatal riding accident. His final words to his bride spoke of his unwavering love. It seemed Lady Marion's affections had remained constant as well, as she had never remarried, despite being presented with those who'd sought her hand and her fortune.

I walked to the nearest bookshelf and began to peruse the titles. The books ranged from scientific to philosophical, and when I mentioned as much to Manning, he only grunted and pressed forward on his toes as if to extend his height.

What a peculiar man. One moment he fit the mold of a dignified butler, and the next he acted like a rooster in a cockfight. I wondered at his behavior but knew that it took a level head and a practiced hand to run such a place as Cattersley. Despite my curious interactions with the staff, the estate did appear well tended and cared for, meaning Mr. Manning and Mrs. Sommers filled their positions well. I found solace in this fact. Confronted with learning all the facets of running the vast estate, I was thankful to have dependable servants.

After partaking of the sandwiches Mrs. Sommers had a maid deliver, I wandered through the upper corridor, peeking into rooms and giving them random monikers in my head. Door after door opened to reveal multiple sitting rooms, a billiards room, a portrait gallery, a chapel . . . how would I ever keep them straight? My situation hit me anew. I was master of this place—this huge, enormous, wealthy estate, and the thought utterly depressed me.

I opened the door of what looked like a music room. With labored breaths I pushed past the draped instruments and furniture and pulled back one side of the heavy brown curtains. My chest tightened as I viewed the vast acreage of grass and gardens and the stableyard. The stables themselves were significantly larger than my childhood home back in Borshire. While learning the responsibilities involved in running the massive property might require my full attention for the upcoming year, I didn't doubt my ability. My fear lay deeper. What if I didn't want to be the owner of Cattersley?

I let the curtain fall closed, and beyond the sliver of light from the partially open door, darkness filled the room. The pounding of my heart thrummed to my head. I'd never aspired to grandeur. I'd not asked for this role. Why had Lady Marion chosen me? I rolled my shoulders and stretched my neck, yet as sure as the blackness surrounding me, my discomfort continued to grow.

I marched to the small column of light marking the exit and threw the door open, the crack of the knob hitting the wooden panels inside the room echoing down the passageway. I extended my arms as I moved down the corridor, running my fingers along the wainscoted panels. The walls were too close, the air too thick. At the end of the east corridor I discovered what appeared to be the servants' staircase. I followed the stairs to the lower level and found myself in the kitchen. Mrs. Sommers immediately scuttled to my side.

"Is there a problem, Mr. Wilkins?"

"It is nothing." I looked over her head at the dozen kitchen hands, each going about their prescribed duties. I needed to get away. I needed to focus on something beyond the massive unknown looming before me, around me. Roaming through the house only served to reinforce how minuscule I was. A lone ant in a rainstorm.

"If you have a moment, could you review these expenditures?" Mrs. Sommers asked. Before waiting for my answer, she stepped into what I assumed to be her private quarters and returned with a ledger in hand. She held the tablet in view, and the raindrops began to fall around me like shrapnel from artillery fire. "I know you are just getting settled, but since you're here . . . Johnson twisted his ankle on the stairs. He's laid up for a few weeks, thus Tisdell is covering Johnson's duties as well as his own. Of course, Mr. Manning will calculate the change in wages, but we did need to send for the doctor. Johnson has been recuperating in the servants' wing; however, due to a leak in the roof, he had to move in to share Hooper's quarters." Her finger tapped the next item on her list in time with my throbbing head. "I was hoping you might approve the purchase of new furniture for the extra rooms in the servants' quarters so if something similar happens in the future—"

My hand sliced through the air. "Enough!" I had not intended to speak with such force, but the commotion in the kitchens was reminiscent of a drilling army camp, and my training kicked in. The kitchens fell quiet, and Mrs. Sommers paled. I pressed my hands to my temples and exhaled a heavy sigh. Too many eyes turned to me in expectation. Only six months ago I'd felt at ease mingling with the other classes. Now my inheritance had built a great barrier between us. "Excuse me," I said and marched directly out the kitchen door to the grounds beyond, donning neither my hat nor gloves.

I'd spent much of my time in the army out of doors, drilling in open fields and marching through the French countryside. Normally I found solace atop Barkley, but I'd been on her back for far too many hours. I opted to wander the grounds near the main house on foot.

My tired legs moved instinctively. Marching days and nights had conditioned me to press through exhaustion. But this was something more. During a march or a campaign, we were assigned a mission. The objective was finite. My inheritance was something I could only quantify in monetary terms.

I stormed toward the vast field that spanned the west side of the property, determined to punish myself appropriately for my outburst. My legs burned, my tired eyes stung, and my chest heaved with frustration. I marched until my temper had cooled, and then I turned around to admire Cattersley from afar. There was an enormity to the place that I could not measure and, with it, a new front. I'd chosen to be a soldier so I could defend my family, my freedom. I had no direction in this new battle, no orders from a superior commander.

But one thing I'd learned early on was that a successful regiment was built on trust. I needed to trust my men, and they needed to trust me. My outburst at Mrs. Sommers had violated that trust. No more than three hours after my arrival, I'd offended my housekeeper. I was not a fool, though I currently looked like one. With a deep sigh of resignation, I accepted my fate. An apology was in order, and I planned to make one directly, for if there was one soldier I needed to win over, it was the housekeeper.

# Chapter Two

## MISS ABIGAIL RUTHERFORD

THE BATTLE OF TRAFALGAR HAD cost me my father and mother. I was six years old when Father had returned home, broken in more ways than one, and drunk himself to death. My mother had died this past November, a broken shell of the woman she had once been. She'd always loathed Father's drinking, but not long after he passed, she had taken up his banner and turned to alcohol herself. But prior to her passing she'd secured a future for my siblings. Benjamin, the eldest, had been sent overseas to live with our uncle in America. Louisa worked nearby as a governess, and the local vicar had only to settle me somewhere. I would have liked to become a governess as well, and the vicar did try; however, my propensity to tangle my letters when I spoke hindered any chance of my finding a household that would take me.

The vicar had determined that my grandmother would provide a home for me and I would be a companion for her. Thus, seven months ago, in late December, I had come to live with my grandmother, Mrs. Josephine Baker, at her home, Fern Cottage.

I'd worn my best black dress, as I was in mourning, kept my posture erect, and spoken slowly to correctly pronounce every letter of every word. The letter *r* had always been the most difficult. Despite my efforts, however, my nerves hindered my tongue, and when I curtsied and said, "Hello, Grandmother," the *r*'s fell out of the beginning of the moniker so that it sounded like *Gwandmother*.

"Oh, heavens!" Grandmother had said, her fan whipping frantically through the air. "How old are you, child?"

Grandmother's abruptness had rattled my nerves—words were always more difficult when I was shaken. "Eighteen. But my berfday is next month."

I'd bitten down on my lips, wishing I could calm myself and try again, for I knew I could say the words properly.

Grandmother had cried out, "Gwendolyn has sent me a dumb child!"

Of course, it hadn't been my mother who'd sent me—the vicar's wife had purchased my ticket for the mail coach—and I was hardly dumb. But I didn't say a word. Instead my eyes turned to the floor. If only I could have responded, told Grandmother my mind was clear and functioned fully. Only my speech faltered now and again. Mother had taught me French, which I spoke fluently. I could moderately play the pianoforte and easily memorized my pieces. Benjamin had met with his tutor in the Morning Room, and while Louisa and I worked on our embroidery, I had oft listened in. I could calculate numbers much faster than both my brother and his tutor. But despite wanting Grandmother to know all these things that she might have a favorable opinion of me, I knew not to contradict my superior. Thus, I had remained still—shoulders tall, head bowed—as Mother had taught me to do.

Grandmother had tsked and paced, then ranted, and eventually collapsed into a chair—my mother had been every bit her mother's daughter—and I had stood quietly through it all, knowing that despite my hopes for a new beginning and the possibility of acceptance, my situation had not changed at all. All that had changed was the roof I would sleep under.

Grandmother's cottage was not large, but it adequately provided for the two of us. She even employed two servants. Mrs. Bearsly remained with us full time. She cooked, cleaned, and managed the laundry. Mr. James Craven was a local lad who came by twice a week. Grandmother set the sixteen-year-old to chopping firewood and tending to any duties requiring more strength then we women could manage. Grandmother often set Craven to rearranging the furniture. In the seven months I'd resided at Fern Cottage, he'd moved the oversized sofa no fewer than eleven times. Mrs. Bearsly assured me Grandmother's indecision on furniture placement was nothing new. Grandmother oft claimed the aura of a room was not balanced. I thought of suggesting a potpourri mixture—I'd seen them in the shops in Plymouth—but in the end, I'd said nothing and simply offered Craven a grateful smile.

I rose early this morning, and after a quick breakfast, I helped Mrs. Bearsly with the mending. Grandmother rang for her, and Mrs. Bearsly set to preparing a tray. Before Mrs. Bearsly had a chance to pull the kettle from the fire, Grandmother rang again.

Mrs. Bearsly sighed and wiped an arm across her brow.

"I'll take it to her," I said.

"Are you certain, miss? She's like to be cross with ya." Mrs. Bearsly quickly added a plate with a boiled egg, toast, and a slice of cheese to the tray.

I stepped beside Mrs. Bearsly and lifted the tray. "I insist."

The bell rang again, and my shaky fingers rattled the tray for a bit before I could still them. The route to Grandmother's room was not nearly long enough. As I climbed the stairs, I silently recited a list I'd compiled of words that had always been difficult: *great, breath, ring, rabbit, roses, grandmother, married, rain, brother, broom.* I practiced them in hopes that I might improve, or at least limit my blunders.

With a nudge of my hip, I pushed the door open. "Here you are at last!" Grandmother's fisted hand slammed down on her comforter. "I began to think you wanted me to starve."

The teacup rattled again. I held my breath until I had placed the tray on the bedside table. "There you are, Gwandmother." I should have practiced pronouncing the word aloud. The words never sounded wrong to me. It was only after my speech faltered and disappointment trickled through the creases around Grandmother's eyes that I realized I'd mispronounced her name again. I clasped my shaky hands together and stepped back.

In these moments she appeared the precise replica of my mother. Benjamin had inherited their curls and hazel eyes. Louisa boasted the same sculpted cheeks and brows. I took after my father: plain features, brown eyes too large for my face, and straight brown hair that matched the ale my father drank. And when I misspoke, Mother would redden with embarrassment or anger and with a single look shame me for my weakness, exactly as Grandmother did now.

"If a little child can speak properly, why can you not do so?" Grandmother asked.

"I do try. It is not my intent to upset you. Please forgive my imperfection." I clenched my hands tighter. "I will stwive to do better." Oh why could my mouth not form the words as I heard them in my mind?

A cry escaped Grandmother's mouth. She leaned back against her pillows and pressed the back of her hand to her forehead. "Do you mean to torment me?" She rolled her head toward me and swept her hand forward. "Be gone with you."

I dared not speak again. I quickly curtsied and ran to my room to fetch my bonnet and dark-gray spencer. My fingers fumbled with the buttons, and I almost tripped in my rush down the stairs. I headed directly for the kitchen door, and without offering an explanation to Mrs. Bearsly, I exited the cottage, hoping to reach the shelter of the forest before my tears began.

My outings had become my refuge. Trees ranging from saplings to monarchs surrounded Fern Cottage. It wasn't a large forest, but it provided plentiful space for my walks, and the edge of the wood served as the boundary between Fern Cottage and the imposing beauty that was Cattersley. There was ample speculation about the new owner, who was due to arrive any day. The chatter about him, Craven said, varied from tales of a hardened but decorated war hero to an awkward, dimwitted relation. I knew how tales spread. Rumors and I did not get along, and I felt a wave of sympathy for the stranger.

Lady Marion had passed away shortly after my arrival at Fern Cottage. I never had the opportunity to meet her, but I had become friends with Mr. Tucker, her groundskeeper. My walks often intruded on Cattersley's vast anchorage, and one morning Mr. Tucker had found me admiring his honeysuckle hedge. After speaking together briefly, he had invited me to walk the grounds as often as I desired.

"Are you certain?" I had spoken slowly and chosen my words carefully. "I would never wish to intrude." I'd been shocked by his invitation. In my life experience, such kindness was rare.

"'Tis no intrusion at all, Miss Rutherford. And I speak on behalf of Lady Marion as well. Please come visit whenever you desire." He'd plucked a bright-pink honeysuckle bloom and handed it to me. Then, with a tip of his hat, he'd taken his leave and returned to his duties.

My goal this sunny afternoon was to find Mr. Tucker and discover if, despite the new owner, his standing invitation remained. I inhaled the summer air and tilted my head to the warmth of the sunshine. The beauty of the day eased my soul. Speaking always became more difficult when I was rattled, and Grandmother's impatience only fueled my anxiety.

I crossed the field, beginning to feel somewhat cheered by the beauty around me and even skipping a time or two where the wildflowers grew in abundance. If I skipped, perhaps I could shake off some of my inadequacies. Besides, how could one simply walk through a field painted in such glorious color? I made my way around the fragrant flower garden, circling toward the large garden shed and greenhouse, looking all the while for Mr. Tucker.

The man was nowhere to be found. Perhaps his duties had called him to another part of the estate today. No matter; it would only give me the opportunity to return and speak with him another time.

I rounded the house, ready to skip back through the fields and enjoy a final bit of levity before returning to Fern Cottage to face Grandmother and her spiteful tongue. I lifted the hem of my skirt and kicked off with my right foot to skip again.

"Hello." The utter maleness of the voice brought me to an abrupt halt.

My fingers froze, clutching the fabric of my dress, and my throat plunged to my toes. Letters and sounds were not the only things that jumbled when I became flustered. The edges of my bonnet prohibited me from seeing who addressed me, and I could not seem to make my head turn to meet him.

"My apologies for startling you, Miss . . . ?"

Despite my desire to respond, or at least to turn and confront the man, my body refused to cooperate. I pressed my eyes closed and in my mind rehearsed my word list until I was able to gather a bit of my wits. I opened my eyes, resolved to answer for my presence at Cattersley, then promptly return home.

But when I turned around, my tongue paralyzed once again. The man before me was handsome. Exquisitely so. He wore no hat, and his blond hair grew long enough in the back to brush against his collar. His piercing blue eyes transformed his otherwise ordinary face into a work of art. The shade alone was enough to make one stare. It was a clear and rich marine color I imagined existed in the depths of the sea. Startling yet somehow kind, his eyes swept over my face.

I clamped my mouth closed and noted his worn clothing. My mother's insistence that I remain silent had always granted me ample time to observe. This man dressed as a gentleman. The cut of his jacket fit him well, but it was not in the latest fashion. His boots were covered in a layer of dust, and upon looking him over again, I found his face held a weariness.

"Pardon me," the man said, dipping his head. His eyes never quite left mine. He straightened again, and his lips twisted into what I interpreted as mischief. "Well then, as we've no one to introduce us, I'll go first. I'm Captain—" He cleared his throat. "Excuse me. Old habits. I'm Mr. Robert Wilkins."

There was no mistaking his slip of the tongue. This man must be the new owner of Cattersley. And what must he think of me, a silly girl skipping around his estate? Grandmother would be furious.

Despite my shaky legs I curtsied. Once I rose, I wanted to respond, to offer some explanation for my presence . . . but no words would come out.

Mr. Wilkins watched me, his posture perfect and his face as impassive as if he were posing for a portrait.

Like a hiccup, words jumped suddenly into my throat. "Good day, sir. I'm Miss Abigail Rutherford." I'd trained my tongue to at least pronounce my surname properly. Thankfully, it only slipped a bit in my introduction, and Mr. Wilkins's expression did not change. "I live at Fern Cottage and came to call upon Mr. Tucker." I could at least feel fortunate that *r*'s were difficult only when placed at the beginning or middle of words.

"I've only just arrived and have not yet met all of the staff. Tell me, who is Mr. Tucker?" The man's smile remained fixed.

"The gwoundskeeper, sir. A very skilled artist. He gwanted permission for me to come to the gardens, but that was before, with the late Lady Marion." I bit my lip, hoping he wouldn't comment on my mispronunciations. He stood silent, his smile still in place, so I pointed toward the greenhouse and continued. "You see, that's why I've come today, to see if I may still walk the gwounds when the new owner—that is, you, yourself—have arrived. And now you're here, I think—I assume you are the new owner, owing to your prior military title and such . . . sir." I felt the urge to salute but instead covered my face with my hands. The constitution of my problem lay in the fact that I switched from one extreme to the other. Silence was demanded by my mother, so when I was told or expected to speak, my mouth could not immediately form the words. But once they came, they came in a deluge, a tidal wave of nonsense pouring out.

"Miss Rutherford?" The note of concern in Mr. Wilkins's voice pulled my hands from my face.

I pushed past my embarrassment, needing to know. "Are you indeed the new owner of Cattersley?"

Mr. Wilkins took a deep breath and looked over his shoulder at the large house. "Yes." The simple reply landed heavily over both of us.

I spoke slowly. "My condolences for Lady Marion. I understand she was quite adored, although I did not have the privilege of her acquaintance." Relief flooded me that my speech did not falter again.

"Yes, well"—a sigh escaped him—"that makes two of us."

I jolted a bit at his words. "You did not know her?"

Mr. Wilkins shook his head.

"Then, how . . . ?" I turned in a slow circle, breathing in all the grandeur and beauty and promise of the estate.

I completed my rotation and found Mr. Wilkins watching me. "It is rather unfathomable, isn't it?"

Shock ran deep, and I let it settle.

"Lady Marion was my great-aunt." Mr. Wilkins's rigid posture remained. If I had not known him to be a soldier, I would have guessed as much by now. "We met when I was still in the nursery, and thus I have no tangible memory of her."

"Yet she named you benefactor of"—my hand swept wide—"all of this?"

"Indeed." One side of his mouth twitched upward, along with his eyebrows.

"Are you not pleased?" I trained my eyes on his boots, hoping he would not consider me impertinent for asking such an intimate question.

"I am honored but, admittedly, a bit overwhelmed."

"Your aunt is lauded by many. Certainly she took great consideration in choosing an heir." With a breath I paused and formulated my sounds. "You are very fortunate." I would gladly keep his secret about being overwhelmed in exchange for permission to walk the grounds.

His smile slipped. "It would seem so."

I raised my head and regarded him. My skills of interpretation failed me. I could not account for Mr. Wilkins's sullenness. I stared at him, wondering if his blue eyes might give me a clue. And he stared directly back. It wasn't nearly as threatening as a standoff with Grandmother. The thought of her forced my surrender. I blinked free from Mr. Wilkins's gaze and curtsied. "Forgive me, sir. My grandmother will wonder where I am." With gratitude that I had tempered my tongue, I made to leave.

"What about Mr. Tucker?" Mr. Wilkins asked.

I turned around, glad to reclaim some of my earlier levity. "I will return and speak with him another day . . . oh . . . I mean, I will send a note."

Mr. Wilkins smiled again, and this time the gesture was sincere. It lit his entire face. My, he was a handsome man. "Miss Rutherford, you are welcome to call upon Mr. Tucker as you wish."

I felt my cheeks warm, flustered as I was by Mr. Wilkins's good looks. "You have my thanks. I shall weturn tomorrow." I ducked my head in a bow, hoping to cover my flush of embarrassment as my pronunciation skewed again, before turning and heading toward home.

Mr. Wilkins's low chuckle sounded in my ears, but I could not face him again to determine whether his laughter was at my expense. I marched back through the wildflower fields. No matter. Whatever Mr. Wilkins's intent, he'd granted me permission to see Mr. Tucker and Cattersley's expansive gardens. That was all I required from the man, and now that he'd come to claim his inheritance, I doubted I would ever see him again.

# Chapter Three

## MR. ROBERT WILKINS

I RETURNED HOME IN A much-improved mood. Whether the fresh air or a particular young miss could claim credit, I could not rightly say, but when Manning tsked that Monsieur Gastineau would have my dinner prepared in thirty minutes, I clapped him on the shoulder and told him I would be cleaned up and ready. After a quick change I requested Mrs. Sommers join me in the library.

I paced before the tall windows. Mrs. Sommers entered the room and shifted her weight between her feet. "You asked for me, sir?"

I walked to where she stood and bent over in a deep bow. "I beg your forgiveness, Mrs. Sommers." I waited another few moments before rising to my full height.

"Oh . . ." Mrs. Sommers fiddled with the cuff of her long sleeve. "Well . . ." Her eyes shifted between me and the curtains behind my back.

"My fear has been that Lady Marion erred in selecting me as her heir. My behavior toward you was inexcusable and proves my fears were justified." Here Mrs. Sommers dropped her hands to her side and met my gaze.

"Forgive me for saying so, but I disagree, Mr. Wilkins. Lady Marion did not do anything on a whim. She was precise and thorough, and the fact that I'm standing here makes me think her selection of an heir was no different."

I swallowed and nodded understanding.

"You've had a long journey. All's forgiven. Now, come and fill your stomach so you can rest." Mrs. Sommers turned, and I followed her from the room.

Monsieur Gastineau either had not received my request for a simple meal, or he'd chosen to ignore it, for he'd prepared a splendid spread. I felt ridiculous sitting alone at the long banquet table that would easily serve thirty, and afterward I insisted that Manning and Mrs. Sommers serve future meals in the west library when I was dining alone.

The following morning Manning arrived in my bedchamber to introduce me to the footman he had selected to serve as a temporary valet.

A young man with a rectangular freckled face and curly red hair stood grinning at me. He was not yet taller than my height of six feet, but I guessed he would soon grow into his gangly limbs and surpass me.

"May I present Andrew Graham, sir?" Manning said. "He's a quick learner and has proven competent in his duties."

I would normally have offered my hand, but Graham stood like a soldier ready for inspection.

"Do you deem him acceptable, sir?" Manning asked.

I glanced at the butler's upturned nose, tension rolling through my shoulders. "Yes, yes. How do you do, Graham?"

At my question Manning forcefully cleared his throat.

Graham looked at the butler, then turned to me with a wide smile. "Thank you, Captain, for accepting me. I am well. I'll do my best by you, sir. What would you have me do first?" He followed his introduction with a solid salute.

"We are not in the militia, Graham. There's no need to salute." The irony of my comment immediately settled between us. While not his commander, I was master of Cattersley, and it was Graham's duty to do my bidding. I awkwardly scratched my chin.

"What will you require of your valet, Mr. Wilkins?" Manning again pressed forward on his toes, his gloved hands clasped in front of him.

I had a part to play, and I felt woefully inadequate. "To be frank, Manning, I've been dressing myself for the better part of my twenty-eight years. I've no idea what is required of a competent valet." Manning returned his heels to the floor and looked utterly incredulous. I acquiesced with a shrug and had to remind myself I was in charge. "Perhaps you could offer your opinion."

Manning's shock transformed to a merry grin. He turned to Graham. "Do you know how to take measurements?"

Graham's face lit. "That I do, sir. I've helped me mother plenty o' times when the regimentals come through. I'll just be needin' about thirty minutes with the master." Graham turned to me. "Will that be to your liking, Captain?"

I lowered my brow and glared at Graham.

"Mr. Wilkins, that is . . . sir." Graham bowed quickly and glanced at Manning before granting me a repentant smile.

I had no desire to stand stiffly while Graham and Manning evaluated my person. However, my new position would require a new wardrobe. Best to be done with it. "Where shall I stand?"

While Graham calculated and scribbled down notes, Manning instructed him on the particulars of his new role. A full hour passed before I could politely excuse myself to head out of doors for some fresh air. It took five minutes to walk to the front door of Cattersley—ridiculous enormity of a house. Yet as I approached the stables, excitement stirred within me, and my step quickened.

Two training pens connected to the stableyard, and beyond the smaller pen half a dozen horses grazed in a large pasture. More than two-dozen stalls lined the walls of the stable, and an additional three rooms were filled with harnesses, saddles, brushes, and bridles. The boy who'd taken Barkley the day before led me to her stall. A hand-carved nameplate was affixed to the door, bearing her name. "Did you do this?" I asked Pratt.

He held his hands stiffly against his side. "No, sir. Mr. Twill carves all the names, sir."

"Mr. Twill?"

"Yes, sir. He assists Mr. Kane with the horses, sir." Pratt's head bobbed, but the rest of his posture remained rigid.

I sighed in exasperation. "Why do you keep calling me sir?"

Pratt's eyes bulged wide. "Well, Captain, we thought you being a military man, an officer and all, you would expect it. Sir." Pratt snapped his heels together.

I placed a hand on Pratt's shoulder. "I've resigned my commission and am no longer an officer. Mr. Wilkins will do just fine."

Pratt's head bobbed again. "Yes, sir." Pratt grinned. "I mean, yes, Mr. Wilkins." I lowered my hand and asked the boy to show me the rest of the building.

The stable hands slept on the second floor, and an open area with a long table and various chairs and couches provided room for the men to gather and eat. Mr. Kane was due to return in the morning. Pratt and the others seemed in good spirits and praised Mr. Kane as a competent horseman.

It seemed Lady Marion had kept her finger on every aspect of the estate. The household staff ran the place with precision, the stables were well kept and orderly, the gardens were immaculate, and to top it all off, everyone appeared to be content in their employment. Despite Cattersley's size, it did not feel empty or shallow or cold. Everything from the facade to the smiling faces of the staff evoked a feeling of welcome, yet managing a home full of servants felt more daunting than ordering a forward-charge to battle.

I dismissed Pratt and saddled Barkley myself. I had an appointment with Mr. Horton, Lady Marion's steward, in the late afternoon, after which I anticipated a large headache. I needed at least an hour's reprieve on Barkley's back.

We galloped across the open field toward the line of trees that crept like giants up the rolling hills beyond. Barkley tossed her head, and I reined her in as we circled the border of forest. The expanse of land spread wide, fanning out to showcase the fields of crops and cattle that lay beyond. While I could not rightly name the boundaries of the estate, the enormity before me stole my breath. The livelihood of so many fell to me—a tiny speck in the vast acreage. The freedom I'd felt only moments before turned inside out.

I'd experienced feelings of defeat before. A commission in the army during wartime was not for the faint of heart. But when it had come time to call for a charge on the battlefield, I'd been surrounded by my men. We'd marched shoulder to shoulder. We'd bled side by side for the cause of freedom.

With a sigh I turned Barkley around and noted the empty space. The house sat far away, easily covered by the size of my hand if held on the horizon. During my ride, I'd not seen another individual. No soldier to march by my side. No commander to give me my orders. But as I returned to the house and neared the formal garden, I recognized Miss Rutherford's black bonnet, and my heart lifted the tiniest bit.

Pratt met me at the stable, and I handed Barkley off to his care. I removed my gloves and dusted off my jacket as I circled the outer wall in search of Miss Rutherford. Her lilting hum reached my ears before I found her. I paused for a moment and listened to her voice. The sound soothed my soul.

When Miss Rutherford's voice faded, I stepped onto the groomed path, intent to speak with her. I rounded a vibrant yellow rosebush and found the lady sharing her alluring smile with an older gentleman. He trimmed a pale-pink rosebud and handed it to Miss Rutherford, who accepted the gift graciously. She was dressed in a simple gray gown, causing the pink rose she held to stand out in contrast. The man then spied me standing there. His smile slipped, and he stepped forward.

When she saw me, recognition filled her wide brown eyes. "Oh, Mr. Wilkins." Her cheeks turned the same color as the rose she held. She dipped into a curtsy, and even once she stood her eyes remained fixed on the ground.

I evaluated the man standing before me. He stood even with my height, and his weathered skin sported a fair share of wrinkles and spots. "May I presume you are Mr. Tucker?"

"I am, sir."

I extended my hand in greeting. The older man wiped his hands against his pant legs.

"I don't mind a little dirt, Mr. Tucker."

Mr. Tucker glanced back at Miss Rutherford and only accepted my hand once she gave a nod of encouragement.

"It's a pleasure to meet you, sir," he said.

"You've a talent, Tucker. Cattersley boasts the finest gardens I've ever seen."

Tucker dipped his head. "I find I'm most at peace while tending the plants. Felton, the undergardener, is a great help to me."

I opened my mouth, but Miss Rutherford spoke first. "Have your travels been extensive, Mr. Wilkins?" Miss Rutherford avoided making eye contact. Instead she stared at the rose she twirled in her fingers.

Her shy countenance was refreshing. Many females of my acquaintance were eager to engage in conversation while exercising their eyelashes and offering coy smiles. Especially after my inheritance of Cattersley had been made known. That was another reason I had fled Borshire and come to Cattersley early. "My time in the military provided the opportunity to see much of England as well as . . ." I did not wish to discuss the war. Miss Rutherford seemed far too delicate to expose to the truths of battle, too innocent to know evil. "Well, various other countries."

She glanced up at me then. Recognition of what I did not say shot like a silver bolt through her discerning brown eyes. Perhaps she *had* seen atrocity. The thought pained me. Her lips slowly pushed into a smile, and she touched Tucker's coat sleeve. "You see, Mr. Tucker, Mr. Wilkins has confirmed what I've been telling you this past season. Your work is beyond compare."

The older man glowed under Miss Rutherford's praise, and jealousy whipped through me.

I pointed to the rose in Miss Rutherford's hand. "That is a lovely flower."

Tucker perked up. "It's a special breed I've been working on. Smells sweet as summer dew."

I raised an eyebrow at Miss Rutherford. She extended the rose toward me, and instead of accepting it from her gloved hand, I set my fingers below hers and raised the petals to where I could inhale their fragrance. I released my hold but did not step away as I turned to Tucker. "Impressive indeed. A sweet but subtle aroma."

The man nearly beamed. "I'm naming it Irene, after my dear wife. I lost her last month." His eyes grew moist. "Miss Rutherford here's been keeping me company. I wanted her to have the first rose."

"I'm sorry for your loss, and I am glad Miss Rutherford's visits have provided solace." I turned to Miss Rutherford, who held the pink flower to her nose. The sunlight danced on the leaves of the hedge behind her, while her face remained hidden in the shadow of her bonnet. I had the oddest desire to reach up and untie the ribbons at her throat in order to allow the sun to spill over her whole person. Rather than act on the impulse, I clutched my fingers at my side. Both Tucker and Miss Rutherford looked at me for direction, so I spoke a bit of my thoughts aloud. "I hope you know, Miss Rutherford, that you are welcome anytime." I looked at her and then at Mr. Tucker, trying to convey my assurance that he had my blessing to continue his visits with the lady. As Miss Rutherford politely took her leave and made her way in the direction of her home, I understood how Tucker found hope in the beauty standing before us. It was a hope I longed for, and for the first time I wondered if I might find solace in something as beautiful and simple as a rose.

# Chapter Four

## MISS ABIGAIL RUTHERFORD

My hand still pulsed where Mr. Wilkins had touched me. It was not unpleasant—quite the opposite. His touch had sent a melodious thrum up my arm and into my chest, and I'd smelled the rose again only to hide the blush warming my cheeks.

As I walked toward the cottage, considering how to convince Grandmother I'd discovered the splendid pink rose growing wild in the forest, Mr. Wilkins's footsteps sounded beside me. I glanced at him without pausing my movement. Had he changed his mind about my visits?

"May I escort you home, Miss Rutherford?" he asked.

Shock froze my tongue. I could not recall a time when a handsome gentleman had offered to escort me anywhere, yet despite my desire to agree, I could not. My hesitation lasted too long. Mr. Wilkins's pace slowed. I needed to explain. "I appreciate the offer, sir, but I must decline." I carefully sounded out my words. "My grandmother . . ." I bit my lip and contemplated an explanation. "She's unaware of my meetings with Mr. Tucker. In fact, she does not know I come to Cattersley at all. And if you arrive, as Cattersley's heir, well, she would be most displeased with me." Thankfully, my letters formed their proper sounds.

Mr. Wilkins thought on this for a moment. "But you see, Miss Rutherford, I am not walking you home."

"But I thought . . ."

Mr. Wilkins's eyes lit with mischievousness. "In point of fact, I am simply inspecting my inheritance from my generous aunt. It is important for one to know the extent of their holdings, wouldn't you agree?"

Despite my reservations about my grandmother, a genuine smile tugged at my lips.

"Eventually I will call on all of my neighbors, but for now, I will walk with you only to the border of our properties. Does that alleviate your concerns?"

Warmth filtered through my insides. I nodded and held the rose again to my nose to inhale its sweet fragrance.

We walked in silence for several minutes. My opportunity to converse with gentlemen had always been limited, for while I was the daughter of a gentleman, I rarely spoke with the gentry. Mother had forbidden it. I spoke freely with Mr. Tucker and Craven, but I hardly knew where to begin with Mr. Wilkins.

He and I walked side by side across the dotted canvas of the meadow. I paused to pick sprigs of white yarrow and arranged them into a bouquet around my single rose.

Mr. Wilkins cleared his throat. "Have you lived with your grandmother long?"

"These seven months past. Ever since my mother passed away." I held the flowers in front of me, thinking back to my arrival at Fern Cottage and the flood of emotions that had filled me that day.

"I'm sorry for your loss. I'm sure it is difficult."

"Yes." The answer jumped out before I could think on it. "But not in the way you might imagine." I raised my eyes to Mr. Wilkins's. Their depths of blue pulled me in, and I did not feel ashamed of my words.

He held my gaze and, gratefully, did not ask me to clarify. "Do you have any siblings?" Mr. Wilkins asked.

I began walking again. "An elder brother, Benjamin, and a younger sister, Louisa." Thinking of my siblings brought a mixture of sadness and joy.

Mr. Wilkins matched my pace. "Do you favor one another?"

"I'm rather plain in comparison. Louisa is a beauty and Benjamin is far too handsome. He's always drawn the attention of others. Whenever we journeyed to the market, ladies would make eyes at him." I laughed lightly at the memory.

"And do they live with your grandmother also?" Mr. Wilkins asked.

I shook my head and watched the hem of my skirts brush over the tips of my boots. "Mother had been ill for almost a year. The summer before her passing, she sent Benjamin to live with my uncle in the Americas. Not long after, she secured a position for my sister as a governess. Louisa worked for a nearby family, and while she was frequently able to visit, her work did not allow her to assist in Mother's care. Therefore, I remained home and took care of Mother until she passed the following winter. Then I came to my grandmother at Fern Cottage." We neared the edge of the wildflower meadow, and I spied the perfect fern leaf to complement my bouquet. I stopped to pick it, then admired the contrast of the deep green, the white, and the pink. Nature produced such wonders.

"You've an eye for beauty, Miss Rutherford."

If Mr. Wilkins only knew how attractive I thought him to be. Heat filled my cheeks. I focused on the bouquet. "It is only a rose." I lowered the arrangement to my side.

"But you've chosen the perfect companions to accentuate its beauty." Mr. Wilkins reached forward and placed a single finger on my wrist to raise the flowers between us. "How many would admire only the rose without consideration of how the beauty of the rose enhances everything it surrounds?"

I'd not allowed myself to feel anything for a long time. Feelings only led to hurt. But Mr. Wilkins's words stirred something within. A tiny flame in my heart and emotion I had thought long dead.

"Abigail!" Grandmother's voice cut through the air, instantly dousing the growing embers.

I gathered my skirts and offered a quick curtsy. "Thank you, sir."

"Miss Rutherford?" The timbre of his voice made me pause. "Tucker has agreed to give me a tour of the grounds. Perhaps you might join me?"

"I would be delighted, sir," I said.

His smile twitched. "And please call me Mr. Wilkins."

I ducked my head and nodded as Grandmother called for me again. "I must go." I rushed into the woods, and in that moment I made a decision. I would honor his request and address him as Mr. Wilkins, but I would think of him only as the man with mystic blue eyes who had once upon a time escorted me home.

Grandmother and I entered the church and sat at our normal place in the third row of pews. The Cattersley pew was on the front row and had sat empty since Lady Marion's passing. I wondered if now that Mr. Wilkins had returned, he would fill it once again.

I did not have to wonder for long. The murmurs and chatter of the congregation suddenly ceased, and I turned to see the man himself standing in the doorway of the sanctuary. The whispers and open gawking did not seem to disconcert him. Perhaps his time in the military had made him indifferent to the opinions of others. Mr. Wilkins looked about the room. His butler soon joined him, leaning near and pointing to the bench assigned to the grand estate. Mr. Wilkins gave a slight nod and walked to his seat.

He didn't acknowledge me as he passed—I was grateful he'd remembered my fear of Grandmother discovering my visits to Cattersley—but I couldn't help but notice him. The entire congregation did. Mr. Wilkins commanded attention.

He was followed by Mr. Horton, whom Grandmother knew, as he'd served as the late Lady Marion's steward. The gentlemen took their seats, and Mr. Wilkins retained his rigid posture throughout the sermon. My attention bounced between the soldier sitting in front of me, and the handsome vicar, Mr. Mead, who currently preached about the dangers of worldly possessions. Eloquent words floated easily from his lips, and the timbre of his voice lulled me into a peaceful trance.

Mother had been a faithful churchgoer. We'd attended weekly until she became ill. I had never particularly cared for the ceremony, as I'd regularly received sideways glances and overheard whispered mockery.

*"Such beauty lost on a stupid child."*

*"Her mother forbids her to speak, for she is an embarrassment."*

*"'Tis a pity she is dumb; her siblings are quite accomplished."*

I'd heard multiple variations of the same insults my entire life. The hypocrisy of the treatment I received from those who sat within the walls of the chapel was especially brutal.

How could one spew offenses while claiming to worship a deity who forbids mockery? Hypocrisy had surrounded me for as long as I could remember. It was a companion to judgment, another of the very things the Lord warned against.

The congregation here in Henwick mirrored the one in Plymouth, but there were decidedly fewer parishioners. Grandmother had spouted multiple excuses for not attending Sabbath worship for the first two months following my arrival. But I knew it was because she was ashamed of me. Afraid of the whispers. Grandmother had allowed me to escort her to town shortly after I'd come to live with her. We'd stopped at the apothecary, where Mr. Mallory, the owner, had greeted me warmly. When Grandmother told him of our relation, Mr. Mallory had expressed sympathy for my mother's passing. His wife had joined him and asked, "Is Henwick to your liking?"

"Very much so," I'd answered. My words had been clear, and I should have stopped speaking. But in my enthusiasm I'd continued. "The twees are so vewy grand. I believe I prefer the fowest of Herefordshire over the seas of Plymouth."

My exuberance hindered my tongue, and Mr. and Mrs. Mallory had stood in shock. Grandmother's face had darkened, her lips pinched tight. After a long moment, she spoke. "Such doltishness. She is a willful child."

Mrs. Mallory had touched Grandmother's arm. "At least you may take solace in her beauty."

My heart and hopes had wilted then and there. Grandmother had forbidden me from joining her on her errands after that. When she insisted I accompany Mrs. Bearsly one afternoon to purchase sundries in town because Grandmother was not feeling well, we'd happened upon the vicar. Our introduction and exchange had been brief, but the next day Mr. Mead had called. I had not been invited to join the conversation, but over dinner that evening Grandmother had told me how Mr. Mead had chastised her for neglecting her worship. He'd insisted both of us attend the following Sunday. That was when I first knew I liked the gentleman.

Grandmother had heeded his admonition and even allowed me to rejoin her in her visits to town. We had entered the chapel that Sabbath morning to see Mr. Mead sitting on the dais, with golden sunlight spilling through the windows behind him. His dark hair had glowed with a halo-like sheen to complement his handsome features, reminding me of Benjamin. The vicar's handsome eyes resonated a confidence I longed to feel. They, too, were dark and had vacillated between determined passion and sincerity for the message he shared. His cheeks were defined, his jaw solid, and the tone of his ardent sermon had touched my soul. I'd estimated he stood only a few inches taller than myself, but his figure was strong and solid, a commanding presence.

He'd sought me out that first Sunday, commending Grandmother for attending and asking my opinion on his discourse. Then he'd called at Fern Cottage that very week and every week since. This had become a tradition, and though the whispers had not diminished, Mr. Mead's fellowship provided a defense, for no one would outright mock me in his presence.

Sunday worship provided me a reprieve from the monotony of everyday life at Fern Cottage. I breathed a deep sigh of contentment. Sitting in the chapel with Grandmother, behind a handsome captain, while admiring the words and face of the equally handsome vicar, made church quite appealing.

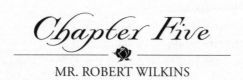

## Chapter Five

### MR. ROBERT WILKINS

PEOPLE WERE PREDICTABLE—WHETHER BY THE fear slinking through the lines before battle, the courage they had to continue fighting despite watching a comrade fall, or the way the mother of a single miss eyed a bachelor who has recently come into his fortune. The reaction of the congregation upon my entrance was no exception. Hands shielded whispers and eyes widened with blatant stares—things I had expected from the townsfolk of Henwick, and they did not disappoint.

In time, the shock would wear off. In time, I would learn my role and convince my neighbors of my intentions to maintain Cattersley as a prosperous estate. And hopefully, in time, I would have friends and acquaintances with whom I could converse and socialize.

I was grateful Mother and Hazel would be joining me soon. I missed Mother's steady perspective and Hazel's cheerful demeanor. I missed conversation in which I was called Robert, son, or brother.

At least Miss Rutherford provided a friendly face. I didn't dare acknowledge her since she had made clear her concern over her grandmother's censure, but I felt a bit of comfort knowing she was one of many staring at the back of my head.

I'd meant to introduce myself to the vicar, but my intentions to call had been thwarted when Manning had insisted I needed to be fit for new boots. Thus, my first impression of the man was when he stood to deliver his message.

He was younger than the pastor in Borshire, and I thought he must be closer to my own twenty-eight years. Manning had told me Lady Marion had welcomed Mr. Mead as the vicar five years ago. Lady Marion had been dear friends with Mead's grandmother. When my great-aunt had heard Mead desired a parish of his own, she'd immediately offered him the dwelling at Mayview Cottage and promised her patronage. The previous vicar had been anxious to retire, so in a matter of months, it was all arranged, and Mr. Mead had come to reside.

Knowing that aspect of the estate was resolved lessoned my burden and I looked to the pulpit, anxious to listen to the sermon. Eloquent words flowed easily from Mead's lips. He read the Lord's Sermon on the Mount, expounding especially on the verses that admonished nurturing the less fortunate. It was a stirring reminder of the benefit of my new circumstance. With my new position and wealth, I could bless many. I determined to discuss various options with Horton when next we met.

When the meeting ended, I took a deep breath and stood, ready to feign a confidence I had not felt since before my arrival at Cattersley. A crowd gathered near the doorway. I steeled myself, then met Miss Rutherford's gaze. She held steady for only a moment before casting her eyes to the floor, but her cheeks lifted a tiny bit, and I knew she was as aware of me as I was of her.

Manning pushed through the crowd, inserting himself before me. "Your coach is ready, sir."

I raised my hand. "I shall be a minute or two, Manning. Thank you."

Horton's knowledge had proved invaluable. I turned to him and spoke softly. "Horton, would you be so kind as to make introductions? I believe the neighborhood knows my name, and I cannot reciprocate. I'd hate to appear at a disadvantage."

Horton tipped his head, and a brief smile touched his lips. "Of course, Mr. Wilkins."

I'd learned in my early days in the military that first impressions could determine loyalty or perfidy. While my role in Henwick was different from my military service, it was also very much the same. Gaining support from the locals would not affect my livelihood, but it could easily determine my success and happiness.

I did not need physical support or comradery, but respect—I'd worked hard to build an honorable reputation. It had been vital with my men, and it gave me peace of mind to know I'd conducted myself in a manner worthy of distinction. The merits of wealth or rank meant nothing to me. I needed only acknowledgment that I would work hard and stand as a man of integrity.

We stepped up to a broad man, and I wondered if his thick side-whiskers and moustache were as itchy as they appeared. "Mr. Lane, may I introduce Mr. Robert Wilkins?" Horton said.

"Yes, yes." Mr. Lane extended his hand. "How do you do, Wilkins? I'd heard you'd arrived."

"Pleased to make your acquaintance." I shook his hand.

Mr. Lane introduced me to his very forward daughter and his wife, a petite woman with an intricate coif, and then he rambled on about his long-standing friendship with Lady Marion. "You know I've a knack for investing in sound ventures. I'd be happy to advise you on such matters. Cattersley's coffers provide a nice little nest, eh?"

I glanced at Horton and offered the barest of replies. "Excuse us, Lane." The man's eyes darkened, and his joviality fled. I had a feeling I'd just made an enemy.

Horton then introduced me to Mr. Edwards. "I'm glad to meet you, Mr. Wilkins." Edwards bowed. He stood even with my height, though he appeared to be a few years younger than I was. His wore his long brown hair tied back, and his jacket was of fine wool, albeit in a conservative style.

"Likewise." I nodded. "I apologize I have not had time to call on all of my neighbors."

Edwards chuckled. "I find it quite magnanimous that you attended church so soon after your arrival."

I glanced around the chapel. "It is rather a gaggle, isn't it?" I laughed.

"Do you ride, Mr. Wilkins?"

"Indeed I do."

"I've only a small holding, south of Cattersley, but perhaps we may ride together once you are settled."

"I would enjoy that," I said sincerely. Edwards then excused himself, and I thought he and I would get on well.

I met several more gentlemen, along with their spouses and young daughters. After bowing to half a dozen sets of batting lashes, I was ready to depart. A headache pressed against my temples, and I began the trek to my carriage. Without a word Manning stepped in front of me and led me to the door. His short stature did not deter him from blazing a path through the parishioners.

In the welcome fresh air I realized I had not obtained the one introduction I wished for. I searched the crowd for Miss Rutherford and found her and an elderly woman I assumed to be her grandmother standing near the corner of the church, under a large oak tree, speaking with the vicar. Miss Rutherford smiled at something he said, then ducked her head, and a wave of jealousy swept over me.

In my time on the battlefield I had learned the importance of decisive action, so I left Horton and Manning and walked to where the group stood.

"Thank you for your words today," I said to the vicar. "Mr. Robert Wilkins." I bowed briefly, then stood tall. "I apologize I have yet to call at Mayview Cottage. Assuming the management of Cattersley has taken my time."

"Not at all. Mr. Daniel Mead, at your service." The vicar bowed, and when he stood, I looked at Miss Rutherford. She did a commendable job of pretending curiosity. Mead followed my gaze. His eyes narrowed, but he quickly continued. "Ah yes, may I introduce you to Mrs. Josephine Baker and her granddaughter, Miss Abigail Rutherford?"

"How do you do? Mrs. Baker. Miss Rutherford." I bowed to each in turn.

Mrs. Baker cleared her throat. "I must confess, it is a surprise to see you at church, Mr. Wilkins."

"Why is that? I understand my great-aunt attended regularly." I looked between Mrs. Baker and the vicar.

Mrs. Baker pressed her hand to the lace at her throat. "Yes indeed! Lady Marion was very devout in her worship." Her eyes first flicked toward the vicar, then at something behind me before her gaze once again returned to mine. "I just assumed, given your former occupation. Forgive me."

"There is nothing to forgive, Mrs. Baker. A life in the military will lead one to call upon God or to forsake him. I've found better success with the former." Prayers had often filled my quiet moments on the front lines. The not so quiet moments as well.

Mead evaluated my words. "And what did you think of today's discourse?" he asked.

"I enjoyed hearing the words spoken by the Lord. His sermons are concise and speak to the finer points of doctrine. Do you agree, Miss Rutherford?" I loved the way her eyes brightened when I said her name. But instead of answering, she bit her lip and looked to her grandmother.

"Abigail thought the sermon delightful," Mrs. Baker answered in her stead. "She regularly tells me how she enjoys the Sabbath, for then we have the pleasure of hearing Mr. Mead expound the scriptures."

"You are too kind," Mr. Mead said. He smiled widely and appeared to relish the praise heaped upon him, which I found amusing, considering he had initially posed the question.

"Horton informed me your property neighbors mine." A small fib, as Horton had not mentioned such a thing. "Tell me, Miss Rutherford, have you ever had occasion to visit the gardens of Cattersley?"

Miss Rutherford's cheeks pinked, but it was once again Mrs. Baker who answered. "Abigail would never presume to intrude. We keep to ourselves, Mr. Wilkins."

"Do you ever venture from Herefordshire?" I looked at Miss Rutherford. "Perhaps to participate in the offerings of London?"

Again she was not able to respond as Mead asserted his opinion. "Not everyone is drawn to the enticements of Town," he said.

"I should like to have gone," Mrs. Baker said. "I imagine lavish dinners and the opera." She leaned forward and whispered conspiratorially, "But there is no hope for a journey now that Abigail has come." Color flooded Miss Rutherford's cheeks as she ducked her head and held her tongue. Mrs. Baker stood back at her full height. "I have put the inclination behind me, and as the vicar mentioned today, I am determined to succor those in need."

Frustration welled inside me. Was this normal for Miss Rutherford, to stand silently while those around her bantered and conversed at her expense? Did her grandmother require such submissiveness? Or was she simply bashful in the vicar's presence? For she was neither mute nor dim-witted. She was delightful. I had witnessed her intelligence and her charm and become quite smitten.

I remained for only a few minutes more before offering my excuses. Of all the residents of Henwick, there was only one lady, thus far, whom I wished to know better. But that was an impossible task if she would not, could not, speak. On the short ride home I decided to call at Fern Cottage as soon as I was able. I would employ diverse tactics to engage Miss Rutherford in conversation. If her grandmother prohibited her responses, then I would work to make her blush, for that would be entirely acceptable as well.

## Chapter Six

### MISS ABIGAIL RUTHERFORD

Upon my arrival in Henwick I had felt like a tenuous leaf. Gusts of whispers and hawkish observance waited for my disgraced tongue to provide a bit of entertainment. But after Mr. Mead had welcomed me with his dashing smile, I no longer took notice of the gossips. At least, not so very much.

When Grandmother had first summoned me to join her and Mr. Mead in the sitting room, it had taken a full five minutes for my shock to wear off. The vicar had greeted me with a warm smile and kind conversation, but I hadn't dared reply. When Grandmother answered in my stead, Mr. Mead had simply looked my way, granted me a flash of his dashing smile, and then continued with his next question.

He paid call every Wednesday at precisely three o'clock. I looked forward to his visits, for they provided a welcome reprieve. Not only was his a handsome face, but Grandmother would flit her eyelashes and turn her attentions to him rather than to my poor posture, speech, or presumed lack of intelligence.

And Mr. Mead was kind. Despite the fact that I rarely contributed to conversation, he made subtle references to include me. He would remark how the color of my eyes matched the coat of the fawn he'd seen grazing near the churchyard. Or once, he spoke of how nice it was to have my voice contribute to the congregational hymns sung on the Sabbath. Being noticed was an entirely new sensation, and I enjoyed Mr. Mead's attentions. Beyond that, Grandmother had begun allowing me to contribute to conversation on a more regular basis.

This Wednesday unfolded as any other, until the conversation turned to Mr. Wilkins's arrival. "What is your impression of Cattersley's heir?" Grandmother asked Mr. Mead.

The vicar tsked and raised his dark brow. "My housekeeper, Mrs. Morse, happened upon one of the scullery maids from the estate. Mrs. Morse reports that the girl was not impressed with her new master, especially after he snapped at Mrs. Sommers in front of the kitchen staff."

Contrary words flowed from Mr. Mead's mouth as he told Grandmother of Mr. Wilkins's domineering personality. I tried to remain impassive. During Mr. Mead's visits he oft related tales of others' woes. As I did not know very many people, I had always assumed he spoke the truth; however, his condemnation of Mr. Wilkins's manners seemed unbelievable or, at the very least, exaggerated. Nothing in Mr. Mead's description of the man paralleled the traits I'd witnessed the week before. Beyond Mr. Wilkins's kindness to me, he'd also been kind to Mr. Tucker. Certainly his generosity was not a charade, for Mr. Wilkins had had every reason to chastise me. I'd invaded his home and distracted Mr. Tucker from his duties. Yet Mr. Wilkins had been a perfect gentleman. He had even walked me home, or at least to the end of his property.

Grandmother pointed out the east window. "I've a bit of a view of Cattersley myself." Mr. Mead walked to stand next to her. "See there." She directed the vicar's gaze to the same high rooftop she'd shown me numerous times. Grandmother liked to boast a connection to the grand estate, even if it were only a section of white gable. She left Mr. Mead at the window and returned to her seat next to me on the sofa.

"Mind your posture," Grandmother whispered.

I took a sip of tea, careful not to rattle the cup on the saucer.

"Were you anxious to meet the man, Miss Rutherford?" Mr. Mead asked as he retook his seat.

"I . . . well . . ."

"Speak up, child." Grandmother frowned at me, then turned with a crooked smile to Mr. Mead. If only she would make up her mind. Should I speak or remain silent?

I took a slow breath. I could not reveal that I'd previously spent a very pleasant hour in his company. I selected my words with care. "I found him to be evewyfing a gentleman should be." I blushed at my pronunciation and the way I'd jumbled the other letters together. Grandmother pressed her eyes closed, dropped her head, and sighed. I would do better if she did not put me on the spot. When I had time to prepare my thoughts, I could speak clearly. But she so rarely included me in conversation or expected a reply that I had little practice. Added to that, her expectation of perfection set an impossible standard.

"Well, I hear he is making the rounds to all of the neighbors. I only hope he does not consider Fern Cottage below his new social rank. One moment he's a soldier; the next he's a wealthy heir. No wonder he's high in the step," Mr. Mead said.

Mr. Mead's inclusion of me had led me to believe he varied from the hypocrites I oft witnessed on the Sabbath. But his assessment of Mr. Wilkins directly contrasted what little I knew of Cattersley's heir. I stilled my hands in my lap and slowly vocalized the question floating through my head. "Is there something particular in his behavior that bothered you?"

Mr. Mead straightened in his seat and brushed an imaginary piece of lint from his trousers. "Well, I've not witnessed his loftiness myself, but I understand he was quite curt with Mr. Lane. And I've heard others talk of his self-importance."

My response tumbled unfiltered from my mouth. "I did not think you would give consequence to wumors. Especially after your splendid sermon a few weeks past. What was the quote in Psalms? 'Whoso privily slandereth his neighbor, him will I cut off'?" I was proud I'd only bumbled once.

"'Twas the hundred and first Psalm, and I'm honored that you remember my words, Miss Rutherford." Mr. Mead's tightened jaw contradicted his compliment.

His sermons were always succinct and doctrinally based, but perhaps he needed a further study of the hundred and first Psalm or to revisit the Lord's admonition to judge not. This was a side of the vicar I had not previously witnessed.

I looked to Grandmother. Her lips pinched tight, but I continued to concentrate carefully. "If you recall, my initial introduction in the village was quite tumultuous. I was beyond grateful when you took the time to call upon Grandmother and myself to sort it all out." My words did not stutter, and my chest swelled with gratitude that I could express my thoughts. "Your attentions helped silence many whispers."

Mr. Mead reached across the space between us and covered my hand with his own. "I simply wanted to know you better."

After my blundered introduction to Mr. and Mrs. Thorpe, blatant stares, snide comments, and open speculation had followed our every move. I'd grown accustomed to judgments and misplaced assumptions. Errors in pronunciation did not equate with intelligence. But when others refused to converse on the topic, it was impossible to convince them of their false beliefs. I'd hoped Henwick would be different from Plymouth. After that initial visit to town, I knew it was exactly the same, with whispers meant to be heard, taunts, and jeers. Ever since Mr. Mead's first visit, our forays into the village had improved. I did feel indebted to the man.

His fingers were cold against my skin, and I was grateful for the timely knock at the front door. I pulled my hand from Mr. Mead's and stood. "I'll tend to that."

Mrs. Bearsly was faster. She stood in the doorway gawking at Mr. Wilkins, who looked even more handsome than I remembered. He wore a dark-green jacket of the finest wool atop a cream-colored waistcoat with blue stripes. Dark-brown breeches and black Hessians completed his ensemble. I guessed the garments were new, as they were much finer than the clothing he'd worn upon our first two meetings.

His eyes flicked to mine, and I couldn't help the lift in my heart at the sight of him. "Welcome, Mr. Wilkins," I said. Mrs. Bearsly practically bowed as she stepped aside to allow Mr. Wilkins's entrance.

I led him back into the sitting room. Grandmother and Mr. Mead watched me curiously, but there was no time for them to question me before the man we'd just been discussing stepped fully into view. I wondered for a moment if perhaps his inheritance *had* gone to his head. But when Grandmother welcomed him with barely concealed skepticism and Mr. Wilkins offered a genuine smile and humble reply, I knew my initial impression of the man to be correct.

I'd been an observer for a long time. Sitting on the outskirts had given me practice in deciphering authenticity from flattery. Despite the loftiness of his new wardrobe, Mr. Wilkins's replies rang with sincerity. Mr. Mead, on the other hand, said all the proper things, but his eyes lacked their usual warmth.

Grandmother asked Mrs. Bearsly to prepare a fresh pot of tea. "How gracious of you to pay call to our cottage. We feel honored to be able to gaze upon the great estate of Cattersley." Grandmother walked to the window as she'd done moments earlier and bid Mr. Wilkins to follow. "As you see, we have a view of the house itself."

Mr. Wilkins looked to the place Grandmother indicated. "So you do."

Grandmother seemed appeased by his assessment, and she walked back to her place on the couch. "Please be seated." She indicated a squat armchair, and Mr. Wilkins sat after she had settled herself back beside me.

"If I remember correctly, Lady Marion graciously called at Fern Cottage on occasion," Mr. Mead spoke to Grandmother directly. "One rarely felt themselves beneath her notice."

I inwardly cringed at the vicar's slight, but Mr. Wilkins seemed unaffected. "I am learning a great deal about my aunt. I wish I'd had the opportunity to know her better," he said. "I understand Lady Marion was a great patroness of your parish."

"Indeed she was." Mr. Mead pulled his shoulders taut and raised his neck an inch or so.

"As I meant to call next at Mayview Cottage, perhaps I might ask you now if you would be agreeable in allowing me to continue as benefactor in my late aunt's stead?" Mr. Wilkins leaned back in his chair. He glanced down at his jacket as if just remembering he wore such a fine garment. Then, without pause, he met Mr. Mead's narrowed gaze.

"I find the suggestion quite agreeable, Mr. Wilkins." Mr. Mead leaned forward and lowered his voice to nearly a whisper. "To be honest, I was rather concerned about the matter."

Mr. Wilkins's face revealed nothing; however, his hand wiped across the top of his leg as he leaned forward to match Mr. Mead's posture. "No need for concern, Mr. Mead. Cattersley is prosperous enough to bless us all."

A smile flickered at the edge of my lips. I'd not considered the advantage of Mr. Wilkins's experience on the battlefield. Mr. Mead's playing field was limited to Henwick. He was no match for Mr. Wilkins's wit and subtle intelligence, and I knew if it came to battle, Mr. Mead would lose to the handsome captain every time.

# Chapter Seven

## MR. ROBERT WILKINS

THE OPPORTUNITY TO SEE MISS Rutherford was the only benefit gained from my visit to Fern Cottage. She sat next to her grandmother, quiet and proper, with her hands clasped on her lap. Several times during my short visit, I thought I felt her eyes on me, but when I looked her way, she appeared to be focused on whomever was speaking at the time. I longed to engage her in conversation, but her grandmother and the vicar allowed me no opportunity.

If a prize were given for spewing false platitudes, Mrs. Baker and Mr. Mead would share the reward. The man's dislike of me was evident from the moment I arrived.

Life was both easier and harder in the regiments. A man was judged for his fortitude in battle, his ability to command among chaos, and his willingness to fight alongside his comrades. I'd hoped the same approach might help me gain acceptance in Henwick, but thus far my fortitude was not enough.

I untied Barkley and wedged my left foot into the stirrup, staring at my newly fitted boots. They were far more comfortable than the standard-issue military footwear, yet I longed for the familiarity of my old, dusty, worn boots.

After hoisting myself into the saddle, I began the ride back to Cattersley. I thought I could make Lady Marion proud, that I could discover the reason she'd chosen me to follow in her benevolent footsteps. But I floundered like a fish in a net, not certain how to function or even fill my lungs with oxygen. Perhaps life as a distinguished gentleman was beyond my reach.

Guilt loomed like the summer clouds overhead. What sort of man would wish away such vast wealth? I kicked Barkley into a trot, determined to stop brooding and make the most of my great-aunt's gift. She'd trusted me to carry on her legacy, to respect her title, and to nurture her home. I gripped the reins tightly in my hand and determined then and there that I would meet the challenge head-on.

I spent the next few days with my steward, Horton, reviewing accounts and familiarizing myself with the goings-on at Cattersley. He was a middle-aged man who had served Lady Marion faithfully for the last fifteen years. His guidance and knowledge proved invaluable. At Manning's insistence, Graham also fitted me for an additional nine jackets: a hunting jacket, a new greatcoat, a dinner jacket, formal wear, and numerous colored garments for daily wear. When I questioned the need for such an expansive wardrobe, Manning simple pushed up on his toes, narrowed his eyes, and told Graham to continue his task.

Thankfully, when my mother and sister arrived the following week, Manning's stern demeanor softened. While I'd lived independent of my mother for the last twelve of my twenty-eight years, her presence brought a measure of solace.

"My memories did not do justice to the grandeur of Cattersley." Mother stood with Hazel and me on the terrace, looking over Tucker's masterpiece gardens.

"It is overwhelming," I admitted.

"La! It's a dream," Hazel said and clasped her fingers together in delight.

Mother placed her hand on my sleeve. "It is all very new. Lady Marion was a wise woman, and I've no doubt she named you as her heir for a reason."

"We'd never shared so much as a conversation." I inhaled deeply.

"You'll be splendid, Robert." Hazel skipped to my side. "You're sensible and hardworking."

"I believe you are referring to our elder brother," I said and winked at Hazel.

"John works hard as well, but his temper flares far too often," Hazel said. She gave me a knowing look. We'd both witnessed John's foul moods.

Mother did not acknowledge Hazel's comment beyond a soft tsk. "Each of you children has different strengths. Your father oft spoke of how proud he was of all of you, and I quite agree. Cattersley simply provides a new opportunity for you, Robert. The livelihoods of many depend on you, and I have no doubt you will rise to the occasion."

That was exactly what I feared. The war with Napoleon had forced decisions based on the good of England. Men's lives had been in my hands.

Many had died. But they'd given their lives for the cause of freedom. When confronted with a madman intent to take over the world, my commands had come of necessity. Now lives again depended on me. Children, women, and the men who loved them depended on the crop yield, the negotiations and decisions I would make, and the rain I could not control.

Hazel swayed her hips and somehow managed to shrug her shoulders gracefully. "Perhaps you would like someone to assist in the running of the household." She batted her eyelashes prettily.

I looked skyward and heaved an exaggerated sigh. "I've no idea whom I could burden with such a task."

"Robert!" Hazel's lips pressed into a pout. "You are teasing me."

I chuckled.

Mother smiled. "Managing a household of Cattersley's size will take far more exertion than your current pursuits, Hazel. Are you certain you're up to the task?"

Hazel's eyes widened. "I can work just as hard as my brothers. I am not lazy, Mother." She turned her nose up and huffed as she crossed her arms.

Mother laughed and slipped her arm around Hazel's. "That you are not. Only consider how the management of Cattersley would hinder your current pursuits. You may scarce find time for your music."

"Not to mention your pursuit of a husband," I added.

Hazel leaned toward me. "That is none of your concern, Robert." Then she spun back to Mother. "And my newest composition is nearly complete." Hazel took a deep breath, then another. Her shoulders relaxed. She stepped away from Mother and turned around to admire the grand home. A smile touched her lips. "Besides, if I can manage Cattersley, it will show any potential suiters that I am capable of running a home." She looked back at me. "What say you, Robert? May I try?"

"You are in earnest?" I asked. Hazel nodded quickly, her curls bouncing on her head. "Very well." She clapped her hands, and I held up a finger in warning. "Only if Mrs. Sommers agrees and you will allow her and Mother to mentor you."

"I will. Oh, thank you, Robert." Hazel pressed up on her toes and kissed my cheek.

"'Tis only a trial, Hazel." I tried to sound firm, but my lips twitched. It seemed I could not maintain my military bearing with my sister.

Hazel poked a finger against my chest. "Which I will pass with top marks."

I looked over the gardens again. A familiar black bonnet peeked just above the boxwood hedge before turning left and disappearing from my sight. I extended my arm to my mother. "Would you care for a closer look?"

"I'll need to retrieve my bonnet," Mother said.

"Very well. I'll wait here while you and Hazel gather your things." I glanced toward the boxwood in vain. Miss Rutherford had not reappeared.

"And then you'll talk to Mrs. Sommers?" Hazel asked.

I agreed to Hazel's request, and the moment Mother and Hazel stepped inside, I hurried down the steps toward where I'd last seen Miss Rutherford. Giddy anticipation, like that of a schoolboy at Christmas, pulsed through me. I rounded the boxwood, then the lily garden, and then the roses. I didn't have much time before Mother and Hazel reappeared and questioned my absence. I circled the hanging honeysuckle arch, noting the sweet fragrance and the lack of Miss Rutherford's familiar face. Where could she have gone? The greenhouse, perhaps?

The greenhouse was on the far side of the gardens. I would not have time to investigate and return to Mother. It took only a moment to devise an acceptable solution. Mother and Hazel would investigate with me. It seemed some command decisions were easier to make than others.

I retrieved the women, and together we ventured into the gardens. Mother held my arm. Hazel preferred to offer a close inspection of every variety of bush and bloom and so skirted around us as we walked down the path. I did not reveal our destination. Subtlety was vital in battle.

The greenhouse came into view, but the sound of voices rang from our right. I led Mother and a flitting Hazel toward the conversation.

"So I want to trim here?" Miss Rutherford's voice rang sweetly.

"Precisely. Now, see? The new shoot will grow here." We rounded a shaped hedge and came upon Tucker and Miss Rutherford. Felton was working nearby, digging about the base of a neighboring rosebush.

Tucker spotted us first. "Mr. Wilkins." He nearly jumped to attention. Felton climbed out from under the bush and stood, brushing his hands against his trousers.

Miss Rutherford straightened as well. Rather than the pleased expression I'd hoped for, her eyes widened, and this time she used Tucker's form to shield herself.

"Hello, Miss Rutherford. Tucker. Felton. May I introduce you to my mother, Mrs. Geraldine Wilkins, and my sister, Miss Hazel Wilkins?" I motioned to each in turn, then looked at Mother. "Tucker is the gardener, Felton is the undergardener, and Miss Rutherford is our neighbor."

Miss Rutherford curtsied, and Felton remained behind and offered a simple bow. Tucker pulled his cap from his head, turning it in his hands as he also bowed forward. "How do you do, madam? Miss Wilkins?"

Mother smiled in her graceful way. "Are you responsible for these splendid gardens?" she asked.

Tucker's mouth twitched with a barely suppressed smile, and a flush of red moved up his neck. "Felton and I do our best, madam. I'm glad you are pleased."

"Your work is beyond pleasing, Mr. Tucker. Surely the heavens approve of your masterpiece." Tucker's flush spread to his cheeks at Mother's compliment.

Hazel leaned her head to peek around Tucker's shoulder. "And how do you do, Miss Rutherford?"

Miss Rutherford looked at me. Her posture reminded me of a frightened rabbit. She clearly wished to be anywhere other than under the scrutiny of my sister.

"Miss Rutherford lives in a nearby cottage," I offered, and Miss Rutherford quickly nodded her head in agreement.

"Truly?" Hazel asked. "In which direction is your home?" Hazel began scanning the horizon as if she could see the silhouette of Fern Cottage from her vantage point. She had yet to comprehend the massiveness of the estate.

Miss Rutherford swallowed and raised her hand to point west.

Hazel was gracious and kind, but her confusion at Miss Rutherford's lack of words surfaced on her face for a quick moment before she reschooled her features. Gratefully, Mother drew our attention back to her. "Miss Rutherford, do you reside with your family?"

Miss Rutherford's brow furrowed. She spoke slowly. "My parents have both passed. My brother has sailed to America, and my sister is a governess in Plymouth. I live with my grandmother."

"You have been fortunate to live so close and enjoy the pleasure of these gardens." Mother was ever so tactful. She turned to Tucker. "I'm sure I will spend many hours wandering the flowered paths."

Miss Rutherford nodded her head once before looking at Tucker and giving him a pretty smile. "I should be on my way." She lifted her dark hem away from the dirt where she stood and curtsied to Mother, Hazel, and me.

She took a step away, and the commander in me wanted to order her to stop. Thankfully, my mother's breeding superseded my military training, and instead of shouting a command, I spoke her name at a rational level. "Miss Rutherford?" She paused and turned toward me. "Next Wednesday evening I'm hosting a dinner to introduce my mother and sister to my neighbors. Will you and your grandmother attend?"

Miss Rutherford's eyes lit for only a moment before she began to shake her head. "My grandmother . . ."

Understanding dawned. Mrs. Baker remained unaware of Miss Rutherford's visits to Cattersley. My recent introduction to the woman was enough for me to know Miss Rutherford could not reveal her secret without repercussion; therefore, she could not extend the invitation herself. "Would it be suitable to call later this week to issue the invitation?"

Miss Rutherford's lips turned up in a genuine smile. It was a moment of contentment, when the clouds parted to reveal sunshine. "Indeed," she said. "It's been a pleasure, Mrs. Wilkins. Miss Wilkins." Then she turned and hurried on her way.

# Chapter Eight

### MISS ABIGAIL RUTHERFORD

DINNER? AT CATTERSLEY? WOULD MR. Wilkins truly come and extend the invitation? Of course he would. He was a gentleman of the best sort. I'd observed enough men to know. Not only had Mother interpreted my faulty speech as stupidity but men did as well. And a stupid girl made for easy prey. Fortunately, I'd escaped the unwanted advances of Father's and Benjamin's friends. Simply faking a cough and then rehearsing how the doctor had assured me the cough would clear, along with my contagious rash, had quelled the lust in their eyes. All but once.

Mr. Thatcher had been too drunk for any words to halt his wandering hands. Thankfully, I'd been able to prevent the situation from growing dire. I'd been grateful for Benjamin's brief belief that he might pursue a study of medicine, for I'd read every book I could find, including his text on human physiology that had explained the sensitive points of both male and female anatomy. A swift knee to Mr. Thatcher's groin had put an end to that encounter, and the man had never bothered me again.

When Mr. Mead arrived for tea on Wednesday, it was a welcome relief. For the entirety of the morning Grandmother had Craven swapping tables of every size and shape in a space near the stairs. She'd given so many demands that I was impressed she had not lost her voice. I was even more impressed that Craven chose to remain in Grandmother's employment.

Grandmother settled on a small two-door rosewood chest with claw feet. She had dismissed Craven only moments before Mr. Mead's arrival. The vicar boasted his usual handsome smile, and my nerves began to settle.

Mrs. Bearsly served tea and lemon tarts. I indulged in the sweet pastry, for the dear woman did not make them often. Mr. Mead covered all the topics of pleasantry and complimented Mrs. Bearsly's tarts. "You seem to enjoy them," he said to me.

I licked the flaky crumbs from my lips and nodded. Grandmother scowled, and I ducked my head. I liked the tarts; should I not get to enjoy them? Silence cocooned us until impatience triumphed.

"Have you yet prepared your sermon?" I asked Mr. Mead.

Grandmother's raised eyebrows confirmed her discontent, but I'd asked nothing improper. In fact, it was a question she posed on a weekly basis.

Mr. Mead cleared his throat and set aside his teacup. "I have."

I smiled and straightened in my seat. "And what will you be pweaching about?" I clasped my hands in frustration at my skewed letters.

Mr. Mead stretched his neck. A muscle in his jaw twitched, and he then resumed his smile. "My discourse is taken from the book of Matthew, chapter thirteen."

"One of the parables, then?" I asked, and Mr. Mead's brows rose. I continued slowly. "That particular chapter offers quite a selection of the Lord's teachings."

"You know this?" Mr. Mead's shock was evident.

"Yes." I smiled and continued to concentrate on my words. "My love for reading provides ample opportunity to read the Bible. I am quite familiar with its teachings."

Mr. Mead crossed his left leg over the opposite knee. "This is splendid news indeed." He glanced at Grandmother, who was busy pouring a second cup of tea. He then turned and winked at me. My stomach tumbled, and my cheeks warmed. Did he mean to flirt?

Grandmother sat back in her seat with her beverage and sighed loudly. "Yes, reading is how Abigail passes much of her day—her books and her walks."

"Both commendable leisure pursuits," Mr. Mead said. "And you are indeed correct. I have written my sermon specifically to the parable of the wheat and the tares. I fear there are those who would sow the tares among us. I hope to admonish the congregation to not be deceived."

"Very admirable of you, Mr. Mead. Admirable indeed." Grandmother sipped her tea.

"I think it is important that we do not assume those around us wish us well," Mr. Mead said.

Grandmother set her cup on the table beside her and cut in. "The devil in sheep's clothing—you've spoken on that before." She wagged her finger.

I thought on the analogy. It was one I'd always found difficult to relate to. Certainly the idea was sound, but I believed that even dressed in fluffy wool, it would be quite easy to discern the devil from a ewe. When I opened my mouth to share my observation, a knock sounded at the door.

I recognized the gentleman's voice at once. Mr. Wilkins. He held true to his word. And he was not alone. Mrs. Bearsly announced Mr. Wilkins and his sister. We stood when he walked in the door, and his eyes immediately found mine. He turned to Grandmother and bowed in greeting. "Lovely to see you again, Mrs. Baker. Miss Rutherford." Then he turned to Mr. Mead and granted him the same courtesy.

Grandmother placed her closed fist against her chest. "Mr. Wilkins, I did not expect you would return to our humble home."

Mr. Wilkins pulled his gloves from his hands and then motioned to his sister. "My sister arrived on Monday, and I wished to introduce her to you and your granddaughter. Mrs. Baker, Miss Rutherford, Mr. Mead, may I introduce my sister, Miss Hazel Wilkins?"

Grandmother blinked wide and fingered the beaded necklace she wore as she dipped into a curtsy. Miss Wilkins's blonde hair matched her brother's. Her eyes held more green than blue, but they were happy and bright. "How do you do, Mrs. Baker? I'm so pleased to make your acquaintance." She curtsied gracefully. "Robert told me about your lovely property, and I just had to see it for myself." Her flattery quelled Grandmother's fluttering.

Miss Wilkins turned to Mr. Mead and curtsied. "I very much look forward to your discourse on Sunday. I've been told you speak very eloquently." Miss Wilkins grinned at her brother before turning back to Mr. Mead.

Mr. Mead bowed his head, then stood tall. "I am indeed blessed to be able to share the Lord's good word. I hope I shall meet your expectations."

Miss Wilkins then looked at me. "And Miss Rutherford, what a pleasure to meet you." She curtsied again to me. Her impressive performance caught me off guard. Grandmother cleared her throat, and I bent my knees to curtsy in return. When I raised my eyes back to hers, Miss Wilkins smiled mischievously. "I begged Robert to find me a friend. Please forgive my presumption." She stepped forward, grabbed my hands, and held them between us. "I do hope we can be dear friends, Miss Rutherford. I plan to remain at Cattersley for a long while, and Robert will only entertain me for so long." She grinned at her brother over her shoulder before turning back to me. "What do you say, Miss Rutherford? Can we be friends?"

I liked her forward demeanor, and even more, I liked the fact that she did not let my lack of conversation at our earlier meeting deter her enthusiasm. "I would like that," I said.

"You don't know how pleased that makes me." Miss Wilkins dropped my hands and returned to her brother's side.

Mr. Wilkins chuckled softly and turned to Grandmother. "We also came to extend an invitation to a dinner party for you and Miss Rutherford." Turning to the vicar, he continued. "We are making the rounds to all of our neighbors. You, of course, are included in the invitation, Mr. Mead. We hope an evening of dinner and cards will help us become better acquainted with everyone."

Grandmother studiously watched the vicar. Only once he accepted the invitation did she.

Miss Wilkins clapped her hands together. "Oh, I can hardly wait!"

Mr. Wilkins grinned at his sister before turning his bright eyes on me. My lungs refused to function as he held my gaze. It seemed that an entire hour passed in that moment, and I did not suffer for want of air. The pulsing of my heart was enough to sustain me.

Mr. Mead coughed, and the sound pulled Mr. Wilkins's eyes away. Mr. Wilkins turned his attention to where his sister had placed her hand on his sleeve.

Miss Wilkins tilted her head, evaluating her brother. "Shall we continue our calls?"

"Of course." Mr. Wilkins bowed to Grandmother, myself, then Mr. Mead. "We shall take our leave."

Mr. Mead and I retook our seats and remained in the sitting room while Grandmother escorted our guests to the door. When she returned, she crossed one arm across her stomach and pressed her other hand to her collarbone. "Well, that was unexpected," she said.

Mr. Mead looked at me. His eyes narrowed in calculation. "Yes," he said. The single word sounded more like a curse. "Unexpected indeed."

He took his leave shortly after, and for the first time since my arrival to Fern Cottage, I was happy to be left alone with Grandmother.

# Chapter Nine

## MR. ROBERT WILKINS

I'D TOLD MOTHER AND HAZEL very little about the residents of Henwick. I'd introduced my family to the household staff, and beyond our visits to extend invitations to dinner, the majority of our time had been spent at the estate. We'd also taken a quick trip to town, where Mother had met a widow named Mrs. Christiansen. They'd formed an immediate friendship, and I'd insisted Mrs. Christiansen join our dinner party.

Our arrival at church caused quite the tumult. It reminded me of my first visit to the parish. Mother met the stares with confidence, her chin held high and a gentle smile on her face. Hazel's confidence faltered. There was a slight tremor in her hands, and her usually rosy cheeks now reminded me of a snow-topped hill. She followed Mother and me to the Cattersley bench, and before she sat, she noticed Miss Rutherford and gave a small wave.

Miss Rutherford smiled back, and with Hazel's next breath, the tension in her shoulders released. Mead pontificated on Christ's parable of the wheat and the tares, and while I wondered at the gentleman's cold reception in personal conversation, I found no fault with his sermon.

Mother met Mrs. Christiansen after the service, and they walked arm in arm out the door. I began to follow but was stopped by Mr. Adams. "Cheers, Wilkins. Say, do you plan to continue Lady Marion's tradition of hosting a pheasant hunt for the local gentry?"

The Adamses had been quick to introduce themselves. Mr. Adams had called two days after my arrival to welcome me, and when I returned the call, I'd met his wife and daughter. Miss Adams was a pretty girl. Her features were sharp, similar to her father's, but she had her mother's almond-shaped brown eyes. She'd also inherited her mother's ability to smile constantly, regardless of the conversation.

"Won't you do us the honor of dining with us?" Mrs. Adams had asked, but I'd been unable to do so, as I'd had an appointment with Horton.

Hazel and I had called upon the Adamses after our visit at Fern Cottage. Miss Adams's smile had grown wide as she flitted about and served the tea. "I've been so excited to meet you, Miss Wilkins," Miss Adams had said.

Hazel had been everything polite but did not return the exuberance Miss Adams had heaped upon her. "She wore the same expression for the entirety of our visit," Hazel had later confided. "I cannot discern whether her sentiment was real. In truth, I find her constant jollity a bit frightening."

I had not wanted to sway Hazel's impression and so had said nothing. Now, as Mr. Adams stood in the aisle of the church and proceeded to give a detailed description of the previous year's hunt, I noticed his daughter moving to approach Hazel.

Miss Adams greeted Hazel with a boisterous laugh, touching her shoulder and smiling wide. Hazel stood like a startled deer. I prepared to excuse myself from Mr. Adams's description of the colored armbands Lady Marion used to separate the hunters into teams to make the hunt a fun-spirited competition, but I halted when Miss Rutherford approached my sister.

She curtsied to both Hazel and Miss Adams, and a genuine smile spread over Hazel's face as Miss Rutherford said something. Miss Adams smiled, but it appeared to be forced, for her eyes had narrowed and she focused solely on Miss Rutherford's mouth.

I numbly acknowledged something Mr. Adams said, and he launched into admonishment of how best to word invitations for the hunt, if I should choose to follow in my aunt's fine footsteps.

Across the room, Hazel dipped her head, then slipped her arm through Miss Rutherford's, and the two of them left Miss Adams standing alone with a pasted smile on her face. I knew my fledgling reputation in Henwick could not survive a scuffle with one of the county's most prosperous families, but my gratitude for Miss Rutherford swelled. I excused myself from conversation with Mr. and Mrs. Adams, promising to give consideration to their recommendations.

I found Hazel and Miss Rutherford standing with Mother and Mrs. Christiansen near the coach. All four women were valiantly trying to suppress their giggles, but with Mrs. Christiansen's next words, laughter rang out.

I soaked in the sound. "I regret I am not privy to your great joke," I said, stepping near my mother.

She pulled out her fan and began to wave it rapidly near her face. "Mrs. Christiansen was telling us about her late husband's aversion to crickets."

"Crickets?" I repeated, and all four women burst into another fit of laughter.

Mrs. Christiansen laid a hand on my arm. "Not to worry, Mr. Wilkins. At the suggestion of my lady's maid, we acquired four kittens. The cricket invasion did not last long against the felines."

"Oh dear." Mother closed her fan and sighed. "Thank you for the jovial tale. May we see you home?" she asked Mrs. Christiansen.

"Abigail!" Mrs. Baker's voice shook the smile from Miss Rutherford's face. The older woman bustled over. "There you are, child. I've been looking everywhere for you." Mrs. Baker seemed to realize she had an audience. "Oh, gracious," she said as her cheeks colored.

"Good day, Mrs. Baker," I said. "May I introduce you to my mother, Mrs. Geraldine Wilkins? You are acquainted with Mrs. Christiansen and my sister."

"How do you do?" Mrs. Baker curtsied, then stood, twisting her hands. "I'm sorry for Abigail's intrusion. She knows it is best if she remains with me." Mrs. Baker's pinched scowl and look of reprimand did not go unnoticed.

Mother's chin raised only a fraction, but it was enough. Mrs. Baker took a half step backward. "Miss Rutherford is a delight," Mother said.

Hazel grabbed Miss Rutherford's hand and squeezed before releasing it. "Thank you for your kindness today, Miss Rutherford. I shall call upon you soon." Hazel's smile fell, and she turned toward Mrs. Baker. "If that would be acceptable to you, of course."

Mrs. Baker fingered the pendant of her necklace. "Yes . . . yes, of course you may call. It would be an honor, Miss Wilkins." Her lips pushed up in a limp smile as she looked at each of us in turn. "Come, Abigail. Mr. Mead has offered to escort us home." Miss Rutherford joined her grandmother, and they walked back toward the church. That man seemed to be present wherever Miss Rutherford was. I watched Mead greet the women; Mrs. Baker began talking at once, and Miss Rutherford remained silent beside her. Mead motioned toward the road, and when he touched Miss Rutherford's elbow, my spine stiffened and I had the oddest desire to march forward and forcefully remove Mead's hand from Miss Rutherford's arm.

"Robert?" Mother called.

I inhaled deeply and turned to assist Mother, Hazel, and Mrs. Christiansen into the Cattersley carriage. Once the coachman urged the horses forward, Hazel leaned near and whispered in my ear, "I'm exceedingly fond of Miss Rutherford."

I spoke quietly, matching Hazel's hushed tone. "I am still coming to know her, but from what little I know, life has not been easy for her."

"Mrs. Baker seems incredibly difficult to please." Hazel pursed her lips. "I think it would be difficult to be so removed from my siblings, yet Miss Rutherford has endured it well."

"Indeed. She retains a smile and a happy countenance. Besides that, she seems to possess a keen mind." The lady's traits continued to impress, but I could not shake from my mind the image of Mead guiding her to the road.

"Don't forget she is quite adorable," Hazel added with a mischievous smile. "I think you are exceedingly fond of her as well."

I cleared my throat. "I wonder if she has an attachment with the vicar."

"Mr. Mead?" Hazel exclaimed before clamping a hand over her mouth. Gratefully, our timely arrival at Mrs. Christiansen's home prohibited the matrons from questioning her outburst.

"He is handsome," Hazel whispered near my ear. "But no." She shook her head. "Miss Rutherford's eyes light when you are near. She does not have the same reaction to Mr. Mead. I think you are only jealous." Hazel crossed her arms and offered a look of challenge.

I knew I admired Abigail. Her rescue of Hazel from Miss Adams warmed my heart, as did her sweet disposition. And the realization had surprised me. Only a number of months before I had courted a lovely woman, Miss Leah Hastings, with the intent of asking her to be my wife. However, when her childhood sweetheart realized he might lose her, he'd confessed his love, and the two were due to be married in a few short weeks.

Miss Hastings had not intended to slight me. In fact, it was I who'd ended our courtship. I could see her feelings for her now-fiancé and knew I could never hold her heart as strongly as he did. Thus, I'd walked away and left them to their happily ever after.

I'd learned two things from that experience. First, I'd decided marriage would suit me. Many of my fellow soldiers had sworn off the ritual, claiming eternal bachelorhood instead. But I thought I would like the companionship of a partner committed to our union and our future family. Marriage would require more effort than bachelorhood, but I'd never been one to shy away from hard work.

Second, I would never ask someone to be my wife who did not utterly adore me. Selfish? Yes. But such devotion would make life much simpler and certainly more joyful. I'd seen too much hate and devastation in my short time upon the earth. I had no desire to battle emotions and jealousy in my marriage. Wanting peace, bliss, happiness did not seem too much to require. When I asked for a lady's hand, I intended to make sure she gave it freely, gave herself freely, and was as devoted to our union as I would be.

I stepped from the carriage to assist Mrs. Christiansen and tried to shake off my sister's words, but the pull in my gut confirmed that Hazel's assertion was absolutely true. I *was* jealous of the vicar, for I wanted to claim all of Miss Rutherford's attention for myself.

# Chapter Ten

### MISS ABIGAIL RUTHERFORD

TUESDAY MORNING, AFTER HELPING MRS. Bearsly weed the vegetable garden, I carefully re-pinned my hair and changed into a clean dress. Not long after I'd finished, I heard voices downstairs. Mrs. Bearsly appeared as I left my room and informed me that Grandmother wished for my presence in the sitting room. I'd awaited Miss Wilkins's promised visit eagerly, and I secretly hoped her brother would call with her.

My smile spread too wide for such a simple occasion, but it could not be helped. Mr. Wilkins's handsome appearance and kind demeanor stirred plenty of happy feelings each time I saw him, and beyond that, he noticed things. He noticed me. And his sister seemed sincere in her request for friendship. It warmed my heart, for I had not had someone to call a dear friend since I was last with my sister.

Mr. Wilkins did not chastise my reticence. He never chided me for my poor pronunciation; rather, he directed questions and conversation so I might be included. Louisa was the only other person who had ever treated me as an equal, and now she was far, far away.

I whispered my list of words to myself as I made my way down the stairs. "Grandmother, brother, broom, marriage . . ." The very thought of a happily ever after brought a smile to my lips.

I skipped down the final step and entered the sitting room. My elation deflated as I saw Mr. Mead, not Miss Wilkins and her brother, sitting across from Grandmother. My step faltered, but practicing my words paid off. "Good afternoon, Mr. Mead." I dipped into a curtsy, wondering what would require the vicar to call a day early.

He stood and bowed. "Miss Rutherford. You look especially lovely today."

"Thank you, sir." At least my efforts to look presentable were noticed. "To what do we owe the pleasure of your company?"

Mr. Mead retook his seat, and I moved to the worn armchair, although Grandmother had had Craven move it last week, so it now sat opposite the couch and nearly beside Mr. Mead.

"I've just heard the most unsettling bit of news," Mr. Mead said.

This piqued Grandmother's interest. "Indeed?"

Mr. Mead scooted forward to the very edge of his seat. "Were you aware that Miss Wilkins plans to remain at Cattersley and assume Lady Marion's role in running the great house?" When Mr. Mead's eyebrows shot to his hairline, his handsome features contorted. "The girl is merely a fresh debutante. What experience does she have with such things?"

Grandmother placed a hand at the base of her neck. "I cannot say. She seems eager enough. Tell me, Mr. Mead, what do you make of it? Do you still plan to join the dinner party?" Grandmother asked. Despite his perceived misgivings, I knew Mr. Mead would never turn down such an invitation.

"Certainly I shall attend. It will be Miss Wilkins's first event as hostess. We will see if she is up for the task, though it is quite bold of her to presume she is prepared for the great responsibility of running Cattersley. Perhaps naivety is a family trait." Mr. Mead leaned back in his seat and crossed one leg over the other.

I remained quiet. Grandmother and Mr. Mead discussed who else might be in attendance, and I mentally added my name to the list.

When Mr. Mead stood to leave, I stood with him, but Grandmother remained in her seat.

"Abigail, would you please see Mr. Mead out? I'm afraid I have overextended myself today," she said.

I nodded in response to Grandmother's request and wordlessly led Mr. Mead to the entrance. I pulled the door open and turned to find Mr. Mead standing too close, with a wide grin spread across his face.

"Thank you for being so hospitable, Miss Rutherford. I find I quite look forward to our visits." Mr. Mead leaned forward, forcing me to press my back against the wall.

His eyes met mine, and my stomach stumbled, along with my words. "Thank you for coming today," I said, dropping letters and sounds in every word.

In one swift move, Mr. Mead scooped up my hand and raised it to his lips. He pressed a soft kiss to my bare skin. "Until next time." He looked at me with a twitch of a smile before releasing his hold. Then he placed his hat atop his head and stepped out the door.

My mouth hung ajar, and a full minute passed before I regained my senses and closed the door. I stared at the place Mr. Mead had kissed. What did his actions mean? The vicar had always been kind in his attentions, but I knew this was more. Did he wish to deepen our acquaintance? I couldn't decide if I liked the feel of his kiss or if I wished to wipe it from my hand.

"Abigail," Grandmother called. "Where have you gone?"

"I'm here." I returned to the sitting room but stood unconsciously tracing the back of my hand with my finger.

Grandmother looked me over with a huff. "Well, don't just stand there. Come pick up your needlework." She collected her sampler, and I slowly gathered mine before sitting again.

I absentmindedly picked at a knot in my work, my mind feeling as tangled as the threads. My walks frequently included daydreams of a handsome man flirting or sharing furtive glances with me. I sometimes imagined my heart set aflutter with a wink or gentle touch exactly like the way Mr. Mead had just taken my hand. But as I analyzed my feelings, I knew my heart had not fluttered. Mr. Mead's touch was neither cold nor hot, and I was more shocked by his actions than gratified. And should I not be flattered by such a gesture?

I rethreaded my needle and pulled the pink thread through the fabric. The mindless action appeased my grandmother, but my mind was far away from my stitches. Tomorrow was the appointed dinner at Cattersley. My anticipation for the event had grown as the day neared. I'd thought on what to wear, how to arrange my hair, and how Mr. Wilkins's kind words might send a blush to my cheeks. It was the handsome captain I pictured in my mind, not the vicar. Never before today had I felt awkward in Mr. Mead's presence, but after his overly friendly farewell, I knew I would not feel at ease when I saw him on the morrow.

Rather than being able to experience an evening filled with laughter and friendship, I would now spend the time observing Mr. Mead's every word and action. I would not be able to simply enjoy my first opportunity to enter the grand doors of Cattersley. Whether the vicar intended his simple kiss to prelude something more or intended nothing by it, I did not know. But now that it had happened, Mr. Mead's actions changed everything. And I found I quite resented him for it.

I attempted three different coifs before finally settling on a simpler arrangement with two braids twined into a knot on my head. I was quite skilled at styling hair. I'd been doing it my entire life. Given the apathy of my parents, I'd often taken solace in the room I'd shared with Louisa. I read and, on occasion, practiced styling my hair and hers.

Only once before had I asked Grandmother if I might wear half-mourning attire. She had never answered beyond a scathing glare. It seemed dinner at Cattersley had changed her mind, however, and I was grateful, for black and gray were such dreary colors. I hadn't attended many private functions—certainly nothing as fine as dinner at Cattersley was sure to be—and I was grateful when Grandmother ordered Mrs. Bearsly to lay out my lavender gown.

I had just finished dressing when Grandmother knocked on my door and then entered. "Mr. Mead will be escorting us to dinner this evening." She looked over my person. "Ensure you are prompt, and do not embarrass me tonight." This announcement added to my trepidation, but it was better to allow Mr. Mead's escort than to fake an illness and forgo the event.

I smoothed my hands over my skirts and, with a deep breath, concentrated as I spoke. "I shall do my best to not embarrass you, Grandmother."

Despite my proper pronunciation, Grandmother scowled. "Perhaps it is best if you do not speak at all. I would insist you stay behind if Miss Wilkins had not invited you as her particular friend."

"I will make you proud, Grandmother." It was a promise I intended to keep.

Mr. Mead's carriage was stuffy and smelled of the pomade he'd applied generously to his hair, but thankfully, Cattersley was only a short distance away. I exited last, and Mr. Mead held my hand for much longer than necessary. I deeply breathed in the fresh evening air and pulled my fingers away. "Thank you," I said.

Mr. Mead inclined his head and then offered his arm. He did not comment on my reluctance but stood, with his handsome smile, waiting for my fingers to cover his sleeve.

"Go on, Abigail!" Grandmother waved for me to accept the invitation.

My appetite fled as I slipped my arm through Mr. Mead's. Perhaps I would not have to fake an illness after all. I truly did not feel well.

With another deep breath, I looked forward, determined to enjoy the blessing of being included this evening. I'd memorized the layout of the doorways, windows, and gables from the vantage of the gardens, but I'd yet to examine the front facade. The absolute splendor stole my breath. The setting sun cast pale orange light on the stone walls, bathing them in a welcoming warmth. Windows speckled the building upward, including one set of glass panes that appeared to rise two stories high and another that had been set with a colorful flowered mosaic.

I could have stared for another hour, but Mr. Mead tightened his hold and led me to the massive front door. We walked up the steps to where a footman greeted us. The young man stood ramrod straight and looked directly forward, avoiding eye contact. I had the strangest urge to whisper a joke into his ear, but instead I simply smiled in greeting as we walked past.

As another footman took our things, Grandmother leaned close. "Remember, not a word."

Mr. Mead offered his arm again, and we were led to a finely appointed drawing room—the very room I'd admired from the outside, with the tall, soaring windows. My eyes traced them to the high ceiling and followed the intricate carvings in the dark wood that circled the room. Grandmother hissed from beside me, and I snapped my eyes forward. I realized we'd been announced, and numerous faces now watched us. I found Mr. Wilkins at once. He wore a fine black jacket and matching pantaloons, with a striped waistcoat. His simple look varied greatly from Mr. Mead's dark-maroon jacket and brown pantaloons, and I thought his subtle dress matched his personality.

Mr. Mead smiled widely, and his neck seemed to lengthen as he dropped my arm. His thick dark hair was slicked back with so much pomade that it hardly moved as he bowed to the room.

Miss Wilkins stepped forward, dressed in a lovely pale-blue gown. "Welcome to Cattersley," she said.

Mr. Wilkins joined his sister. "Good evening, Mead, Mrs. Baker, Miss Rutherford." When he said my name, he captured my gaze and did not look away.

I curtsied, hoping the warmth spreading to my cheeks was not apparent.

Grandmother curtsied also. "Thank you for the thoughtful invitation. And thank you for offering the use of your carriage."

I startled and looked at Grandmother. I was unaware of Mr. Wilkins's offer.

"Alas, there was no need, as I'd made arrangements to accompany Mrs. Baker and Miss Rutherford," Mr. Mead said. "I consider their comfort my duty."

"You are very good to us." Grandmother beamed at the vicar. "Abigail and I are in your debt."

Miss Wilkins glanced at her brother. His jaw tightened, and his piercing gaze landed on Mr. Mead. Miss Wilkins's lips twitched. "Mrs. Baker, you look lovely in blue. Wherever did you find such a beautiful shade?"

"Mr. Thorpe ordered it from London at the request of his wife," Grandmother said, clearly pleased by Miss Wilkins's praise. "She has a keen eye for such things. I often wish I could go to Town, if simply to peruse the dressmakers."

In the course of her compliment and Grandmother's response, Miss Wilkins somehow made her way to my side. "I should like to meet Mrs. Thorpe," she said. "Mother promised me a new gown. Perhaps Mrs. Thorpe may recommend something equally divine for me." Miss Wilkins looped her arm through mine and gave a gentle squeeze. She turned to Mr. Wilkins, Mr. Mead, and Grandmother. "Please excuse Miss Rutherford and me. I wish to introduce her to our other guests." I found myself pulled away before Grandmother could utter a reply.

Once there was some distance between myself and the vicar, my stomach began to settle. I dared a glance over my shoulder and was surprised to see Grandmother's lips lifted in a smile. My excitement plunged as truth sank in: the thought of Miss Wilkins befriending me pleased Grandmother. To be welcome guests at Cattersley, to form any kind of attachment to the estate or the owner, would elevate Grandmother's pull in Society. Even in her small social circle, boasting such a thing placed her as chief among a ring of gossips. The thought boiled my blood. Grandmother thought only of the benefit to herself, not the joy I felt to be wanted as a friend. Such feelings of inclusion were entirely new to me.

Miss Wilkins introduced me to Mr. and Mrs. Lane, whom I had seen numerous times at church. The Lanes spent summers at their nearby estate, Mortley Manor. Next I met Mr. Horton, who served as Mr. Wilkins's steward, and Mr. Edwards, who was spending the summer at his family's hunting lodge on the far side of Henwick. We gave only a brief greeting to

Miss Adams before moving to converse with Mrs. Wilkins and the widowed Mrs. Christiansen, whom I'd met previously at church. I spoke no more than a few words, worried Grandmother might overhear or my tongue would tangle. Thankfully, Miss Wilkins was not deterred. She cheerfully greeted each individual by name and either paid a compliment or asked a pertinent question.

Dinner was announced, and I stood watching the company, hoping to know how to proceed. No one moved. Instead it seemed the guests had been transformed into statues. Miss Wilkins's happy smile fell.

Her brother cleared his throat. "Thank you all for joining us this evening. As we are anxious to become acquainted with each of you, Miss Wilkins thought it best that we forego rank and dine as friends." A wave of hushed whispers rippled across the room. "Mother, will you please lead us to the dining room?" Mrs. Wilkins smiled and followed the straight-faced butler. "Shall we?" Mr. Wilkins indicated we should follow his mother. I quickly looked at Grandmother and Mr. Mead. Their smiles now drooped, but Mr. Wilkins did not let that deter him. He held his head high and escorted his sister from the room.

The guests followed, mumbling their discontent. I stepped behind Grandmother, who pinched her lips as she listened to Mr. Lane express his shock at the lack of formality.

"Lady Marion would be disgraced at such an idea," Mrs. Lane said in agreement with her husband.

Things grew progressively worse. Miss Wilkins's decision against a traditional seating arrangement necessitated that guests sit near someone they wished to become acquainted with. Not one guest chose the empty seat near her. The moment I realized the slight, I walked to her side and claimed the place for myself.

Tears gathered in sweet Miss Wilkins's eyes, but the tiny lift of her mouth let me know I'd done the right thing. She held her tears at bay, but only until we began the second course. Miss Wilkins had opted to serve only three courses. After the soup was consumed, the footman cleared the bowls and the remaining sampling of fish, vegetables, and pies laid before us.

Mr. Lane picked up his fork and poked at the cooked fish. He glanced at his wife, who grimaced at the offering, and said, "Most interesting choice, Miss Wilkins." He set his fork on his plate and clasped his hands. "Have you dismissed Monsieur Gastineau?"

Mr. Lane's question was directed toward Mr. Wilkins, who rather than answer, gave Mr. Lane an incontestable look of warning. His eyes reminded me of a roiling storm, and I thought Mr. Lane would certainly heed the caution, but the man seemed to have a thick skull or an abrasive personality, for he continued his complaint. "Your late aunt, Lady Marion, generously hosted us for dinner on numerous occasions. Monsieur Gastineau always prepared a delectable feast."

"As is laid in front of you this very moment." Mr. Wilkins served Miss Wilkins a helping of fish, then served himself as well. He speared a piece of meat on his fork and lifted it to his mouth, daring Mr. Lane to speak again.

As whispers grew louder, Mr. Wilkins valiantly tried to direct the conversation to other topics, but the cynical group would not have it. Mrs. Christiansen held her tongue, and unsurprisingly, Mr. Horton and Mr. Edwards entertained Mr. Wilkins's altered line of conversation, but the Lanes, Mr. and Mrs. Adams, and Mr. Mead felt the need to subtly comment on the break from the traditional fare of roasted meat. Truth be told, it wasn't subtle at all.

It seemed the guest list consisted of daft neighbors, for Mrs. Adams opened her mouth. "Surely Monsieur Gastineau didn't recommend serving this." Her hand flitted over the dish in front of her.

"I believe Miss Wilkins altered the menu on my behalf," Mrs. Christiansen said. "I find I often have an upset stomach after I consume beef. Unfortunately, this has caused some alterations in my meals. I revealed as much to Miss Wilkins when the dinner invitation was extended."

"Hazel has always been a thoughtful girl." Mrs. Wilkins gave her daughter a warm smile.

Mr. Lane had sat directly across the table from Miss Wilkins. He leaned forward until he caught her attention. His tone could be described as a whisper, but his abrasive voice carried to the entire party. "Miss Wilkins, this combination of dishes is most unusual, and while I commend your consideration of Mrs. Christiansen, I, too, dined frequently at your late aunt's table—enough to know that serving fish alone as your main course is simply not done. More is expected of Cattersley. For future engagements, my wife would be happy to assist you in such matters"—his voice lowered the tiniest bit—"so you don't embarrass yourself further."

Miss Wilkins had bravely weathered the criticisms of her guests, but Mr. Lane's comment proved to be too much. She swiped the first tear from her cheek, then pushed back in her chair. A footman immediately appeared to assist her, and all the gentlemen stood.

She spoke only to her brother. "Forgive me, Robert. I find myself unwell and shall retire for the evening." And as the next tear fell, she quickly made her exit.

The gentlemen retook their seats. All but Mr. Wilkins. He remained standing, a muscle working in his jaw. The fury in his eyes conjured up images of a stormy sea—waves and froth and power. I understood how he would have been a force on the battlefield.

Mr. Lane's ears turned red, and he focused on his food.

"Robert," Mrs. Wilkins softly called.

Mr. Wilkins sat, but he did not touch his food. I felt for my new friend. I'd read enough books to know the dictates of Society. I also knew rules were modified time and again, sometimes out of necessity and sometimes to establish oneself as unique. I didn't think either reason had motivated Miss Wilkins. She had been thinking of Mrs. Christiansen and wished only to become acquainted with some families in the neighborhood.

As I thought on this, my anger brewed, and my lips opened of their own accord. "I feel grateful to be included in the invitation to dine at Cattersley." My speech stumbled a bit on the word *grateful*, but the pleasure I felt in defending Miss Wilkins trumped everything else.

Grandmother's scoff resonated across the table. I dropped my eyes to my plate and furiously cut a piece of potato and popped it into my mouth. I didn't understand the complaints about the food. It was far finer than anything Mrs. Bearsly had ever prepared or anything Mr. Mead had offered on the one occasion we had dined with him.

"I wondered if it was your first time at Cattersley's tables, Miss Rutherford. I understand you often keep to Fern Cottage. It must be a delightful home to so occupy your time," Miss Adams said.

I swallowed the bite of potato and looked up to see Mr. Wilkins watching me. A flood of retorts came to mind, but I only said, "It is."

Grandmother coughed awkwardly. "Abigail very much enjoys her walks about our property. I prefer a simple companion."

"Simple indeed," Mr. Adams said. His wife smiled prettily at him before raising her glass to her lips.

Mr. Wilkins slammed his hand onto the table. Plates and utensils shook, and all attention turned to him. His angry breaths filled his chest, and he skewered first Mr. Adams and then the man's wife with a look that could clear a battlefield. He beckoned to one of the footmen. When the lad drew near, Mr. Wilkins said, "Please clear the card tables from the drawing room. We will no longer be needing them tonight."

Silence reigned over the remainder of the meal, until the Lanes quickly gave their excuses and bid farewell. The Adamses followed shortly thereafter.

Grandmother twisted her hands, glancing continuously at Mr. Mead. I believe she, too, wished to depart, but Mr. Mead was busy evaluating every twitch and tremor of those present. Mr. Edwards and Mr. Horton bid goodbye, and only Mrs. Christiansen remained when Mr. Mead finally stood from his seat and addressed Mr. Wilkins. "Please pass our concerns and well wishes on to your sister. I do hope her ailment—"

"Good night, Mr. Mead," Mr. Wilkins snapped. His scathing glare halted Mr. Mead's words.

The vicar gave a curt bow, and Grandmother and I stood. Mr. Wilkins stood as well, and two footmen stepped forward to hold our chairs. Grandmother curtsied at her place, and I mirrored her movement. Both of us remained silent. Mr. Mead turned and walked from the room, and Grandmother followed. My heart hammered quickly in my chest. I ached for Miss Wilkins, her brother, her mother and, selfishly, for me. The night had not transpired to anything I had imagined, and instead of a lingering happy memory, disappointment and sorrow filled its space.

With my doused expectations I turned to join Grandmother. I'd barely exited the dining room when I heard my name. "Miss Rutherford?" Mr. Wilkins called.

I turned around and found him walking toward me. He stopped a mere foot away, and I watched the knot of his cravat rise and fall with his breath. "Miss Rutherford," he said again.

My eyes lifted to meet his. His expression held a mixture of regret and solace, like a lake shrouded in fog.

"Thank you," he said on a whisper.

A bit of my sorrow washed away with his words. My lips could not remain still, and I covered my smile with my hand. I nodded and looked down at my skirts.

Footfalls sounded behind me. "Abigail, the carriage awaits," Grandmother snapped.

I dipped a hasty curtsy and walked to the front door to quickly gather my things. Mr. Mead guided me into the equipage, and I sat beside Grandmother, pondering how the very end of the evening was my favorite memory of all.

## Chapter Eleven

### MR. ROBERT WILKINS

I'D NEVER BEEN MUCH FOR social engagements. Mother had been shocked when I'd suggested hosting dinner for our neighbors. In truth, Hazel had wanted to entertain, and I'd hoped to get to know my neighbors better—at least, one particular neighbor. I'd thought a simple dinner with several of the local gentry would gently ease Hazel into her desired role. I'd thought wrong. I'd met prisoners of war who acted with more decorum than our guests had.

As I watched Mr. Mead hand Mrs. Baker and her granddaughter into his carriage, I pitied Miss Rutherford that she found herself in such close quarters with the vicar. But the moment the carriage pulled away, I hurried to Hazel's room and knocked on the door.

"Hazel?"

No answer came.

"Hazel?" I called again.

Mother appeared behind me and placed a hand on my shoulder. "Robert, let her be."

"How did it all go wrong?"

"People are callous. You've witnessed it firsthand through your experiences, but Hazel has been sheltered from such things." My mother moved her arm and slipped it through mine. "Come. Give her some time." Mother led me away from Hazel's bedchamber. "Tomorrow will be a new day. We will discuss everything then."

Sleep did not come easily. I worried over my sister and inwardly chastised myself for not insisting Hazel follow the expected social norms. Mrs. Baker had been quiet; she'd seemed intrigued by the mounting tension, but she'd offered no opinion, either in rebuke or defense of Hazel.

I thought on Miss Rutherford's few but pointed words. They were the only solace I found in the evening.

When Hazel did not come down for breakfast, my anxiety regarding her wellbeing multiplied. I ate very little before leaving the table in search of a distraction. Horton had informed me of the average yield and variety of apple, pear, plum, and apricot trees, but I had yet to make an inspection of the orchard.

I exited through the kitchens, recalling the first day I had lost patience and snapped at Mrs. Sommers. Thankfully, she had readily forgiven me. I did not think I could so easily forgive those who had offended my sister.

Frustration pulsed through my veins, and I stomped more than walked southward, toward the orchard. The trees were planted in straight, uniform lines, reminiscent of military ranks standing in formation. On the battle-field the enemy was known. I clenched my fists and admitted to myself that I did not know how to defend myself, nor my family, from the attacks of those I'd hoped to befriend.

The orchard was beautiful. At least one hundred trees stood with green leaves and budding fruit. I wondered if Tucker and Felton were responsible for maintaining the orchards as well as the gardens, for the trees were immaculately trimmed and pruned. Horton had informed me that once the staff had cleared the fruit they needed for canning and preserves, Lady Marion had designated a day for her tenants and neighbors to come gather any remaining harvest from the trees. They preserved the fruit, and it became a staple for the families during the cold winter months.

It seemed the tenants, villagers, neighbors—everyone—praised and honored my aunt. I meant to carry on her traditions, her charity, her legacy, but my inadequacies continued to hinder me at every turn.

I paced up and down the rows of trees. Anger thrummed through me, and I could not separate reason and malice. Rounding the end of the orchard, I intended to repeat my paces, but when I looked up, I spied a familiar figure crossing the meadow.

Miss Rutherford wore her gray gown with a blue bonnet. She walked a step or two before pausing and bending low to the ground. The distance between us was too great for me to determine her purpose. I immediately changed course and walked toward her. My head seemed to clear or at least push my anxieties to the far corners of my mind. My focus turned to curiosity. What was Miss Rutherford doing?

She stepped forward and turned her back to me. Her skirts flowed in tandem with her movements. She bent her knees and again seemed to examine something on the ground. Not wishing to startle her, I opened my mouth to announce my presence. At that moment, she stood and spun in my direction.

"Mr. Wilkins." She appeared to be surprised to see me, but not displeased. She glanced down at her hands, where she clutched a variety of flowers, and then she dipped into a quick curtsy.

"Good morning, Miss Rutherford." I bowed, and when I stood, a smile split my lips. "Gathering flowers?"

She glanced again at the bouquet she held. "For Miss Wilkins." She held the arrangement up for me to see.

"You picked flowers for my sister?"

"I hope you don't mind. I felt picking flowers from the meadow was safer than disturbing Mr. Tucker's beds." She pulled a flower from the center of the arrangement and moved it to the outside.

I stepped near. "You're right. Although, I believe Tucker would allow you to pick anything in his garden. He enjoys your company." Miss Rutherford's cheeks turned a delightful shade of red. "You are very kind to think of Hazel," I said.

Miss Rutherford's brown eyes met mine. "They were wrong."

The fierce determination of her words, her posture, drew me even closer. "But they were also right."

Miss Rutherford looked at me in confusion. She slowly shook her head. "No. There I cannot agree."

"We did not follow convention. I'd hoped once they realized Hazel's intentions, it would quell their censure." I inhaled deeply, then raised my shoulders. "I assumed wrong."

"It should not matter," Miss Rutherford said.

"There we are in agreement. Perhaps once they come to know my family, to better know me . . ."

"I knew upon our first meeting what type of man you are. They are blind if they cannot see as well." Miss Rutherford held my gaze.

Curiosity again pulsed through me, and my heart picked up cadence. "And what type of man is that?"

Miss Rutherford bit her lip. "Well . . . you are a respectable gentleman; that much is obvious."

"Is it?" My lips twitched.

"Yes." Miss Rutherford's hand dropped to her side. "Lady Marion would not select a cad as her heir."

I laughed aloud. "One would hope."

Miss Rutherford tipped her head the tiniest bit. "You are also sensible and even-tempered. You are fiercely protective of your family, or at least your sister, and you must be very brave, having served as a captain in His Majesty's army."

Her praise spread like a serum through my battered soul. "You deduced all of this upon our first meeting?"

She blinked prettily and glanced at the flowers in her hand before returning her gaze to mine. Her words came slowly, thoughtfully. "You did not rebuke me for wandering on your land, and you granted permission for my visits to continue. Of course, I did not know of your devotion to Miss Wilkins until her arrival."

It took all of my energy to resist the pull of this woman. "May I share my first impressions of you?" I asked.

Miss Rutherford's eyes widened, and she shook her head. "I wish you wouldn't."

I smiled. "But how else will you know how delightful I found your smile and the blush that oft touches your cheeks?" Miss Rutherford raised her free hand to her face. "You quickly deduced that I was the new owner of Cattersley, which led me to know you've a quick mind."

"Please . . ." She looked down at her handful of flowers again.

"Shan't I go on?" I asked with a light laugh.

"No. You've embarrassed me quite enough." Her eyes met mine again. The smile spread across Miss Rutherford's face contradicted her words.

"That was not my intent. I only wished you to know my opinion of you," I said. Hazel had not yet ascertained the connection between Miss Rutherford and the vicar. The stirring in my chest ached for me to ask. "Mr. Mead—"

"I, too, found myself disappointed in his lack of censure. His hypocrisy is upsetting." Miss Rutherford cut in. She sucked in a deep breath and returned her gaze to her flowers. "Their words were cruel and far too harsh."

"If only they'd been directed at me instead of Hazel. She should remain innocent in all of this. My inadequacies deserve rebuke. But my sister . . . I wish I could shield her from their condemnation."

"It seems we both would sacrifice for our siblings. Your family has been everything kind and welcoming. The Adamses, the Lanes, and Mr. Mead—they were . . ." She bowed her head. "It wouldn't be proper for me to say."

I laughed again, and Miss Rutherford's pretty mouth twitched up in a smile. "So you picked flowers for Hazel?" I asked again.

"I wish I could do more." Miss Rutherford continued to rearrange the flowers.

"May I see?" I stepped forward and cocked my head first to one side and then the other as I admired the offering.

Miss Rutherford pointed to each flower. "Daisies, delphinium, phlox. My sister loves daisies, but this wild thyme is my favorite." She pointed to a flower with a small pink head attached to a scraggly stem. "It smells divine."

She lifted the bouquet to my face, and I inhaled the warm, grassy, lemonlike scent of the wild herb.

"I like this one." A single blue bell hung over the side of the bouquet. As I reached to point it out, my finger brushed against Miss Rutherford's gloved hand. The emotion that accompanied that simple touch made me want to take her hand in my own.

My fingers dropped away, and we did not speak. Birdsong rang from the trees beyond, and for a moment, voices could be heard from the direction of the stables. Then it was silent, until the cool morning breeze whispered the possibility that perhaps Miss Rutherford felt a bit of the same tendresse that currently pulsed through my veins.

"Would you please give these to your sister for me?" She extended the bouquet toward me.

"No," I said softly. Miss Rutherford startled a bit. I offered my arm. "You should give them to Hazel yourself."

"I wasn't sure if she'd be receiving visitors today," Miss Rutherford said. "It might be best if you give them to her."

"Please. She needs a friend." I reached forward and took Miss Rutherford's free hand, selfishly fulfilling my need to touch her again. I pulled her arm through mine, and before she could refuse, I began to walk toward Cattersley.

Miss Rutherford walked in silence. I shared several random facts I had learned about the estate in my short time as its master, and as we neared the doors, I realized my mood had quite improved from when I had left an hour before.

Upon our return to the house, I learned Hazel had taken refuge in the east library. I was proud I could escort Miss Rutherford to the door without turning down a wrong passageway. I knocked and then guided her into the room. She gasped. Her eyes traced the rows of books up to the ceiling and back to the floor. I stood a happy observer of her myriad expressions.

When Hazel said my name, Miss Rutherford and I turned to where she sat on a long yellow chaise lounge. Miss Rutherford dropped into an awkward curtsy, as her arm was still woven through mine.

"Miss Rutherford has come to call on you, Hazel." I released my hold on Miss Rutherford's arm, immediately missing the feel of her fingers there.

Hazel set her book aside and stood. "Hello, Miss Rutherford."

"Hello, Miss Wilkins." Miss Rutherford looked at the wildflowers and then extended her arm. "I know it isn't much, but I picked these for you."

A smiled touched Hazel's lips. She stepped forward and accepted the bouquet. "They're lovely." She sniffled and swiped a finger beneath her eye. I offered my handkerchief to my sister. "Thank you, Robert." She wiped her eyes again and then exhaled loudly. "Oh, it's so silly. I should have known better and followed stuffy old protocol."

Miss Rutherford stepped forward and placed a hand on Hazel's arm. "I thought your choice of menu and attention to Mrs. Christiansen's needs commendable. Is it really a bad thing to be slighted by the Adamses or the Lanes?"

A pout spread across Hazel's lips. "But the vicar—"

"Needs to revisit his holy scriptures," Miss Rutherford said. Hazel laughed, and Miss Rutherford continued. "You mustn't let their short-sighted opinions worry you, Miss Wilkins."

"Please, call me Hazel." The duo began to walk back to the yellow chaise lounge.

"Then, I insist you call me Abigail," Miss Rutherford said.

I thought it an angelic name.

Knowing my sister would be well cared for, I quietly exited the room. It seemed Miss Rutherford—Abigail—had brightened not only my day but my sister's as well.

# Chapter Twelve

## MISS ABIGAIL RUTHERFORD

MISS WILKINS OFFERED USE OF the carriage home, but I refused. Grandmother would make enough of a fuss over the book Hazel insisted I borrow. Arriving in the Wilkins's carriage was not an option. Besides, the walk back to Fern Cottage allowed me to prolong the feelings happily bubbling inside of me. Miss Wilkins had claimed she needed a friend. I acknowledged I did too.

My sister and I were amiable, but we had never shared our secrets or dreams, successes or failures. We commiserated with each other in our situation, and Louisa and I had tried to look out for one another. But I'd always considered our relationship as much a sisterly duty as a friendship. Except for once.

Near the end, on Mother's hard days, Louisa would watch as Mother ordered me around, making demands that were near impossible to meet. Then Mother turned to drinking. After watching Father's decline, I could not understand why Mother would take the same path. She used to comment on how the alcohol had changed my father, turned him into a man she didn't recognize. Her pain was so fierce at the end that I believe she didn't want to recognize herself. She only wanted to escape.

One day things were especially bad. I had returned home from the market, and Mother had beckoned me to her. When I took too long to deposit the parcels in my arms, she'd sworn and thrown an empty plate across the room. It was then I'd noticed the bottle of wine sitting by her side, but I didn't say anything. I'd hardly spoken at home anymore by that point, for my slurred letters seemed to aggravate Mother's temper. And after that day, I never spoke to my mother again. I stood silently as she rebuked me, cursed me, and wished me dead. I had known the wine had hold of my mother's tongue. She'd never been warm, but she had taken the time to educate me, to provide for my needs, and I considered that many were not as fortunate.

Mother had pointed to a place in front of the fire. "Stand there and repeat these words." Ironically, her speech had slurred. I'd thought she might faint at any moment. In truth, I'd prayed for it to happen.

"Rain is a withering type of weather," she'd said with a smirk, her glassy eyes daring me to disobey. "Say it!"

I'd repeated the phrase, hoping if I was agreeable, she might dismiss me. "Rain is a withewing type of weather."

Mother had laughed, callous and loud. "Say it again!" she screamed.

"Wain is a withewing type of weather," I had said with my stumbling tongue. I had become frustrated, and my letters had blended in awkward combinations.

"Now say, 'I really want a horse for Christmas.'" She then swilled again from the bottle.

Over Mother's shoulder I'd seen Louisa sitting on the stoop, her legs pulled into her chest and her eyes wide with fright. I had repeated the words, simply to shield my sister from witnessing Mother's drunken wrath.

From my lips the sentence fell. "I weally want a hoase for Chwismas." Despite speaking the words slowly, my efforts had failed.

"Ha!" Mother had rocked back and forth in her chair. "Stupid, stupid girl."

She continued to harangue me with criticisms and insults, making me stand and repeat nonsensical combinations of words and phrases for the better part of an hour. Louisa had remained hidden on the stairs, tears running down her cheeks. Whether she was humiliated for me or because of me, I did not know. I had never asked because I didn't care to know. But that night, after the wine had numbed Mother to sleep and I'd climbed into bed, Louisa had tiptoed across our room and wrapped her arms around me. I had sobbed into my pillow and wet the top of her head, and she'd held on tight. We'd fallen asleep that way, and when I woke in the morning, she was gone. She was my sister, and on that night, she had truly been a friend.

Miss Wilkins, on the other hand, had embraced me from our first introduction. Today we'd talked of favorite pastimes, hobbies, preferences on literature, Seasons, and the clothing hues that best highlighted the colors of our eyes. She had never criticized my speech, nor made mention of our vastly different situations. My visit with her had been a rare delight.

When she called at Fern Cottage the following day, I could not contain my excitement.

"I've come to invite you to tea, Miss Rutherford. Does tomorrow at three o'clock suit?" Hazel asked.

I looked to my grandmother. "Would that be acceptable to you, Grandmother?"

She fiddled with the lace at her throat. "I'm afraid not. I need you to go to Mr. Thorpe's shop. I ordered some ribbon several weeks ago, and it should have arrived by now."

Hazel clapped her hands together. "Oh, 'tis perfect!" she said. "Mother needs some new trimmings as well. Perhaps she can inquire after your ribbon while she is on her errand?"

Grandmother's hand dropped from her neck. Red splotches appeared on her cheeks. "I suppose that will suffice."

"I do thank you, Mrs. Baker." Hazel smiled prettily and swept away.

The next day I emerged from the woods, and for the second time in my life, I made my way to the grand front door of Cattersley. The butler welcomed me and told me Miss Wilkins waited for me in the drawing room. I felt privy to a great secret, knowing I'd been given liberty to call her Hazel.

Mr. Manning led me to a beautifully sunlit room. Maroon furniture dominated the space, accented with cream and blue adornments. Cream curtains framed tall glass windows, and a woven rug, combining all three colors, was spread out between the sofa and two sets of chairs.

"Oh, Abigail! You've arrived." Hazel hurried to me and took my hands. "Mother will join us soon. I hope you don't mind, but once I showed her the beautiful bouquet you arranged, she insisted you teach us."

The thought did rattle my nerves a bit. The women in my life had inflicted some of the worst scars. But Hazel was a delight, and on the few occasions I'd visited with Mrs. Wilkins, she, too, had been kind and inclusive.

Hazel and I chatted amiably until a maid delivered the tea tray. Mrs. Wilkins arrived shortly thereafter. "Where is Robert?" she asked.

"I've not sent for him. Should I have?" Hazel's eyes widened, and her fingers began to tangle in her lap. "Oh, I shall forever be blundering propriety."

Mrs. Wilkins laughed. "I only thought to invite him so he might say hello to Miss Rutherford. You know I don't give a fiddle about propriety. Oh, and Miss Rutherford, your grandmother's order is wrapped and waiting in the entrance. Manning will ensure you have it when you leave."

Hazel's posture relaxed, and she called for a servant to ask her brother to join us.

When Mr. Wilkins arrived, I thought him the handsomest man I'd ever beheld. His hair was slightly disheveled, as if he'd just returned from a ride. His green jacket fit him well with his buckskin breeches and black boots. His cravat was a bit askew, but I found him all the more handsome for it. My cheeks warmed, and I looked away.

"Good afternoon, Mother, Hazel, Miss Rutherford." He walked to Mrs. Wilkins and kissed her cheek.

"What have you been up to this morning, Robert?" Mrs. Wilkins asked.

"I've just returned from visiting several tenant farms. I asked Horton to show me the smallest farms first. I want to make sure we've made all necessary repairs before the weather turns." Mr. Wilkins sat across from me.

Hazel poured out. She added only a touch of cream to her mother's cup before passing it over. "See, there. Just as I like it." Mrs. Wilkins accepted the tea from Hazel. "You are everything proper." She added with a smile.

Pink tinged Hazel's cheeks. "Thank you, Mother." She then prepared and passed her brother his tea. "And how do you prefer your tea, Abigail?"

"Just a touch of sugar, please," I said. Hazel made easy conversation while preparing my cup. I envied the ease with which she served and smiled. Frequent thoughts flowed through my mind, but unlike Hazel, they rarely sounded eloquent when I spoke.

"Do you correspond with your siblings?" Mrs. Wilkins asked.

"Louisa and I wite every now and again. Her duties occupy much of her time, so I don't hear from her as often as I would like." While I dropped a few letters, I was tremendously pleased that the majority of my sounds formed correctly. "I've not heard from Benjamin since he sailed to America."

"That is a dreadfully long time." Hazel pressed a hand to her heart. "I don't know that I could stand to be away from either of my brothers for such a prolonged period."

"Even a contrary one?" Mr. Wilkins teased.

"Even a contrary one." Hazel punctuated her words with a deft nod.

Mrs. Wilkins smiled at her children before returning her attention to me. "How do you enjoy living with your grandmother?" she asked.

I knew not how to respond. Grandmother was not nearly as harsh as Mother had become in her final weeks; she shushed me at certain times and begged for company at others. I decided to answer in truth. "I miss my siblings, but I do prefer Herefordshire to Plymouth. Trees make better company than wowdy sailors." I clenched my fist in frustration at the slurred *r* in rowdy. When speaking with Hazel two days prior, there were letters that had slipped, but she did not comment, nor had my blunders deterred our conversation. Her acceptance of my deficiencies was one of the many reasons I'd decided we would be fast friends. But now I'd embarrassed myself and possibly Hazel. I pressed my eyes closed and forced my mind to my memorized list of practice words.

A teacup chinked, and I opened my eyes to see Mr. Wilkins setting his tea aside. He then helped himself to several small cakes before turning his attention to me. "I quite agree with you, Miss Rutherford," he said. "The bustle of the city is exciting for only a moment. The pace never slows enough to allow one to think."

"But what of the soirees, balls, and card parties?" Hazel asked. "Do you not miss those, Abigail?"

I looked between the siblings, disbelief certainly evident in my face. Neither of them commented on my ill-trained tongue. Instead they both awaited my answer. I set my tea aside and answered slowly. "If I ever have the occasion to attend, I shall let you know." Invitations to such things had not been extended to me.

Hazel's jaw dropped. "You have not been? But—"

Mrs. Wilkins cut her off with a wave of her hand. "You aren't missing much, Miss Rutherford. I prefer a small country gathering myself. Thankfully, my late husband was sensitive to such things. We rarely traveled to Town."

"What about you, Robert?" Hazel asked. "You've spent time in Lincolnshire, London, Derbyshire, and even the Continent."

Mr. Wilkins grew solemn. "My time in France was hardly a holiday."

Hazel waved away her brother's somberness. "Oh, I know. I only wonder which you prefer."

"You know the answer to that, Hazel." Mr. Wilkins sat back in his chair. "I prefer peace and quiet."

"Then Cattersley is perfect for you," I said. The words surprised me. But the excitement of knowing Mr. Wilkins would be in residence for a long while was not such a shock.

Mr. Wilkins laughed lightly and crossed one leg over the other. "If only the neighborhood agreed with your sentiment, Miss Rutherford."

He held me in a hypnotic spell, and I could not look away. I did not want to. He drew me in with every breath, every second ticking on the clock nearby. "In time they will see your goodness," I said softly.

His eyebrows twitched. "Are you certain?"

I thought on my response. How could I know? I'd known the man for only a matter of weeks, but I'd been watching people for many years. Mr. Wilkins embodied goodness. His care for his mother and sister, his desire to know his tenants and ensure their wellbeing, his commitment to his country—all spoke of his fine character. But his humility confirmed his goodness in my eyes. I did not get the opportunity to convey my conviction, for Mrs. Wilkins coughed, a subtle reminder that Mr. Wilkins and I were not alone.

"Hazel," her mother said, "I believe Miss Rutherford is right."

As I'd not said much, I shared a look of confusion with Hazel. Mrs. Wilkins continued. "It will take time for the neighbors to accept Robert and his newly acquired wealth. They do not know him as we do, so we must provide an opportunity for them to know him better."

"What are you suggesting, Mother?" Mr. Wilkins dropped his foot back down to the floor and placed his hands on his legs.

"Why, you must host another event, of course." Mrs. Wilkins stood and rubbed her hands together. "Something not too grand."

"Or too unique," Hazel added with a frown. "Nothing that will cause an uproar." She tapped her finger against her cheek. "A musicale?"

Mrs. Wilkins walked in a circle around us. "Not a bad thought, but I was thinking a picnic might be in order—a more casual affair that will allow for conversation."

"And I shall let Monsieur Gastineau determine the menu, as long as there are samplings for Mrs. Christiansen." Hazel clasped her hands primly in her lap.

"Are you certain, Hazel?" Mr. Wilkins asked.

Hazel glanced at her mother and nodded. "I will not let them affect me, Robert."

Mr. Wilkins looked between the two women. "Very well. May I ask when this picnic is to take place?"

"Thursday of next week." Hazel jumped up from her seat and grabbed my hands. "Come, Abigail. We've so much to do." She began to verbalize her list as she led me toward the door.

I looked over my shoulder, hoping for a chance to bid goodbye to Mr. Wilkins and his mother. Mrs. Wilkins stood with a wide smile, watching her son. Mr. Wilkins also smiled, though his eyes were on us or, more accurately, me. He gave a lighthearted salute, and Hazel pulled me from the room.

I'd only picnicked one other time in my life, two weeks after Father died. Rain had fallen every day after he was buried—until that morning. The sun had broken through the clouds and shone brightly in the sky. Mother's crying had lessened, and when we all woke to the glorious light, she'd declared there would be no more moping. She'd then asked our housemaid, Trudy, to prepare a picnic for us and instructed each of us children to dress in our best mourning attire. I had secured Louisa's hair into a fabulous twist and pinned my own into a perfect knot. Mother had handed the picnic basket to Benjamin and led us to the park that was situated on the hillside north of Plymouth. We'd sat on the grass and watched sailors work the sails on tall ships as they moved in and out of the port. We talked of many things that day, but not once did we discuss my father, his death, or anything of real significance, and I'd always found it odd that I considered that day to be one of the happiest of my life.

Hazel put me to work writing invitations. She thought it best to invite all the guests who had come to her dinner party, to show no ill will. And she determined to include several other neighbors as well.

I completed only six invitations before I took my leave. Grandmother had insisted I return to Fern Cottage before supper, and I did not want to cross her and risk being excluded from the festivities.

Grandmother usually demanded my silence during our private meals. Today, however, from the moment I took my seat at the table, she peppered me with questions. "In which room did you take tea? Did Mr. Wilkins or his mother join you? Did they ask about our living expenses? How many varieties of cakes were offered?" And my favorite, "Did they make you serve them?"

I answered each of Grandmother's questions in truth. But when she asked if I'd been relegated to the hired help, I couldn't help but laugh.

Grandmother glared at me. I calmed myself before I spoke. "They were really very kind, Grandmother. They are adjusting to their new roles the best they can."

"Do they plan to remove to London for the Season? I've heard Miss Wilkins ordered an entire new wardrobe." Grandmother speared a bite of beans. "I should like to order new dresses and prance about Town." She ate the bite on her fork.

"I don't know anything about that. But I can tell you that today Miss Wilkins wore her rose-colored day dress—the exact one she wore when she first called at Fern Cottage."

"Hmm." Grandmother swallowed and picked up her drink. She eyed me over the top of her goblet.

"If she had ordered a dress, or even two, would you fault her for it?" I hoped to better understand Grandmother's reasoning. Where she once boasted of Cattersley's past owner, she now appeared to spurn Lady Marion's chosen heir while simultaneously coveting a closer connection to the estate.

"I suppose if Miss Wilkins is truly going to run the household, she should dress the part," Grandmother said, raising her glass in a faux toast before taking a drink.

Her admission surprised me, and I decided it would be best if I remained quiet throughout the remainder of the meal. Too many times I had hoped my mother would change, soften her disgust of my impediment or favor me as she had Louisa. Even during Mother's final months, as I'd cared for all of her needs, she had remained distant. But maybe Grandmother would soften. Her acknowledgment of Miss Wilkins's dressing and looking the part of a grand lady was a promising step. I hoped it was the first of many.

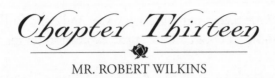

## Chapter Thirteen

### MR. ROBERT WILKINS

HAZEL'S EXCITEMENT FOR THE PICNIC spread throughout Cattersley. The staff smiled more, Monsieur Gastineau experimented daily with new dishes to be served at the event, and I even caught Manning whistling a happy tune.

The morning before the appointed day, Graham finished tying my cravat, and with a final tug, he centered the knot on my neck. "There you are, sir," Graham said.

I slipped my fingers under my collar in the hopes of loosening the infernal thing.

Graham laughed. I shot him a look of warning, but it did not deter him. "You'll be seeing Miss Rutherford today, right, sir?" I narrowed my eyes, but Graham simply shrugged. "You want to look your best for the lady."

He was right. Abigail—Hazel spoke of her so often using her Christian name that it was how I had come to refer to her in my mind—would be joining my mother and sister to make final preparations for the picnic. It would be her third visit this week, and I rather enjoyed seeing her with some degree of regularity. She brightened Hazel's mood, and while I'd allowed myself only a brief greeting on Abigail's last visit, I'd offered her free rein of the library. She'd been extremely pleased, which had only led me to consider what more I could do to win her favor.

I shrugged my shoulders forward and straightened my sleeves. "What do you know of it?" I asked.

"Miss Rutherford's a pretty miss, sir. I'd be wanting to look my best too." Graham pulled at the end of his coat and peeked into my tall standing mirror.

"Graham," I said sternly.

He turned and faced me. "Oh, it's not just me, sir. Everyone's talking about it."

"Everyone?"

"Well, everyone belowstairs. We agree you and Miss Rutherford would make a fine couple." I could tell from the expression on his face he was in earnest.

No need to admit I'd come to the same conclusion. "And here I thought my staff was loyal."

"Oh, we are, sir. Never said we liked that batty old Mrs. Baker." Graham started tidying my things. "And we don't think Miss Adams suits you at all. None of us pay heed to what those haughty neighbors say. You've a bit more to learn, but we believe you're a fine master. Lady Marion chose well. We all agree."

I walked to the window that overlooked the gardens. Abigail had come. Mother and Hazel stood talking with her near the topiary garden. Hazel grabbed Abigail's hands, and Mother laughed at something she said.

"See, there. Your mum likes her too," Graham said over my shoulder.

"That's quite enough, Graham," I said in my best commander's tone.

"Yes, sir." He gave a cheeky salute and disappeared into the dressing room to attend to his duties.

Graham's enthusiasm was only a sliver of my own. I was excited to see Abigail. I left my room and headed toward the gardens. However, due to the enormity of Cattersley, it took far too long to reach the topiary hedge, and once I arrived, the women were gone. I looked skyward. Nature had provided another beautiful day, and there was work to be done. Miss Rutherford would be present at the picnic on the morrow; I could wait until that time to see her.

I entered the house through the music room on the east side and headed toward my office. Horton had designated which tenants had the most need, and together we had formulated a plan to ensure they received ample provisions to see them through the winter. Today I was to ride with Horton to visit three widows. Each had lost her husband in the war. I hoped a personal visit would assure them Cattersley would provide for their families.

Before battle I had often rehearsed the words I wanted to share with my troops so that when the time came to encourage and prepare them for what lay ahead, my thoughts would be centered, concise, and meaningful. I found myself following the same protocol now, considering how to voice my condolences and reassurances to the widowed women.

I walked past the east library, and from within came a thump followed by a small screech. I quickened my step and passed across the threshold to see Miss Rutherford in a heap on the floor. She didn't notice me and instead shook her head and shifted her legs so she might stand.

Perhaps I should have thought on her embarrassment and excused myself without her knowing I was witness to her fall. But she looked adorable; her lips pursed in frustration, and her blue skirts tangled around her. I could not resist the opportunity to be chivalrous.

"Please, let me help you." At the sound of my voice her head shot up and her eyes widened. She scrambled to rise, and I hurried over.

"Why must you find me in such a state?" She placed her hand on her cheek to cover her blush.

"Providence?" I offered and extended my hand.

"Fate does like to laugh at my expense." She slipped her fingers into mine, and I assisted her to her feet.

"On the contrary; I think fate was granting me a favor." I did not release her hand.

"Oh?"

"Don't you see? Now I get to act the part of a gentleman and spend a few moments in your company." I would never be described as a flirt. I usually approached matters head-on. But I intended to hold Miss Rutherford's hand for as long as she would allow and utilizing words to stall our separation seemed the natural thing to do.

Miss Rutherford's blush began to spread. "Hazel allowed me to borrow a novel last week. If you recall, you granted me access to Cattersley's books—"

"Indeed, I did." I couldn't help but smile.

"Well, as I have finished the one, I saw another I hoped I might read." With her free hand, Miss Rutherford pointed high on the shelf near where the rolling ladder rested. "I should have moved the ladder a bit closer."

"You fell from that height?" A tinge of worry pricked my chest. With her hand in mine, I turned Miss Rutherford to face me and looked over her person. "Are you hurt? Shall I summon a doctor?"

"No need. Truly. Only my pride is injured." She blushed once again.

"Come." I led Miss Rutherford to the nearest seat and grudgingly released her hand. "Will you tell me which book you were after?"

"You will only think me sillier." She ducked her head.

I crooked my finger and lifted her chin until her eyes met mine. "Not at all."

Miss Rutherford blinked prettily, then turned her gaze to her hands in her lap. "I hoped to read *Emma*."

"And I shall fetch it so you may." I moved the ladder farther to the right and climbed to retrieve the book Miss Rutherford desired. After a moment of searching in the area she had indicated, I found the book and descended the ladder. "There you are." I handed it over to her, and her lips turned up in a bashful smile.

"Thank you, Mr. Wilkins."

"Are you certain you're not hurt?"

Miss Rutherford nodded her head. "I'm sorry to cause you concern."

I winked. "Fate, Miss Rutherford. Fate."

Hazel scurried into the room like an eager pup. "Oh, hello, Robert. Abigail, did you find what you wished?"

Miss Rutherford stood with the book in hand. "Yes, Mr. Wilkins kindly assisted me."

"How convenient." Hazel smiled at me, then at Miss Rutherford. "Come, we had better hurry along. Mother is waiting in the blue drawing room. We've so much left to do." She slipped her arm through Miss Rutherford's, and while I would have much preferred to escort her to her destination, I knew it was past time for me to meet Horton. There were some benefits to being master of such a grand estate—no one would chastise my tardiness.

It was approximately two in the morning when lightning flashed through the sky. Graham asked every night if he could pull the heavy curtains closed, as he claimed it would allow for a more peaceful sleep. But I liked waking to the yawning morning, and now, instead of being awoken by warm sunlight, I was acutely aware of the rain pelting the window. Hazel would be heartbroken. Unless the rain cleared, there would be no picnic, and she'd hoped the outing might redeem her qualifications as hostess of Cattersley. I'd tried to convince her that outside opinions did not matter—the decision for her to remain was entirely mine—but it was obvious she still felt a keen desire to prove herself.

I hoped the storm might pass before sunrise, but as the hours slowly crept by, the rain did not relent. In truth, the thunder seemed to rumble louder, as if to announce its command of the sky.

Graham was unusually quiet as he helped me dress. After assisting me into a new pair of boots, he finally spoke. "I'm sorry you'll not be able to picnic today."

I looked toward the window and pretended shock. "Why ever not?"

Graham eyed me as if I were daft and pointed upward. "The heavens decided to flood the earth today."

"Not to worry. I have a plan." I'd not been able to settle after being woken by the lightning. The solitary hours had provided a chance to think, to plot.

Rain was a common enemy in battle. But it could also be an ally. I recalled a time my superior had given orders to attack a French weapons garrison near the front lines. The fort was heavily guarded by the enemy, and I knew we had little chance of success. My men had murmured, knowing many would end their fight for freedom in an offensive attack destined to fail. But I'd understood the reason for the command. If we could take the French munitions, it would greatly hamper their ability to push their offensive line forward. Only, how could it be done?

I'd spent the day pacing in my tent. Clouds had covered the sky just as the sun had set for the evening. Within the hour a heavy rain had begun, and a brilliant plan began to unfold. I'd roused my troops and explained my idea. We'd worked through the night to reroute a stream. We'd waited for the stream to swell, and at around four o'clock in the morning, we'd broken down our makeshift dam and sat armed and waiting while water poured into the enemy hold. Within thirty minutes the entire enemy regiment had surrendered. Not one shot had been fired. Not one man killed. Several bags of gunpowder had been lost to the floodwaters, but the siege was considered a success. My men had followed me without question after that incident, and I had learned that some battles needed to be fought with weapons while other campaigns could be won with a little ingenuity.

"The ladies are expecting a picnic," I continued. "As are our neighbors." I clapped Graham on the shoulder. "What say you, Graham? Shall we give them a picnic?"

A slow, conspiratorial smile spread across Graham's face. "How may I help?"

# Chapter Fourteen

## MISS ABIGAIL RUTHERFORD

My somnolent mind layered my dreams with raucous laughter and the clatter of horse hooves. Only once light touched the sky did I connect my dreams with the rain tapping against my bedroom window.

I hurried to look outside. The clouds were bathing the entire yard. Thoroughly. My heart broke, not only for my own loss but for Hazel's as well, for surely the rain was too heavy to pitch tents. The picnic would have to be canceled.

I sighed and moped around my room, trying to distract myself in the words of my borrowed novel, with little success. Resigned to spending the day with Grandmother, I dressed and headed downstairs.

Mrs. Bearsly hummed happily in the yeasty-smelling kitchen. She punched down her dough, then wiped her hands on her apron before turning to see me. "Good morning, Miss Rutherford."

"Please, call me Abigail." I'd made the request numerous times before.

Mrs. Bearsly glanced at the door, then back at me. "Mrs. Baker would never allow it." She cupped my cheek briefly before walking past me to the larder. "But I appreciate your kind offer."

I walked to the kitchen table and sat down. She dished me a plate with two boiled eggs and a slice of bread.

I expressed my gratitude, and Mrs. Bearsly pulled a note from her apron pocket. "Now, this is what ya should be thanking me for." Her smile nearly filled her face as she handed the paper to me.

"What is it?" I asked as I took it from her hand.

"Go on." She waved.

"*Dear Abigail, Robert has thought of the most brilliant plan!*" I read aloud. "*The picnic will take place after all, only it will be indoors. Can you imagine? I will send the carriage to retrieve you and Mrs. Baker at noon. I hope you may arrive prior to the rest of the party so I may show you all we have done. Until then, your friend, Miss Hazel Wilkins.*" Hazel had signed her name with a flourish.

"But how?" I asked Mrs. Bearsly.

She leaned forward. "Young Mr. Pratt delivered that first thing this morning. He said Cattersley is abustle. The maids, the footmen, even the stableboys have been called to assist in the effort. Of course, the kitchen staff is helping Monsieur Gastineau with the food, but all others are working under Mr. Wilkins's direction."

"I still don't understand how one can have a picnic indoors." I slowly refolded the note.

"Well, I best not say more. I'd hate to ruin the surprise." She motioned to my plate. "Eat quickly, now. You'll be wanting your energy, and I assume you'll be wanting to change your dress."

A bell on the wall rang, and Mrs. Bearsly looked at it with a frown.

"I'll take Grandmother her tray." Curious excitement had doused my hunger. "I must inform her of the arrangements."

"Very well." Mrs. Bearsly prepared the tray, and I carried it upstairs.

"Enter," Grandmother called when I knocked. I managed to balance the tray on my hip as I opened the door. "Is Mrs. Bearsly ill?" Grandmother asked.

"Not at all." I set the tray on the table beside her bed and then moved to open the draperies.

"Then, where is she?"

"In the kitchen. I offered to bring up your food in hopes that I might discuss the picnic with you." I stood with perfect posture near the side of the bed.

"What is there to discuss? It will be postponed, of course." Grandmother took a bite of her toast.

"Actually . . ." I pulled Hazel's note from my sleeve and handed it to my grandmother.

She scanned the lines, and her eyebrows jumped to her hairline. "What utter nonsense! A picnic in the house?"

I sat on the edge of her bed. "You will come, won't you, Gwandmother?" Her name was one I rehearsed frequently, yet in my excitement, I lost control of my letters.

Grandmother frowned at the sound and flicked my cheek. "Of course I'll be there. The entire neighborhood will come to see the farce. I shan't be left out of the excitement."

I ignored the sting on my cheek and stood and twirled in a circle with my arms spread wide. "I think it sounds splendid. A picnic indoors!" I leaned forward and pressed a kiss to Grandmother's cheek. I'd never done it before, and I wasn't sure what had compelled the show of affection, but shock swept over Grandmother's features and she remained quiet.

"I'm going to change. Do you still approve of the green gown?" I asked.

"Yes, yes." Grandmother shooed me away.

I returned to my room and changed into the dark-green dress I'd saved for the day. It seemed strange to wear the color of half-mourning instead of black on such a dreary day, but I slipped it over my head and then pulled all the pins from my hair to arrange a more intricate coif.

The whinny of horses sounded as I placed the last pin. I gathered my gloves, and Grandmother hollered my name. At the bottom of the stairs Grandmother completed her inspection.

"Will it suffice?" I asked, holding my skirts to my sides.

"That will do," Grandmother said. She slipped into the cloak Mrs. Bearsly held, and I pulled on my long gray pelisse. A red-haired footman held an umbrella in the doorway, and when we were ready, he escorted us to the carriage.

We arrived at our destination, and upon entering the elegant house, I saw that Mrs. Bearsly had spoken true. Cattersley resembled a colony of ants. Servants bustled every which way while Mr. Manning stood in the corridor directing the commotion with stern commands; he took no notice of me. I wondered where I would find Hazel and decided to ask the next maid who scurried past, but then a throat cleared behind me. I turned to find the same redheaded footman who'd held the umbrella smiling down on us.

I found his welcoming grin contagious.

I curtsied. "How do you do?"

Grandmother tsked. "Don't curtsy to the footman, Abigail," she said under her breath.

He kept smiling and said, "I've been instructed to escort you to the picnic." He stepped in front of me and began to ascend the staircase.

"The picnic is upstairs?" I'd wondered all morning where they would have the event. The greenhouse, perhaps? Or the room Hazel had designated as the *Sky Room* because of its tall windows?

The footman led us to the first floor, and when he turned down the east corridor, I knew where we were headed. Cattersley's ballroom was built on the first floor and overlooked the gardens. Grand French doors opened onto a terrace with two staircases winding down opposite sides to the groomed path. I'd walked past the gray stone stairs many times on my way to find Mr. Tucker in the greenhouse, and I'd gazed up at the paneled doors. But never before had I seen the inside of the room.

If the picnic were to be inside, a ballroom would have plentiful space for the guests and allow the staff to serve the food easily. It provided the ideal solution to the rain. As we walked toward the room, I imagined what the inside would look like. Would there be marble columns or stone archways? Perhaps a balcony overlooking the dance floor? Would there be accents of blue or green or yellow? My steps grew lighter, and I realized I was practically skipping behind Grandmother.

We reached a set of tall oak double doors. A large *C* surrounded by delicate vines of ivy had been carved into each of the door's panels. The servant stopped in front of the doors and turned toward us with a sheepish grin spread across his face. Then he knocked on the door three times.

A boy I'd seen working around the stables opened the ballroom door. He bowed low. "Welcome to our picnic, Mrs. Baker. Miss Rutherford."

Grandmother's hand fluttered at her throat. "Th-thank you."

Grandmother stepped into the room, and I followed behind. My breath hitched in my lungs. Whether the floors were wood or marble or imported tile, it mattered not, for they were hidden beneath plush carpets spread like a tapestry of grass, flowers, and forested woodland. Grandmother's jaw dropped open, and her hands fell to her side. Bedsheets had been hung overhead from the ceiling at various heights, creating the illusion of fluffy white clouds. My feet moved forward as I turned and spun in a slow circle to take it all in. Screens, along with various tables and chests, had been artfully arranged to create paths. Greenery of all sorts fanned high and low. Mr. Tucker must have emptied the entire greenhouse, for the room had truly transformed to resemble a luscious garden.

"Abigail!" Hazel wore a bright-yellow day dress. A light-brown bonnet topped with white daisies hung from ribbons in her hand. "What do you think?"

I continued to look above and around me. "How did you manage to do it?"

"Robert took charge." Hazel's eyes took in the scene with delight.

"Mr. Wilkins?" Shock laced Grandmother's voice. I was not so surprised.

Small benches, chaise lounges, and low tables were arranged in clustered groups. A multitude of candles flooded light through the room, repelling the dreary clouds outside the window. "Look here." Hazel pointed to a sign where the word *picnic* had been roughly carved into wood that was still soft, not hardened from time. The placard was attached to a pole and set in a wooden stand. Hazel smiled with pride. "Robert asked Mr. Twill to carve it only this morning."

I reached forward and traced the letters with my fingers. "He thought of everything."

Mrs. Wilkins appeared. "Welcome."

Grandmother and I greeted the matriarch appropriately.

"What do you make of our improvisations?" Mrs. Wilkins waved a hand at the sheets hanging overhead.

I'd never seen such joy upon my grandmother's face. "The room is exquisite. I never could have imagined . . ." Her voice trailed off as she looked again over the decor.

"Come." Mrs. Wilkins motioned for Grandmother to follow her. "Let me show you what Robert is calling the *Grand Arch*." Grandmother's wide eyes revealed her excitement as she allowed Mrs. Wilkins to lead her away.

Hazel leaned close. "Maybe we have won her over."

"How could you not? This is indeed spectacular." I smiled for my friend. Surely those who doubted Hazel would now see her sincere intent to honor her late aunt and the estate of Cattersley.

"Miss Wilkins?" A young girl with flushed cheeks and an apron covered in flour stood behind Hazel.

Hazel turned around and bent her knees to be at eye level with the girl. "Yes?"

"Monsieur Gastineau needs you to come to the kitchen at once." The concern in the girl's expression melted my heart. "There's a problem with the strawberries."

Hazel straightened and took the girl's hand. "Let us not keep him waiting." She looked over her shoulder. "I'll only be a moment, Abigail. Have a look around. The rest of our party should be arriving shortly."

The rain falling outside was forgotten as I walked through the greenery. The foliage and furniture had been situated in artful paths around the room. I could hear voices, but I did not see Grandmother and Mrs. Wilkins. I picked my way through the maze, wandering toward the tall windows that overlooked the outside gardens.

"Miss Rutherford." Mr. Wilkins appeared on my right. "How do you like the arrangement?" Knowing his insistence in holding the picnic and his part in everything surrounding me made my heart flutter with happiness. Or maybe it was simply the man beside me who made my heart flutter. "Does it please you?" he asked.

I again looked overhead, trying to decipher how the bedsheets had been hung from above. When I looked back at Mr. Wilkins, he was watching me. My chest squeezed. "I . . . well . . . I hardly know what to say."

Mr. Wilkins chuckled low and moved to stand closer to me. "We never had the opportunity to tour the gardens together." He clasped his hands behind his back.

"Your efforts today are more than adequate compensation," I said.

We stood in silence, watching the rain that had earlier seemed to spoil the day but now created a symphonious melody.

Every now and again, I glanced at Mr. Wilkins. He stood tall but comfortable. He was neither imposing nor dismissive. With all he had done, all that the day yet held, he chose to stand with me, watching the raindrops patter on the windowpane. I found the scene refreshing. I found him refreshing.

"There's a smile dancing upon your lips, Miss Rutherford," Mr. Wilkins said from beside me.

"I find I cannot help it." Truly, there was no way to dampen my joy. Mr. Wilkins's efforts had ensured it.

"That is excellent news." His own grin spread wide. "I quite enjoy your smile."

My lips were not the only thing dancing. My heart again twirled inside my chest as I held his gaze. It seemed we joined each other in the swaying movements of a dance. He scanned my face while I memorized his features—defined cheeks; playful, happy eyes; and hair I longed to run my fingers through.

"La! There you are." Hazel stepped directly between us and looped her arm through my own. Whether she'd noticed the connection between her brother and myself I could not tell, for she carried on as if all were right in the world. And it was. I stood amid a flurry of bedsheet clouds, artfully arranged plants, and scattered rugs, prepared to enjoy a picnic while the rain continued to fall. And there was no place I'd rather have been.

# Chapter Fifteen

MR. ROBERT WILKINS

THROUGH THE CHAOS OF THE morning Hazel's happiness had served as my original motivation, but as we commenced preparations for the picnic, I realized Abigail would be pleased by our efforts as well. I'd continually anticipated her delight once she could witness the transformation of the ballroom. Truth be told, I hadn't thought to hang the bedsheets until I'd considered how Abigail enjoyed the outdoors. It seemed only natural to recreate billowing clouds overhead.

Seeing her pleasure at the arrangement now buoyed me—more than I thought it would. Standing beside her, witness to her simple joy, I realized I would hang bedsheets from the ceiling every day if it pleased her. How had Abigail's smile bewitched me so? Through all that had transpired with my great-aunt and adjusting to my inheritance of Cattersley and my relief of command, Abigail had resembled a candle. She was not boisterous or assuming. She knew herself, her weaknesses, and her preferences, and she glowed like the warm flame of a taper, giving just enough light to entice. And enticed I was. I wanted to spend the entire afternoon in her presence, even if it meant standing quietly beside her.

Alas, Hazel had arrived, putting an end to our quiet interlude. But Abigail's smile remained fixed, and that was all that mattered.

"Manning has just informed me that the others have arrived. Will you both join me in welcoming them?" Hazel asked.

I shook my head. "You know I support you, Hazel, but as you wish to convince them of your suitability in your new role, I suggest you greet the guests. Miss Rutherford and I will locate Mother and Mrs. Baker and wait for you here in the ballroom."

"Are you certain I must go alone?" The look in Hazel's eyes reminded me of the many times she'd solicited my help in confronting our elder brother.

John had oft assumed a position of authority and bid Hazel to do his will, whether it be to fetch him a drink or return to the house when he believed our boyish antics to be too much for her feminine eyes. I'd defended Hazel in many such situations, much to the ire of my brother.

Abigail took Hazel's hands. "It will be only for a moment. Then you will bring them here." Her eyes swept around the room. "And they will see how brilliant you are. Not many can claim a successful picnic amidst a rainstorm."

Hazel's chin lifted. "Very well. I will return shortly."

Mother and Mrs. Baker waited with us, and we briefly discussed the benefit of the rain to the crops before Hazel rejoined us with the others. I'd assumed the Adamses would be the hardest to please, but they seemed delighted with our alternative arrangements.

"However did you manage in such a short space of time?" Mrs. Adams asked.

I'd hoped for such an opportunity and quickly replied, "Once the idea was agreed upon, Hazel managed the staff with precision. Under her organization and direction, everything came together flawlessly."

Hazel laughed. "It was hardly flawless."

"You are being modest," the younger Miss Adams said with wide eyes. "'Tis exquisite."

A blush spread through Hazel's cheeks as Mead, the Lanes, Mr. Edwards, and Mrs. Christiansen praised her creativity and the decor. A gentleman I had not yet met lingered at the outskirts of the group. I waited for Hazel to lead the others to where the food had been set out, and then I approached him.

"Mr. Nicholas Poppy." The man bowed. "'Tis an honor to meet the new master of Cattersley." He straightened, and I inspected him further. He possessed handsome features and a portly figure.

"Ah, Mrs. Christiansen's brother," I realized. Hazel had told me he'd been added to the guest list, and from his snow-white hair I'd assumed him to be Mrs. Christiansen's elder brother.

"Yes, yes. Just arrived from Longsborro, Yorkshire." Mr. Poppy clasped his hands around his lapels and grinned. "Splendid arrangement you have here."

I inclined my head. "The circumstances provided a unique opportunity, I confess, but my sister had her heart set on a picnic."

"The things we'll do for our sisters, eh?" Mr. Poppy said with a laugh.

"Indeed."

Mr. Poppy and I trailed behind the slow procession. Given the multitude of stops and pointing fingers, I assumed the guests were pleased. Among the winding paths through the ballroom, we'd arranged to have the food set out in a large alcove. The smiles continued as all enjoyed Monsieur Gastineau's prepared feast.

Most of the guests spread out across the plush rugs; Mrs. Lane, Mrs. Christiansen, Mr. Poppy, and my mother sat around a small table with their plates piled high. Laughter filled the air, lightly bouncing off the tall glass windows.

I'd hoped to sit near Abigail, but Mr. Mead had claimed the place at her side. Hazel, the Adamses, and Mrs. Baker sat on rugs near them. Abigail nodded politely at something Mr. Mead said. He laughed, and Abigail looked at her lap. She had condemned his actions at the dinner party, and it seemed she had not yet forgiven him. I wondered if I could draw a true smile from her lips.

"Robert, come." Hazel motioned for me to join her.

I prepared a plate for myself and sat across from Hazel, angling myself so I could to see Abigail, and sampled the fare. Monsieur Gastineau had truly perfected his craft. The finger sandwiches, pastries, jams, fresh fruit, ripe tomatoes, and a variety of cheeses disappeared quickly.

Numerous candles had been placed on stands, tables, and pedestals, yet as the minutes passed and the clouds outside thickened, shadows crept through the room. The hung sheets and arranged plants added to the illusion of a haunted, overgrown maze garden.

"Shall we play a game?" Hazel asked.

Mother's brow twitched, but she said nothing.

Miss Adams clapped her hands in excitement. "Charades?"

"Oh, I do love a good game of charades." Mrs. Lane moved from her seat at the table and came to stand near Hazel.

"We can play charades if you wish, but since we have created this imaginary garden, I thought we might try something different." Hazel looked at her guests, a hopefulness in her eyes.

"What do you propose?" Mr. Mead asked.

Hazel shifted. I stood and offered my hand to help her to her feet, and she pressed her hands together as she spoke. "I thought perhaps one of us could hide within the ballroom. We could then count to fifty and spread out to search for the person hiding. Once they are found, we can shout out a phrase—"

"Oh, I know." Miss Adams raised her hand. "We could shout, 'Lark in the park!'"

"Perfect." Hazel clapped in excitement as Miss Adams had done a moment before. "Then we will all return here and begin again."

"I believe I shall remain here and watch the entertainment from afar," Mrs. Christiansen said. Mother agreed, but Mr. Poppy stood and said he would like to join the game for a round or two.

Everyone began to shuffle to their feet. Mrs. Baker cleared her throat. "What is your opinion, Mr. Mead?"

The vicar took his time, clearly contemplating his answer while rising to stand. He straightened his cuffs, then lifted his nose in the air. "As this temporary garden is rather rudimentary and obviously limited to within the walls of the ballroom, I see no harm in the game."

"And there are plenty of us participating, so each turn should end rather quickly," Mr. Lane added.

I did not immediately balk at Hazel's proposal, but when Mr. Mead and Mr. Lane justified the activity, I questioned whether I should call it to a halt. I had quickly learned my opinions varied greatly from those of the two gentlemen. However, when I saw Abigail's face light with excitement, I knew I would not be the one to snuff her smile.

It was decided that Hazel would be the first to hide. "Now, remember, you must count to fifty so I have time to conceal myself. Whoever discovers me first shall hide in the next round." She nearly burst with anticipation. "You may begin your count . . . now!" Hazel dashed around one of Tucker's potted trees that had been brought in for the occasion.

"One, two, three, four . . ." We counted in unison, all but Abigail. She mouthed the words, but I noticed she did not speak them aloud. And rather than glancing around at the others, she tipped her head just a bit to the side, as if listening.

The numbers naturally slipped from my tongue, but I kept my eyes fixed on Abigail. The final number counted off, the Lanes, the Adamses, Mead, Edwards, and Mr. Poppy set off in search of Hazel. Mrs. Baker had decided to remain behind with Mother and Mrs. Christiansen. Abigail looked at me and raised a single eyebrow. Her lips turned up, and she spun on her heel and disappeared around an oriental screen decorated with graceful birds.

Giggles and whispers echoed through the room. It sounded as if all were pleased with Hazel's chosen entertainment. I walked the opposite direction from Abigail, hopeful to circle back and find her. The candles flickered light on the carpets and the bedsheets overhead. In certain sections of the path, the foliage was too thick to allow the light to permeate the growing darkness.

I did not make it very far before a masculine voice called out, "Lark in the park!"

"Return to the start," someone else shouted.

I wound my way back to our meeting point. Hazel's arm was wrapped around Mr. Poppy's. "You almost walked right past," Hazel said with a laugh. "What gave me away?"

Mr. Poppy tapped a finger against his temple. "I've a sense about these things."

"Oh, hush!" Hazel smiled. "You heard me giggle."

"Indeed, my dear. Indeed." Mr. Poppy patted her hand.

"You are next to hide, Mr. Poppy," Mrs. Lane said. "Shall we begin our count?"

"Right you are." Mr. Poppy shuffled to where the manmade path disappeared. "You may need to count to seventy-five. I'm an old man."

"Seventy-five it is!" Hazel declared.

And then we began another round. Again Abigail tilted her head and listened instead of counting audibly. Mother laughed as we scattered different directions in search of Mr. Poppy. The old man had a few tricks up his sleeve. A full ten minutes passed before a shout of "Lark in the park!" rang out.

I recognized Abigail's voice at once and made my way back to the group with a smile. I walked near the windows, noting that rain no longer fell from the dark clouds.

Mr. Adams's voice sounded nearby. "Not even her beauty can compensate for a lame tongue."

"Poor Mrs. Baker. But I wonder that Miss Wilkins has taken a liking to the girl," Mrs. Adams said. "It is not good for her reputation."

"Indeed," Mr. Adams replied. "Come. They'll wonder where we are."

My fists clenched as their steps faded away. Such presumption! Such gall! Blind and prejudiced. Why had Hazel insisted on inviting these people again into our home? I returned my gaze to the window and seethed with the storm clouds.

"Mr. Wilkins?" Miss Adams's singsong call only irritated me further. "Mr. Wilkins, the round is done. Where are you?"

I inhaled deeply, determined to rein in my temper until I could find Hazel and put an end to the game.

"Ah, there you are." Miss Adams held a candle aloft. "Did you not hear? Mr. Poppy has been discovered. Miss Rutherford shall take a turn now."

"I think I've tired of this game," I said.

"But I've yet to hide." Miss Adams fluttered her lashes and placed a hand on my arm. "I've discovered the perfect hiding place." Her fingers closed around my sleeve. "Shall I show it to you?"

I pulled my arm away. "We should return to the others." I stepped past her and marched back to the group.

"Ah, there you are," Hazel said, blissfully unaware of the insults I'd overheard. "Are you ready, Miss Rutherford?"

I meant to open my mouth to put a stop to the silly game. Hazel's picnic could be considered a success. There was no need to continue, no need to impress, for those she sought to please would never be pacified. But when I turned to Abigail, my protest died on my tongue. Eager excitement lit her eyes, and I did not want to be the one to quash her enthusiasm.

At Hazel's command Abigail dashed away and the count began. I took a lesson from Abigail, and rather than count, I listened. Her footfalls were faint, but I could hear them. The enormity of the room bounced the sound around, and by the time the count of fifty rang out, I thought I had pinpointed her location to the far-right corner. I waited until the others left before I moved in that direction.

When I neared the area, I slowed, scanning each nook and crevice. The assortment of plants really did make for a labyrinth of leaves and shadows. I thought I spied movement in a small recess, and I crept in that direction.

A whispered laugh sounded behind me. "Mr. Wilkins. We meet again." Miss Adams sidled up next to me. She whispered in my ear, "Shall I show you my hiding place now, while the others are distracted?"

I opened my mouth to quell her brazen assumption when a cry sounded. It was not a call of success but a fearful scream. My blood turned cold as I recognized Abigail's voice yelling, "Fire!"

# Chapter Sixteen

## MISS ABIGAIL RUTHERFORD

I'D DISCOVERED THE PERFECT HIDING spot while searching for Hazel. When I had the opportunity to hide, I'd been ecstatic. Then Mr. Mead found me. Rather than call out to the group, however, he laid a finger across my lips and pressed himself into the small space.

"Let them search a little longer. There's no need to spoil their fun." He stepped forward, closing me in.

My back pressed against the wall. My breath quickened, along with my pulse. The levity of the game diminished, and all I wanted was to be away. In the darkness, Mr. Mead ran a hand down my arm. I closed my eyes, at the same time praying someone would come upon us and that we would not be discovered in such an intimate condition. In the next moment, Mr. Mead made his true intentions known. His gentlemanly guise was a ruse. He leaned his body nearly into mine and whispered near my ear. "You are beautiful, Miss Rutherford."

The heat of his breath moved across my cheek, and I knew he meant to kiss me. He drew closer still, and despite the confines of the space, I shoved him back and wiggled myself free. I jumped back into the wider walkway and, in my haste to be away, knocked over a candelabra. Then I saw the flame skimming across the top of a cream-colored woven rug.

Mr. Mead stepped from the shadow, and I didn't know what to fear more—the spreading flame or the stoked fire in Mr. Mead's eyes.

"Fire!" I shouted.

And then I ran . . . straight into the arms of Mr. Wilkins.

"Miss Rutherford." He pulled me to his chest, and I could feel the beating of his heart beneath my hand. It matched the rapid pace of my breaths. The peace of his embrace lasted for only a few seconds. His hands moved to my upper arms as he pulled back. "What happened?"

"Th . . . the . . . candle fell." My words quaked along with my body. I looked over my shoulder. Mr. Mead was nowhere to be seen.

Mr. Wilkins brought my attention back to him. "Miss Rutherford, you must get to safety." Mr. Poppy appeared then, along with Hazel. "Escort the ladies away," Mr. Wilkins instructed Mr. Poppy. Then he rushed toward the flames.

The smell of burned carpet and the crackle of the growing flame grew as Mr. Poppy steered us to the main ballroom doors. I clasped Hazel's hand, and we ran. Servants passed us, heading for the danger. Calls for water and buckets sounded as the smoke thickened.

Hazel shouted for her mother, and through the haze we saw Mrs. Wilkins, Grandmother, and Mrs. Christiansen exit the room. We followed, gathering with the other women in the corridor before rushing down the stairs to the front hall. Mr. Mead stood there, placating the others, offering a scripture about peace and holding Mrs. Adams's hand in what seemed to be compassion. I wanted to retch.

In fact, my entire body began to protest. I shook violently, from my knees to my fingertips. Hazel led me to a chair, but the enormity of what had occurred continued to rake over me.

Voices turned muffled. Words like *traumatic* and *weak* flitted around me. I was led to a carriage. I knew it to be Mr. Mead's, and I wanted to scream, to renounce the man. But words would not form, and I was forced inside.

I looked out the carriage window and saw Mr. Wilkins emerge from the house. He had shed his jacket and wore only his waistcoat and shirtsleeves. His hair was tousled, and his chest heaved. He looked over the assembled guests, searching faces until his gaze met mine. I raised my fingers to the small pane of glass, and he nodded once.

Grandmother sat down beside me on the bench. Then Mr. Mead sat on the opposite side, and the horses lurched forward.

Fog consumed my mind, and the world seemed to tilt. Once the carriage stopped, I opened the door, stepped down, and walked directly to my room, for there, I knew, Mr. Mead could not follow. I collapsed onto my bed and let the tremors wash over me until I fell asleep.

❧

I woke to Mrs. Bearsly's kind ministrations. She set a tray of bread and a cup of tea near my bed and pulled open the curtains. The night had passed, but storm clouds still veiled the sky and a light rain pattered on the windowpane.

I sat up abruptly. "The fire!"

Mrs. Bearsly stepped to the bed and arranged the pillows so I might lean against them. "Don't you worry, Miss Rutherford." She picked up the tray and moved it to my lap. "Mr. Wilkins came this morning to inquire after you. Said the damage was minimal. Lost only a few rugs, and a bit o' the floor was burned."

"Was he very upset?" I asked.

"Upset? Ha." Mrs. Bearsly chuckled. "Not at all. Didn't even mention Cattersley until Mrs. Baker insisted he relate the details. He only asked after your wellbeing."

I raised a hand to my head. How had things spiraled so quickly? The game . . . Mr. Mead . . . his breath on my face. "I'm afraid my appetite has waned."

Mrs. Bearsly puckered her lips. "Well, then, just a bit of tea." She moved the tray back beside the bed and handed me the cup. My fingers shook as I took it from her. "Go on, now," she said and watched until I swallowed. "You'll need some nourishment for when that man returns. He's due to arrive any minute."

"Mr. Wilkins?" I asked. My heart fluttered at the thought.

"No." Mrs. Bearsly frowned. "Mr. Mead."

My breath hitched, and my stomach clenched. "Why would he call?"

"Seems *he's* taken a special interest in you as well." Mrs. Bearsly walked to the wardrobe and removed my best day dress—a light-blue muslin with cream-colored trim. She held the dress up. "Your grandmother suggested you wear this."

As much as I longed to wear brighter colors again, I did not wish to do so to impress Mr. Mead. I wanted nothing to do with the man. Perhaps my face revealed my repulsion, for Mrs. Bearsly walked close and laid a hand on my cheek. "There, now. You've endured the vicar's visits before."

"I confess I have previously enjoyed his company. But now . . ." Tears sprang to my eyes.

Mrs. Bearsly rubbed her hand along my back. "Come, dear."

I dressed as slowly as possible, as if I could delay the clock. Despite Mrs. Bearsly's insistence that I receive the vicar, I hoped to convince Grandmother I was unwell. It was the truth.

Mrs. Bearsly then left me alone in order to attend to her duties. Shortly after, Grandmother rapped on my door. "Come, Abigail. You have a visitor." Grandmother walked to where I stood near the window.

"My stomach is unsettled. Surely Mr. Mead will understand." My insides shook, but my voice sounded strong. Too strong, it seemed, for Grandmother dismissed my plea and herded me to the sitting room.

Mr. Mead stood and immediately took notice of my gown. "Miss Rutherford, may I say, you look lovely in that shade of blue."

I mumbled my thanks, and as Grandmother took the seat farthest from Mr. Mead, I was forced to sit near him. On Craven's last visit, Grandmother had insisted all of the furniture be clustered together around the windows. If Mr. Mead extended his arm, he could reach me. Every inch of my skin itched to crawl away from him, to put distance between us. The look on his face made my stomach curl.

Grandmother arranged her skirts. "Mr. Mead does us a great honor, Abigail." When I did not smile, Grandmother tsked. "She's still shaken from the events at the picnic. Thank you again for seeing us home."

"Not at all. 'Twas my honor to escort you both back to Fern Cottage." Mr. Mead smiled at me, and my stomach lurched again.

"You have salvaged our good name, sir, and for that we owe you a great debt." Grandmother's sugary words caught my attention. "Come, you must tell Abigail what you have done."

"If you insist." The vicar looked far too pleased with himself.

Grandmother nodded vigorously. "Yes, go on."

"After escorting you ladies home, I returned to Cattersley to offer my assistance. The fire had been extinguished, but unfortunately a bit of damage was done. I'm sure it is no great expense for the Cattersley coffers, but for you and I . . . well." He raised his hands, then dropped them again. "Mr. Wilkins and his butler were trying to determine the origin of the fire." Mr. Mead turned to me, his eyes drawn down with false empathy. "I knew if you had been present, Miss Rutherford, you would have voiced your part in the tragedy. And as I was nearby and witnessed the event, I spoke on your behalf."

My heart beat loudly in my ears. My chest ached with every breath. Yes, I had caused the fire. I'd knocked the candle over. But only in my efforts to extract myself from Mr. Mead's salacious designs.

With audacious confidence, he continued. "I did, of course, explain that it was an accident, but Mr. Wilkins's anger was palpable. I feared you would suffer greatly from his wrath, so I immediately insisted all expenses for the repair be sent to me." Mr. Mead straightened himself in his seat, preening for the praise he expected me to give. He would be disappointed.

Grandmother's hand fluttered at her neck. "So chivalrous, Mr. Mead. How can we ever repay you?"

"My dear Mrs. Baker, I offer my assistance not in expectation of recompense. We've witnessed Wilkins's wrath before, but I'm afraid this was even more extreme—and over such a paltry sum . . ." Mr. Mead frowned and shook his head.

"You, sir, are too good. Truly the Lord's servant." Grandmother stiffened and looked at me. "Abigail, you owe Mr. Mead a great deal." She waved her hand. "Do not be ungrateful, child."

I had never realized disgust could be such a potent sensation, but every vein in my being seared with the emotion—a combination of disappointment, anger, and sickness I could not ignore. A pounding in my chest, aching to be released. A scream stifled only by my humanity.

"Abigail!" Grandmother snapped.

I looked directly into Mr. Mead's cold brown eyes, the ones I had once thought focused on God's word. "Thank you for the offer, Mr. Mead, but I will happily pay for the damage caused by the fire."

Grandmother scoffed beside me. Mr. Mead's lips turned upward. "Nonsense, Miss Rutherford. It is all settled." He stood as if to leave, then halted and turned to Grandmother. "There is another topic I wished to discuss with you, Mrs. Baker."

"Of course, of course." Grandmother motioned to Mr. Mead's chair, and he retook his seat.

"It should come as no surprise that upon Miss Rutherford's arrival in Henwick, she has been of particular interest to me." He leaned forward. "I admire her a great deal, and as you are her guardian, I would like to ask for your express permission to court her."

I gasped, but Grandmother either did not notice or chose to interpret my reaction as excited awe. "Mr. Mead . . . after all you have done! You honor us greatly, and of course, you have my blessing." Grandmother fairly beamed. Could she not see the feral grin lurking in Mr. Mead's smile?

My disgust turned to despair as Mr. Mead came near and took my hand. He placed a cold kiss on the back of my knuckles and left me sitting speechless and ill while Grandmother led him to the door.

When she returned from bidding Mr. Mead goodbye, Grandmother proceeded to lecture me for the next hour. I remained silent and impassive as Grandmother, in no uncertain terms, demanded I accept Mr. Mead's suit. She covered every gambit of the issue, emphasizing how Mr. Mead desired me for a wife despite my course manners and unrefined speech. "Thank goodness you have inherited your mother's handsome features," Grandmother said. "It is the reason you have caught the eye of such an eligible suitor. And now that you have offended Mr. Wilkins with your clumsy mistake, we shall receive no further invitations to Cattersley. Bless Mr. Mead for paying your debt and bartering his good name to save our own."

When Grandmother finally dismissed me, I returned to my room and paced the short length of my chamber again and again. I wished the rain would relent so I might exercise my frustrations out of doors. But as the sun set, the dreary weather continued.

I refused the dinner tray Mrs. Bearsly brought up. I preferred to feel hunger pains gnawing my stomach over the roiling bile Mr. Mead's request had conjured. I could not think on his words, his haughty attitude, nor his features, which I'd once considered handsome, without nausea welling inside of me.

I woke early the next morning to discover the sun had finally separated the clouds. I left my hair in its braid and threw on my boots, my plain gray dress, and my pelisse, and rushed outside. Despite my desire for the rain to pass, I enjoyed the smell of saturated earth. The soggy leaves dampened the sound of my steps. I circled the perimeter of Fern Cottage, considering Mr. Mead's story. Was there truth to his words—to any of them? Was Mr. Wilkins truly angry? Was that why he had called immediately after the event? To demand payment? But Mr. Mead's words directly contradicted Mrs. Bearsly's report that Mr. Wilkins was not upset in the least. Between the two of them, I knew whom I should believe, but I couldn't help but wonder if Mr. Mead's explanation was an embellishment on a small bit of truth.

Hazel had not contacted me. Oh, the poor girl. Another of her gatherings gone awry, and I was entirely to blame. No wonder she had not been in touch. My heart ached anew, wondering if I'd lost the valuable treasure of her friendship.

I kept to the wooded area behind Fern Cottage. I did not wish to be found if Mr. Mead should call again, and I was not brave enough to venture onto Cattersley land. Walking through the trees, inhaling the clean air, did not bring the usual measure of peace. Grandmother insisted I accept Mr. Mead's suit, while I wanted nothing to do with the man. Could Grandmother force me in this? Could Mr. Mead? What recourse did I have?

Benjamin.

If I could locate my brother, perhaps he would allow me to live with him. America seemed so very far away. I looked up through the branches of the trees. Reaching the sky through the branches seemed as elusive as the hope I clung to. Whether I traveled across the sea or became the wife of the vicar, I would lose Hazel, Mr. Wilkins, and the solace I'd found in Herefordshire. What was I to do?

# Chapter Seventeen

### MR. ROBERT WILKINS

AFTER THE FIRE HAD BEEN extinguished, I'd wanted to rush directly to Fern Cottage and see for myself that Abigail was well. "She was quite shaken," Hazel had explained. "Mr. Mead and Mrs. Baker returned her home so she might rest." Mother had then redirected my focus to our remaining guests.

When Mr. Mead returned and revealed Abigail's part in the fire, I had only desired to hold Abigail close and tell her not to fret. I paid little attention to the obnoxious vicar's offer to pay for the loss of a few rugs and floorboards.

The night had lasted far too long, and when I called at Fern Cottage first thing the following morning, I was told Abigail was still abed. Duties did not allow me to return until this morning. I knew I was taking a chance that Abigail might not yet be awake, so in order to delay my arrival, I walked, rather than rode Barkley, across the estate. My choice proved to be a wise one.

Abigail walked among the sodden leaves; her hair, free of its usual bonnet, swung in a braid across her back. I moved closer, and my movement drew her attention. I swept my tall hat from my head. "My apologies, Miss Rutherford. I did not mean to startle you."

Confusion flitted over her face. She offered a shallow curtsy, and then her gaze bounced between my face and the ground. "I'm truly sorry for what happened," she said.

I shrugged away the apology. "No harm done."

"But the floor, your rugs . . ."

"All replaceable." I smiled and stepped closer, hoping to assure her of my sincerity.

She now met my gaze with determination. "I plan to find a way to pay for the repair."

She was adorable. My lips twitched. "I give you my word it has been handled."

"Yes, Mr. Mead . . ." Her face fell, and she turned away from me and took only two steps before turning to face me again. She tossed her braid over her shoulder. "The responsibility is mine," she said. I wanted to reach around her and pull her hair forward once more.

Desperation clung to me like the moisture hanging in the leaves of the forest. "I respect your integrity and mean no disrespect, but I assure you the cost is minimal." I turned the hat in my hands. "Pray tell, what does Mead have to do with it?"

"He said you agreed that he could cover the cost of my blunder."

The blasted man was determined to interfere. I stepped closer. "He has misspoken. I've agreed to no such arrangement."

Abigail nodded her head. "I shall do it, then. It may take a bit of time, but I can sell a few items, and perhaps there's a family nearby in need of a governess."

"Please, Miss Rutherford, don't you see? I don't want any recompense for damages. No one was hurt, and the fire was quashed rather quickly. Repairs will be minimal; in fact, they are currently underway. My concern is with those involved."

"I see." Her hands fisted at her side.

"Do you?" I stepped forward again and stopped when I stood only three feet away. I needed her to truly understand. "I've no doubt the fire was an accident. In fact, if anyone is to blame, it is I. Knowing the arrangement of candles around the room, I should have dissuaded Hazel from her game. There is no other fault to be had."

"Truly?" she asked.

"Truly. I've come to inquire after you . . . Miss Rutherford." Her nearness scattered every rational thought from my mind.

My eyes never veered from hers, and I could not, did not, resist the urge to lift her hand from where it hung at her side. I uncurled her fingers and placed them in my own. With a gentle squeeze I asked, "Are you well, Miss Rutherford?"

A long minute passed, and her eyes caressed my face, searching for something. "You've not come to chastise me?"

Her words sobered me. How could she suggest such a thing? I looked at her fingers in my own. "Not in the least. When I last saw you, you were fleeing the fire. Your cheeks were flushed, and the reflection of the flames danced in your eyes. It was almost as if the devil himself were chasing you. Once the fire was extinguished, I came to find you, but you were settled in Mead's carriage to return home. I was told you were quite shaken. I only wish to confirm your wellbeing."

"I am well now, Mr. Wilkins." Her eyes wandered to the damp ground. "Or rather . . . I am physically unharmed."

"Physically? Do you mean to say . . . ?"

Abigail pulled her hand free from my grasp. "I am well, sir, and I sincerely thank you for your concern."

Her abrupt change of demeanor rooted me in place. Abigail's slip of the tongue did not go unnoticed. What did she mean she was *physically* well? Was she injured in some other way? To me, she appeared radiant. The sun filtering through the leaves of the trees danced on the crown of her head, and I knew I was a smitten fool. "Will you tell me what happened?" I asked.

In response to my request for an explanation, she began to walk among the trees. I replaced my hat and walked beside her. "When it came my turn to hide, I'm afraid I did not choose well," she said. Her hand trailed along the bark of a pine. "I shifted to get more comfortable and toppled the nearby candelabra." She glanced at me but looked away far too quickly. "I truly am sorry."

Two nights of worry and wonder had tested me. I reached forward to take her hand in mine again but then remembered that she had pulled away the first time. My arm fell back to my side. "I never doubted it was an accident. I'm glad Mr. Mead was able to see you home."

She stopped, and her gaze jumped up to meet mine. The light in her eyes disappeared. "Yes . . . Mr. Mead," she said.

Hazel had always been a sensitive girl. She possessed a tender heart and would often cry at even the smallest critique. I'd learned to recognize the signs of tears: lips pressed closed, fast-blinking lashes, and misting eyes— all things I noticed in Abigail as she stood before me.

I opened my mouth but closed it again. I could not tease her as I did my sister. Abigail was upset. I had upset her, and I knew not how to fix it. "Shall I return you to Fern Cottage?" I asked.

"Thank you, but no. I've been indoors far too long." She offered a pinched smile.

"Then, shall we visit Tucker?" Perhaps talk of flowers and plants would lift her spirits. "Or Hazel?"

Abigail's expression softened. "How is your sister?"

"She's determined to relate the events of the picnic to everyone she sees." I chuckled. "I'm grateful my late aunt employed patient servants." The improvised picnic in the ballroom, Monsieur Gastineau's food, and the culminating fire dominated conversation at Cattersley and I assumed all of Henwick as well.

"I've ruined everything." Abigail sighed and pressed a hand to her brow.

"Not at all. I don't think the servants have been this entertained for quite some time. And I'm certain Hazel will call in a day or two."

Abigail dropped her hand and began walking again. I stepped beside her. "Thank you for calling, Mr. Wilkins," she said.

Disappointment swept through me, but I acknowledged Abigail's dismissal. "I shall leave you to your thoughts." I bowed my head. "Good day, Miss Rutherford."

"And to you," she said.

I touched the tip of my hat and turned away, determined to call again with Hazel on the morrow. Then Abigail would see all was well. But as I walked back through the trees, I considered that something more was amiss. Abigail's contrite apology was no surprise, but she did not seem herself.

Upon returning to Cattersley, I found the household in a frenzy and endeavored to shake myself from my reverie. "Manning, what is going on?"

The butler lifted his chin. "It seems Mr. John Wilkins is due to arrive within the hour, sir."

John? I had not been expecting him until Christmas. "Where is my mother?" I asked.

"She's overseeing the preparation of one of the guest chambers, sir."

"Manning, pray tell, which of the numerous guest chambers?" Manning's lips fidgeted as if he wanted to smile. He did a commendable job of controlling his mirth.

"The Hunting Room, sir."

"Thank you." I handed over my hat and gloves and set off in search of my mother.

She stood straightening one of the cream-colored damask-print curtains in the appointed room. "Where have you been, dear?" she asked when she spied me.

"I called at Fern Cottage." I stepped through the doorway and inspected the room.

"And how is our Miss Rutherford faring?" Mother moved to the curtain on the opposite side of the window and began straightening the folds there.

"She appears to be well, but in truth, I'm not sure." The admission granted relief.

Mother's hand stilled. "What do you mean?"

"She readily accepts blame for the fire, admits she knocked the candles over, but something does not sit well." I walked to the window and looked out at the stables.

"You don't believe her?" Mother asked.

"I don't know." I turned around to face Mother. "I don't believe she lied, but I'm not sure she told me the whole truth." I clenched my fists in frustration. "I assured her the damage was minimal. The cost as well. I meant to assure her that all was forgiven and forgotten, yet she did not seem relieved. She avoided my questions and dismissed me."

"She's embarrassed, that is all." Mother smiled.

"Perhaps." I reconstructed my interaction with Abigail. Her surprise that I had called. Her struggle to hide her tears. And her smile that had been as dampened and wilted as the leaves beneath our feet. But when she'd held my gaze, really looked into my eyes, I thought she'd felt an inkling of something growing between us, until the shift in her eyes when I'd mentioned Mead.

"The gossip will die down in a day or two. Then Miss Rutherford will return to herself." Mother touched my arm, and Pratt entered the room with an armful of wood.

He gave a curt nod. "Pardon me, ma'am. Sir. Mr. Kane asked me to deliver a hearty supply of wood. Wanted to be sure we was ready for the guest."

"Yes. Our guest." Sarcasm laced my words. "Carry on." Pratt finished his task and left the room. I looked at my mother. "Did you know John was coming for a visit?"

She pulled a letter from her sleeve and handed it to me. "This arrived only today."

I skimmed the contents. "Is Hazel aware?" I returned the letter to my mother. It contained nothing that would indicate his sudden desire to celebrate my inheritance.

"She's discussing the menu with Monsieur Gastineau. It seems John intimidates her more than the Adamses do." Mother offered a wan smile.

"If Hazel wants to play hostess at Cattersley, I'm the only one she needs to impress."

Mother touched a hand to my cheek. "Right you are."

"Shall we go await John's arrival?" I offered my arm, and Mother allowed me to escort her to the Sky Room. John rode into view an hour later.

The footmen cleared the final course. There was no reason for John and me to remain; we were all family. We settled in the drawing room, and John shared the happy news that Clara was expecting their fourth child.

"Oh, I can hardly wait." Hazel had always doted on her nieces and nephews.

"How is Clara feeling?" Mother asked.

"She has a strong constitution. Carrying a child requires very little from her," John said. I'd always wondered at John's ability to see things the way he thought they should be.

"I hope your nursemaid is keeping the other children out of trouble. Clara needs her rest," Mother said.

"Actually"—John shifted in his seat and turned to Hazel—"how long do you intend to remain at Cattersley?"

Hazel's eyes widened. "When I left Borshire, I made it quite clear I intended to remain here for the foreseeable future."

"You mentioned your hope that Robert would have need of you. He now commands an army of servants; what purpose might you have here?"

"John." Mother's stern tone gave my brother only a moment's pause.

Hazel straightened in her seat, but her hands were clasped so tightly in her lap that her knuckles began to turn white. "Robert has agreed to allow me to remain as hostess." Her voice dropped to a whisper. "On a trial basis."

John rubbed a hand across his leg. "I've no doubt you enjoy planning dinners with your French chef, but the children miss you dearly. As Clara's confinement nears, we could use your help. It would be nice for the children to be with someone other than Mrs. Henderson. I fear she allows far too much folly. We hoped you might return home with me."

Hazel paled, but she did not look away. "And I them. But I am finding my place here."

John stared at Hazel and did not speak for a long moment. "Clara worried that the grandeur of Cattersley would numb you to reality. I fear she was right." John's hardened eyes either did not notice or did not care about the mist gathering in Hazel's fair blue ones.

But I did. "Hazel is welcome to remain," I said.

John scoffed. "Little brother, you've always been reasonable. Surely you see that Hazel will be smothered here, lost in this vast household. In Borshire she has friends and family who love her. How do you suppose she will make a match if she is busy managing this?" John waved his hand at the ceiling overhead.

I harbored the same concern. I'd told Hazel as much, but she'd promised to return to London for another Season. "As difficult as it is for you to comprehend, Hazel has friends and family here also. It is for her to decide."

John shook his head. "Mother, is my assessment not correct?"

Mother sat with her eyes closed, massaging her temples. "I believe I'm ready for bed." She looked up and studied us each in turn. "It's been a long day, and I think it best if we all turn in for the night." She stood. John and I did as well. "Hazel, will you please escort me to my room?"

Hazel did not look at us as she left with Mother. And I had no desire to continue conversation with my brother. "Good night, John. Let Manning know if you require anything further."

"Still the favorite," John mused as I walked toward the door.

I looked back over my shoulder. "You said it yourself—I'm the reasonable one." I turned back around and headed to my room.

# Chapter Eighteen

## MISS ABIGAIL RUTHERFORD

THE REMAINDER OF THE WEEK passed without a word from Hazel. One moment I worried she'd fallen ill and the next I wondered if she was angry that I had ruined her picnic. I walked out of doors as much as possible to avoid Grandmother and Mr. Mead. He'd called twice since the day he asked Grandmother's permission to court me. Thankfully, both times I'd been unavailable. It was easy to lose track of time while out of doors. Grandmother lectured me on punctuality and insisted I stay nearer the cottage, but she never did make the connection that Mr. Mead was the very reason I stayed away.

Alas, Sunday arrived, and I could no longer avoid seeing the man. At least we would be surrounded by a congregation of worshipers so he could not catch me alone. I hoped to avoid any conversation with Mr. Mead, lest he thought I was encouraging his suit.

Grandmother insisted we arrive early, and we sat in our usual pew. About five minutes before the service was due to begin a great chatter rose from the doorway. I looked back to see Mr. Wilkins, his mother, and Hazel enter, followed by another man. His handsome features left no doubt of his relation to Mr. Wilkins. The family walked in formation past us to their pew and sat silently until Mr. Mead began his sermon.

I had not realized how dearly I'd missed Hazel's company until I saw her again. Did she despise me, or was there still hope for our friendship? I hoped I might catch her eye with a timely placed cough, but when I attempted it, Grandmother quickly hushed me with an elbow thrust to my side.

Once upon a time I'd enjoyed Mr. Mead's sermons. He was well-spoken and versed in the scriptures. However, while his message spoke of truth, I could not absorb it knowing the hypocrisy of the man standing at the pulpit. He said something about duty and marriage and how a union should honor the Lord. Perhaps he had prepared his remarks for me. He would be disappointed to know I filled my head with my thoughts of Mr. Wilkins and Hazel rather than his ramblings. I only realized Mr. Mead had finished his discourse when Grandmother stood.

I shook my head clear, followed her outside, and fiddled with the ribbons on my bonnet, hoping to stall for time so I might have an opportunity to speak with Hazel. Grandmother greeted several neighbors, and I stood silently behind her, searching the crowd for my friend. I spotted the Cattersley coach but did not yet see Hazel.

"Miss Rutherford." Mr. Mead touched my elbow. "I hoped you and your grandmother might remain for a moment. It would be my honor to escort you home."

I meant to decline, but Grandmother answered before I had the chance. "We would be delighted, Mr. Mead. And may I commend you on a brilliant sermon, sir."

Mr. Mead inclined his head. "Thank you, Mrs. Baker. I endeavor only to share God's word. You cannot argue with doctrine."

I wanted to argue his hypocrisy. And I wanted to vomit.

Mr. Mead held his arm out to me. I pressed my lips tight, desperately trying to think of a way to decline his offer. My mind worked too slowly, and when Grandmother cleared her throat, I knew I had to step forward and place my arm around Mr. Mead's. But before I could, Hazel appeared.

"Abigail!" She grabbed my hands. "How I've missed you." She then noticed Mr. Mead. "My apologies, Mr. Mead. I've interrupted."

He bowed his head. "You needn't worry, Miss Wilkins. We are not in a rush."

"La! Are you walking to Fern Cottage?" Hazel squeezed my hands.

"Yes," I said.

She swung our arms between us. "Oh, I was just telling Robert it is a beautiful day for a stroll." She looked first at Mr. Mead, then at me. "Might we join you?"

"Certainly!" My heart lifted. It was the happiest I'd been since the first moments of the picnic. "You don't mind, do you, Mr. Mead?"

He smiled through his tightened jaw. "Not at all."

"Come, Abigail." Hazel pulled my hand. "Let's tell Robert. And you must meet my eldest brother, John."

"Excuse me, Mr. Mead." I practically giggled as Hazel led me away.

We walked toward where Hazel's family stood near their carriage. "I've missed you, Hazel! I thought perhaps you were angry with me," I confessed.

Hazel stopped immediately. "Not at all." Her pretty eyes widened. "After the picnic I was distraught. But not because I was upset with you." She leaned close and whispered low, "I worried the other guests would consider it a failure." Her eyes twinkled mischievously. "I should have known better. The indoor picnic and fire are all the talk." She pulled back. "Robert said he told you."

"He also said you would call." The whine in my voice betrayed me, and I had to turn away.

"I wanted to, believe me. But John arrived, and . . . well . . . he's demanded our time." She began to walk again with my hand in hers. "Come. I'll introduce you."

The stern-faced Mr. John Wilkins offered a cold greeting. Mrs. Wilkins requested her parasol from the carriage, and Mr. Robert Wilkins instructed his driver to meet us at Fern Cottage. Then we began our stroll. Grandmother walked with Mrs. Wilkins at the head of the group, and the rest of us followed behind.

It truly was a beautiful day. The clear blue of the sky enriched the other colors of the earth. The green leaves, the golden fields, even the path we walked upon seemed to breathe in airy conversation with the other elements.

Mr. John Wilkins talked about the success of his crops and the measures he had implemented to improve their yield. I remained silent, content to walk beside Hazel. Mr. Mead engaged the elder Mr. Wilkins in conversation, and both men appeared to relish the attention. Mr. Wilkins animatedly waved his walking stick as he answered Mr. Mead's questions. Mr. Robert Wilkins fell into step with his sister and me.

Hazel wandered to the side of the road and picked a lone white daisy. "Here you are, Abigail." She stepped in front of me and tucked the flower into my bonnet. "What do you say, Robert? Doesn't it look lovely?"

Mr. Robert Wilkins gave a great show of examining the flower. "Indeed. The flower is much improved now that it has the honor to adorn Miss Rutherford's bonnet."

Hazel swatted his arm, and he chuckled. Turning to me, Hazel then said, "Abigail, you must come to Cattersley tomorrow. The most brilliant purple flowers have just bloomed. I know you would love them. And then we could take tea in the garden." She leaned close and whispered, "We'll have a picnic—a proper one—just the two of us."

"I shall try to get away." It had been over a week since I'd wandered through Mr. Tucker's masterpiece. I hoped Grandmother would allow me to go.

"Might I send the carriage for you?" Hazel asked.

"Thank you, but I pwefer to walk," I said. I bit down my frustration at my mispronunciation, but I was determined to continue in the conversation. I spoke slower. "The meadow is a canvas of color and will last only a few more weeks."

Hazel huffed. "Don't remind me. I wish summer would continue on forever."

The lack of a rebuke for my mistakes bolstered my courage. "I do love summer. But to watch the snowfall is a different sort of beauty." I smiled in my success of conveying the thought properly.

"Winter only means I must return to London." Hazel stopped and picked another flower. She twirled it between her fingers for a moment, then walked near and tucked it next to the daisy she had placed in my bonnet.

"Come now," Mr. Robert Wilkins said patiently. "You agreed to a Season when you arrived. We will spend the Christmas holiday together, and then you and Mother may travel to London together."

"I only agreed because you hardly allowed me a choice. You are rarely forceful, so I felt I must comply." Hazel frowned.

"I will not force you to accept a new wardrobe," Mr. Robert Wilkins said with a mischievous glint in his eyes.

"That will be one benefit, I suppose." Hazel clasped her hands behind her and skipped a few steps. Her skipping drew the attention of the others. Mr. Mead and Mr. John Wilkins paused and waited for us to reach them.

"John, do you think Robert should come to London with me? If he insists I have a Season, he should come stand as my guardian." Hazel turned a triumphant smile on the younger brother.

"You would both do well to find a spouse." The elder Mr. Wilkins pointed his walking stick at his siblings. "It's as the vicar preached today: 'A union sanctified in holiness brings blessings.'"

Mr. Mead puffed out his chest and inclined his head. "I am pleased you liked the sermon, Mr. Wilkins." Then he turned to me, a calculating smile upon his face. "What did you think of it, Miss Rutherford?"

Any doubt that he had prepared his words for me vanished. I wondered who knew of his intent to court me. Had Grandmother spread the news to her friends?

My heart sped. "You've a talent for delivewing doctwine in a succinct manner," I said. Mr. Mead's attention flustered me, and my sounds slurred together. No one mentioned my error, but I did not miss the shocked disgust that passed over Mr. John Wilkins's face. I directed my gaze to the path at my feet.

Hazel came to my rescue. "It's not that I don't wish to marry. I am simply not in a rush to do so."

"There will always be a new flock of debutantes to entice the bachelors. You must take advantage of your youth and catch a husband while you are in your prime." Mr. John Wilkins tucked his walking stick beneath his arm. "If you return with me to Borshire, Clara can direct you in the art. She had three men vying for her hand."

"And how did you win her over?" Mr. Mead asked.

"Dogged persistence." Mr. Wilkins raised his chin and grinned.

Mr. Mead laughed. "I shall employ that tactic myself."

My stomach churned with his words and with the thought that Hazel would remain at Cattersley for only a few months more. Mr. Robert Wilkins might be leaving as well, and I would be left to spend the cold, dark winter sitting silently at Fern Cottage with only the snowfall to keep me company.

Grandmother tolerated my outside wanderings and even granted permission for me to visit Cattersley at Hazel's invitation. But Mr. Mead began to call almost every day. His punctuality was my downfall, for Grandmother insisted I be home to receive him. At two o'clock every afternoon he rapped on the door.

My silence was no longer insisted upon. Instead Grandmother directed questions to me, and I could do naught but answer. Mr. Mead's moods varied from gracious to calculating. His veiled references to an impending union frayed my nerves, and I repeatedly dropped my letters in my responses. Grandmother's eyes pinched tight at each of my blunders, but she refrained from commenting in Mr. Mead's presence. Only after he left did she make her displeasure known.

Her lectures lasted for what seemed to be an eternity. "Mr. Mead has singled you out. No other offers will come your way. Love is truly blind— or deaf, rather; why else would he pay you any regard? Practice your words ten times before he calls tomorrow." Again and again I listened in silence, wishing to be anywhere other than confined with my grandmother. I did try, yet I received no recognition for my efforts. Why, then, should I even attempt to speak correctly?

One afternoon, I returned from my walk, resigned to receive Mr. Mead for his daily call. Craven sat scrubbing a large pot, and Mrs. Bearsly's flour-covered hands busily shaped scones.

"Good day, Miss Rutherford," Craven said.

"Hello, Craven." I turned to Mrs. Bearsly. "Do you need help preparing the tea tray?"

"Shan't take me but a moment. With Mrs. Baker gone to town, I don't need to skim fresh cream, as you and Mr. Mead prefer your tea without it." Mrs. Bearsly dusted the flour from her hands and set her tray in the oven.

"Grandmother's not here?" Worry coursed through me like a thorny bramble.

"No, ma'am." Craven poured a pitcher of water into the pot and swished it around. "Had me hitch the horse to the cart an hour ago. Said she needed to visit a friend on the far side of Henwick. Planned to be home late this afternoon." He stepped to the door to toss the water out, but instead of it flying over the step, he dumped it onto his leg, dousing his trousers.

Mrs. Bearsly chuckled. "You didn't account for the rim of the pot." Craven grinned, shook his head, and stepped back inside.

"But what of Mr. Mead's visit? Did she send word for him not to come?" I asked hopefully. Mr. Mead's visits had been torturous enough. To visit with him alone . . . Perhaps he and Grandmother had schemed to make it so.

"I imagine he'll be arriving shortly. Mrs. Baker insisted I use the rose tea service today." Mrs. Bearsly began preparing the tea tray.

My heart began to pound. I could not be alone with that man. "You must tell him I'm not here."

Mrs. Bearsly froze in her task and looked at me. "Is everything all right, Miss Rutherford?"

"No, it is not." I peeked out the open door to see if Mr. Mead had yet ridden into view.

Craven came to stand at my shoulder. He mimicked my posture and scanned the yard. "What are we looking for?"

"Mr. Mead," I said in exasperation. The two servants exchanged a look, and I knew to procure their help, they needed to know the truth. "He's asked to court me."

"Ah." Mrs. Bearsly nodded. "I wondered as much, with his daily visits and all."

"I'm afraid he might wish to make an offer." I pulled the door shut.

"And that ain't good?" Craven scratched his neck.

I shook my head. Mrs. Bearsly offered a sympathetic smile. "He's quite a handsome man, and as Cattersley supports his parsonage, he will provide well for a wife."

"But he . . ." Should I tell them more? Tell them of the liberties he'd attempted to claim at the picnic? "I simply cannot become his wife."

Mrs. Bearsly's lips pushed her cheeks into a full smile, and her eyes lit. "You're in love with another."

"What? No." Horse hooves sounded outside. Time was short. "Please, tell him I am gone!"

A knock sounded, and I didn't have time to run to my room. "Hurry, miss. In here." Craven opened the door to the storage pantry, and I ducked inside.

I held my breath and pressed my ear to the door. Mrs. Bearsly spoke first. "Welcome, sir. Miss Rutherford is not up to entertaining this afternoon."

Then I recognized Mr. Mead's voice. "I insist upon seeing her."

"I'm afraid it isn't possible. She's quite ill," Mrs. Bearsly said.

"Nonsense! I saw her not an hour ago." An hour prior I'd stood at the border of Grandmother's property, gazing across the meadow toward Cattersley. He would only have seen me if he'd been in the forest at the same time, but he had not made himself known. What was he about? My hands began to tremble.

"What ails her?" he demanded.

"A . . . a sour stomach, sir. She's extremely qualmish." Bless Mrs. Bearsly.

"Then I should call for a doctor." Footsteps sounded, and my heart beat so loudly I felt it might knock open the door.

"Good day, Mr. Mead," Craven said. "It's nice to see you again, sir."

Mr. Mead mumbled something I couldn't hear. Then he said, "Either lead me to Miss Rutherford's chamber, or I shall find it myself."

"I wouldn't recommend it, sir," Craven said. "I led her up only a moment ago. Miss Rutherford missed the pot I held for her to retch into and tagged my trousers. I've just now scrubbed them clean." What a quick-thinking lad!

It was quiet for a long moment. "Please inform Miss Rutherford that I shall return," Mr. Mead said. "I am confident she will be improved on the morrow."

"You have such faith," Mrs. Bearsly said, and footsteps followed. Then silence fell.

I stood in the dark and willed my breathing to slow. Finally, Craven cracked open the door. A huge grin spread across his face. "It was close, but we did it, miss."

I exited the closet, grateful for my two allies. "Thank you, my friends." I grabbed one of each of their hands and then turned to Craven. "You were brilliant to show him your wet pant leg."

Craven beamed. "'Twas nothing."

Mrs. Bearsly led me to the kitchen table. I sat, and she carried over her prepared tray. "Come on, Craven." She patted a place beside her, and he joined us. She poured three cups of tea, and after handing me mine, she said, "Now, tell me which lucky man has captured your heart." She took a sip of her tea, and with a chink she replaced the cup on the saucer. "Though, I wager I could guess." The smile on her face told me she knew full well the answer to her question.

Craven scooted forward on the bench. He reminded me of an eager pup awaiting a treat from its master.

I turned my cup in my hands. My heart searched for its rhythm, recovering from the scare of Mr. Mead's arrival and the more-pleasant thought of a handsome captain. "It's true my affections lie elsewhere, though I hardly know when it began."

Mrs. Bearsly scoffed. "It was written on your face the day he first arrived."

I held a hand to my cheek and laughed lightly.

Craven looked between us. "Do you mean to say . . . ?"

"Mr. Wilkins is fortunate to capture our young lady's attention," Mrs. Bearsly said.

Craven hooted and slapped his knee. "I knew it."

My cheeks flushed. "I'm under no illusion that he returns my affection, but I admit I admire him greatly." I set my cup aside and raised both hands to cover my face.

Craven sobered. "But what of Mr. Mead's suit?"

My hands fell away. Craven's question summarized my reality. "Grandmother insists I accept him." I looked at the golden liquid sitting in my teacup. "I've always known a happily ever after was not intended for me."

## Chapter Nineteen

### MR. ROBERT WILKINS

JOHN PLANNED TO REMAIN AT Cattersley for a week. After Mother's and my response to his request for Hazel to return with him, he did not mention it again. Whether Mother had had something to do with him dropping the subject I did not know, but I was grateful he'd reverted to safer topics.

Every day we'd ridden to a separate part of the estate. We'd discussed weather patterns, crop yields, and the best way to manage the ledgers. He'd given me some useful tips, and I'd shared some of the management techniques Horton had taught me.

On Friday afternoon I led John to the west side of the estate, for there I was most likely to see Abigail. It had been five long days since I'd seen her bewitching brown eyes—far too long since I longed to see her every day. Hazel had called at Fern Cottage earlier in the week, but she'd shared very little information about her visit.

I searched the trees and the property border, circling Barkley around for an extra sweep, and was rewarded when I saw a dark-green bonnet moving among the trees. "Miss Rutherford," I called, turning Barkley in her direction.

She waved at me, then looked back over her shoulder. I rode closer, and John followed. Barkley halted on my command. "Out enjoying the sunshine?" I asked.

Abigail gave a small smile. "I haven't been walking as much of late." She then turned again to look behind her.

"Have you been ill?" John asked.

"No, nothing of the sort. I simply . . . well . . ." She extended her arms, and I prepared myself for a great explanation, but before she said more, her arms fell to her side and she bobbed a quick curtsy. "I should be on my way. Good day, gentlemen." She bit her bottom lip and scanned the surrounding trees. But she did not move.

"Are you sure you are well, Miss Rutherford?" I asked.

She nodded but gave no verbal response.

John cleared his throat. His horse skittered beneath him, anxious to return home to his feeding trough. "Are you certain?" John pressed.

"I thought I might have heard something." She looked behind her again. "It is only my imagination; I'm sure of it." Abigail forced another smile upon her lips. Her peculiar behavior concerned me.

"Would you like an escort home?" I asked.

"No!" She answered quickly. Too quickly. "I'm certain no harm will befall me. Fern Cottage is only a few minutes away. Excuse me." She gathered her skirts and turned to walk back into the trees. While her words spoke of confidence, her voice shook and her posture exuded uncertainty or perhaps fear.

"She's peculiar." John frowned at her retreating figure.

"I find her refreshing." I watched Abigail depart, though her behavior evoked concern.

"Robert." John's voice held a note of warning. "Don't tell me you've fallen for the chit. Don't let her pretty face muddle your brain. Miss Rutherford is far below your station, and she's—"

"What? What is she?" I glared at my brother, daring him to continue his thought. I'd not put such force into a look since having to discipline my troops when they'd become drunk after a long day of fighting. One never knew when the enemy would retaliate, and I'd insisted my men be ready for battle at all times. After my stern lecture and glaring reproach, I'd not had a similar instance among my men.

"You know very well what she is." John scoffed. "Her speech is flawed, and she's a poor orphan who has only her beauty to recommend her."

"Enough!" My voice boomed.

John's eyes narrowed. It seemed we had inherited the same withering scowl. "You've been given all of this," he said, jutting his chin toward the great estate. "Don't settle below your station, Robert. You'd be doing yourself a great disservice." He kicked his horse's flanks and galloped away before I could reply. All that was left was to follow him home.

John and I did not talk much as we dismounted and returned to the house. He followed me into my office. I knew I was brooding, and

John would have done well to take notice, but instead he thought it the opportune time to reveal the true intent of his trip. "Do you remember Harlan Briggs? I studied with him at university," John asked as he helped himself to a glass of port before settling into one of the leather chairs.

"No." I wanted time alone to continue fuming.

John licked his lips and leaned forward, propping his arms on his knees. "He was always the brightest in class. Beat us all at hazard. Cleaned us out every time."

"Do you still owe him money?" I sat in the chair opposite my brother. He was not one to make idle conversation, and I began to wonder at his purpose.

"Of course not!" John snapped. He sat up and took a drink of his port. "Although . . ." I looked at my brother and saw his expression laced with hopeful cautiousness. "Briggs has connections, Robert. He's looking for investors. Recent conflicts have opened up opportunities for trade. Tension between His Majesty's army and the Ashanti Empire are mounting. You must have heard something about the colonization during your time in the army."

"I dedicated myself to my troops and our mission. Halting Bonaparte's advance left little time for rumors of other battles." Rumors had only served to unsettle the troops. It had been hard enough to keep their spirits high amid the blood and loss we'd witnessed daily.

John huffed in frustration. "Briggs has connections throughout Europe. He's looking to charter a shipping line based out of Portugal. He lacks only the funds to get started. Within a year we would double our investment."

"This is why you came to Cattersley, was it?" I asked, though I knew the answer. I pinned John with a stare, and the excitement slipped from his face. "Why did you not simply send a letter?" I pushed out of my chair and walked to the window.

"The funding must be secured soon." I heard John sigh. "I hoped we might discuss the idea together. The venture would be profitable, Robert. Briggs has a contact in Portugal, and if we create an international charter, the restrictions will be less stringent."

I turned around to face my brother. "How much?" Inheriting an unexpected sum of money was a funny thing. I either became a friend or an enemy depending on how easily I would empty my pockets. And then there were the neighborhood gentry who seemed to adore my great-aunt and loathe me. Now my brother, who'd questioned my ability to manage such a great estate, wished to draw upon its coffers.

"Fifteen thousand pounds," John said.

I scoffed at the number. "Fifteen thousand?"

"Such a sum is nothing to you."

"Nothing!" How eager John was to spend money he had no claim on. "Whether I am master at Cattersley or not, fifteen thousand is an enormous sum."

"Briggs is searching for other investors," John said.

"Oh, I am sure he is." Sarcasm dripped from my tongue. "And how long after word of my inheritance spread through London did he wait to contact you?"

John leaned back in his seat. "I told you, Robert. He's good at this sort of thing." He took a drink of his port.

"You cannot compare winning a round of hazard to chartering a company. Even if Briggs boasts a superb intelligence, I am not willing to gamble fifteen thousand pounds that he will succeed." I paced to my desk with clenched fists. Frustration pulsed through me. "Does he even have experience in the industry?"

"His uncle sailed with the East India Company." John tapped his fingers against his thigh. "Though, now he runs his own frigate. Briggs has traveled with him several times to Africa. He guarantees there's money to be made."

"And what is there to trade?" I asked.

John looked down at his lap. "There's talk of gold."

"Only talk? You want me to invest fifteen thousand pounds based on *talk*?" The broad proposition did not sit well.

"Our focus would be the gold, but there are also slaves." When John's eyes flashed up to mine, a searing pain tore through my heart. Did my brother not know me at all?

I met John's eyes with sorrow and regret. "Slave trade has been banned for almost a decade."

"In Britain, yes. But not everywhere." John swirled the port in his glass, awaiting my response.

"Your friend," I spat, "will not get one farthing from me."

John stood. "Robert—"

"This conversation is over." I marched from the room.

Dinner was a quiet occasion. John had given me valid suggestions to help grow Cattersley. I'd thought we'd made headway on our rides—bonded as brothers. Disappointment swamped me. When Hazel inquired after the reason for my doldrums, I told her I was overwhelmed with my new responsibilities—a truth but also a lie. There was no need to burden Mother or Hazel with the true purpose of John's visit. The next morning they showered him with well wishes and mournful regret at his parting. I ached with the knowledge that I was glad to see him go.

Once John rode out of sight, Hazel slipped her arm through mine. "I am going to call upon Abigail today. I hoped she might visit the modiste with me next week. Mother said I should begin preparing my wardrobe for the Season, and Abigail is such a clearheaded girl; I value her opinion." Hazel looked at me through her lashes. "Would you care to ride to Fern Cottage with me?"

Here was a sibling who knew me.

We departed for Fern Cottage shortly after noon. Barkley didn't like our sedate pace, but Hazel was not an accomplished rider. And as eager as I was to see Abigail, I did not want my sister to fall from her horse.

Mrs. Bearsly welcomed us warmly, and despite the surprise on her face, Mrs. Baker invited us to sit. Then Abigail entered the room, and the stone that had lain upon my heart since John made his proposal lifted.

"Abigail. You look lovely today." Hazel moved to sit beside her on the sofa, in the place I longed to be.

Instead I sat on a worn wingback chair. "You've rearranged your furniture again, Mrs. Baker," I said.

"The morning sun was blinding. This is a much better arrangement." She shifted in her seat.

"I do have a delightful prospect of the trees from this vantage point," I said. Abigail seemed to barely contain a giggle.

Mrs. Baker followed my line of vision. "Yes, yes. It is ideal."

Hazel chatted about the latest flowers to bloom in the gardens and asked Mrs. Baker's opinion on holding a ball now that the floor had been repaired.

Mrs. Baker encouraged a ball, and when Hazel asked her input on the decor, the woman nearly burst with pride. "The warmer shades of orange and brown, perhaps with a touch of gold, would be ideal."

"Oh yes!" Hazel clapped her hands. "To welcome the changing seasons. You are brilliant, Mrs. Baker." Mrs. Baker blushed. Hazel really knew how to please people. She turned to Abigail. "Your grandmother possesses such fine taste. Tell me, did she aid in the selection of your wardrobe?"

Abigail looked down at her pale-lavender dress. "This one I selected myself."

"Then the talent must run in the family." She took Abigail's hand in her own. "You must come with me to Henwick Tuesday of next week. I have an appointment with the modiste, and I tend to make frightfully poor decisions when it comes to patterns and colors." Without pause Hazel turned to Mrs. Baker. "Would you allow Abigail to join Mother and me? I shall be lost without her."

Mrs. Baker fiddled with the brooch pinned to her dress. "Mr. Mead intends to call after luncheon. He particularly would like to call on Abigail."

That bit of information nettled me.

"I will do my best to have Abigail home in time to receive him. Would that suit?" Hazel affected her most charming smile.

Mrs. Baker was not prepared for Hazel's barrage of batting eyes and sugar-laced words. My sister gave the woman no option but to relent. When all was settled, Hazel suggested a stroll around the cottage.

"Abigail has not been walking for days," Mrs. Baker said.

"You insisted I walk yesterday, Grandmother," Abigail said.

Mrs. Baker pointed her finger. "Right you are, but you returned so quickly and in such haste that I imagined a pack of wolves was at your heels."

"I was anxious to return home is all." Abigail bit her lip and looked at her lap.

"Well, your constitution could use some sunshine. You young people should enjoy a stroll while the weather holds." Mrs. Baker declined joining us and shooed us away.

Hazel spoke of all the dresses she thought she might need in order to have a successful Season. Abigail nodded politely and answered at all the right times, but she kept glancing about.

"Are you looking for something, Miss Rutherford?" I asked.

She startled a bit, then shook her head. "Just admiring the trees."

"You know you are welcome to Cattersley's gardens whenever you wish. I am certain Tucker has missed your company." The trail narrowed, and I stepped aside to let the women pass before following behind.

"Grandmother insists I remain nearby so as not to miss any callers." Abigail turned to glance at me, then searched the trees over my shoulder.

Hazel spun once in the path, then sighed in contentment. "I admit I am not the best at social visits. But I have called upon the Adamses and the Lanes and, of course, Mrs. Christiansen with Mother. But only Mrs. Christiansen has reciprocated. She is such a sweet woman. And her brother shares the most ridiculous riddles. Mother finds them diverting, but my mind does not sort through them fast enough." Hazel stopped and pointed to a pattern in the bark that resembled a smiling face.

We resumed walking, and curiosity forced the question from my lips. "Do you have many callers, then?"

Abigail sighed. "Besides yourselves, only Mr. Mead. But he comes nearly every day."

"Every day!" Hazel said. "I imagine conversation becomes dreadfully dull. What does he mean by calling so often?"

Abigail did not answer right away. She wrapped her arms around her middle and stared at the hem of her skirt. In a voice as light as a breath she said, "He means to carry out his plan."

I wasn't sure I'd heard her correctly and meant to clarify. I opened my mouth, but a call rang through the trees.

"Lo, there!" Mead himself walked toward us. "Mrs. Baker said I might find you here. Mind if I join you?"

If only the answer I wanted to give mattered.

For the remainder of the walk Abigail did not speak a word. I'd seen her acquiesce to her grandmother, and when in a larger gathering she held her words, but she'd never been so silent around me.

We returned to the house, and Mrs. Baker opened the door. "Oh, Mr. Mead. What a pleasant surprise!" The woman fluttered her lashes. "Had I known you were here, I would have had a fresh pot of tea prepared. I shall put Mrs. Bearsly to it at once." Mrs. Baker walked away, leaving the door open wide.

Hazel finalized the details of her outing with Abigail, who nodded but did not seem excited about the prospect.

Hazel and I had no reason to extend our stay, yet I felt hesitant to leave. Abigail stood beside a grinning Mr. Mead, and the air between them stirred with a mixture of frustration and glee. I bowed low and offered a reluctant goodbye. Then I assisted Hazel into her saddle, mounted Barkley, and rode away. Unease beat in time with my heart, but I could not pinpoint the cause.

"It's peculiar, is it not?" Hazel continued before I could reply. "When the vicar came upon us, did he not claim Mrs. Baker had sent him in our direction? But when we returned to the cottage, she seemed surprised to see him."

Hazel's words pricked a spark of worry in my mind. "Indeed, you are correct."

"And Abigail became awfully quiet." The facade of Cattersley began to appear as we rounded a copse of trees. "I hope she returns to herself before our outing, for I am relying on her eye to help select my wardrobe."

I mumbled some nonsensical response, and then we rode in silence. Hazel had solved the riddle I could not. Mead's duplicity could not be ignored. Something was amiss.

# Chapter Twenty

## MISS ABIGAIL RUTHERFORD

The following day, Hazel and Mrs. Wilkins arrived in the Cattersley carriage at eleven o'clock. I wore my light-blue muslin. Grandmother thought my best dress appropriate for the outing, and she herself suggested I wear it.

The modiste doted on Hazel from the moment we entered the shop. Our party was waited upon by no fewer than five servants, who laid a rainbow of colors and patterns before us. Hazel was presented with so many options—puff sleeves, lace, overlays, trims, and ribbons.

She stood on a step while fabrics were draped and pinned all around her. Mrs. Wilkins admired a combination of colors or textures and then turned and asked my opinion, which I really had no business giving. My dresses had all been made by my mother or a neighbor who'd needed the extra income. I did not want to share my opinion because I did not want to be wrong. But I thought it quite obvious that the pale-green and muted yellow did not suit Hazel. When Mrs. Wilkins pressed for my opinion, I told her as much.

Mrs. Wilkins smiled and reached across the space between us to pat my hand. "I couldn't agree more," she said.

"The sapphire satin is stunning though," I said. "And I like the maroon as well."

Mrs. Wilkins stood and picked up the bolt of maroon fabric. She walked near and held it close to my face. "This is the color for you."

"Oh, I did not mean to imply—"

Mrs. Wilkins waved my comment aside. "Hazel, what do you think?"

Hazel turned. "Abigail," she said. "Your eyes are enchanting against the jeweled tone."

I felt my cheeks heat to the same color of red as the fabric.

"Miss Kinston," Mrs. Wilkins called to the modiste. "Please add a gown for Miss Rutherford to our order. Let's fit her for a ball gown in this satin." She set the bolt of fabric against my chair.

When she retook her seat, I leaned close. "Mrs. Wilkins, I do appreciate your offer, but I cannot accept it."

Her eyes widened, and she stared down at me. "Why ever not?"

"It is far too fine for me."

"Nonsense." She shifted in her seat, her posture perfect. "You have been a dear friend to Hazel. Robert will not mind the expense, and now you will have something to wear to the ball."

I'd never owned something so costly. Excitement bubbled in my chest. But what would Grandmother say?

As if she could read my thoughts, Mrs. Wilkins tapped my hand. "I shall tell your grandmother I insisted." Her fingers closed over mine, and she squeezed softly. "She will be delighted."

I doubted that very much. But further argument died away when one of the servant girls came to fit me for the gown.

The afternoon passed in a flurry of color and adornments. Hazel was delighted with every selection, and her mother and I sat enjoying a variety of sweets while Miss Kinston tucked and trimmed and scribbled plentiful notes.

Grandmother was irate that we did not return home in time to meet Mr. Mead. Hazel and Mrs. Wilkins told her they were to blame and asked Grandmother to come to Cattersley the following day for dinner as recompense. As much as Grandmother liked sidling with the gossips and claiming indifference for the new owner of Cattersley, she could not resist the lure of the grand estate. The dinner invitation was accepted.

I slept well and dreamt of twirling skirts and lovely music. Among the flowing gowns in my dream I caught glimpses of a maroon satin dress. I woke with a smile, which continued to grow as the day progressed. The idea of seeing Mr. Wilkins, surrounded by only his family, caused my imagination to conjure visions of plentiful smiles and delightful conversation. In order to ensure I was prepared for such a reality, I dutifully practiced my word list as I went about my morning tasks. *Bright, brilliant, ground, grand, great . . .*

Mr. Mead's visit was blessedly short. We set to dressing immediately after his departure; Grandmother seemed as anxious as I was to arrive at the grand estate. I wore my lavender gown and laced a section of dark-green ribbon through my hair.

Grandmother and I were greeted warmly. Hazel covered her mouth to stifle a giggle while Mrs. Wilkins showered Grandmother with compliments. Mr. Wilkins stood across the room, looking debonair with a smile as tempting as Mrs. Bearsly's tarts. We did not have much time for conversation, for we were seated for dinner shortly after our arrival.

I dared not mention the gown Mrs. Wilkins had insisted I order. I knew not how to tell Grandmother, and in the end, I did not need to. After the main course had been cleared, Mrs. Wilkins and Hazel began to talk about the ball.

"Mrs. Baker suggested orange and brown decor, with a hint of gold," Hazel said.

"What a divine combination. It shall be warm and welcoming, and the gold will add elegance to the evening." Mrs. Wilkins smiled and enjoyed a bite of her dessert.

"My thoughts exactly." Grandmother beamed.

"When exactly will this ball take place?" Mr. Wilkins asked.

"I thought the thirteenth of September would be ideal," Hazel said. "Monsieur Gastineau said he could obtain all he needs by then, and four weeks allows us ample time to address the invitations."

"And whom do you plan to invite?" Mr. Wilkins asked.

"Everyone." Hazel clapped her hands together, and her shoulders swayed from side to side. "How else will they get to know the generous new owner of Cattersley?"

"They could attempt friendly conversation. It seems that is the recipe you and Miss Rutherford employed, and now you are barely separable." Mr. Wilkins looked first at Hazel, and then his gaze settled on me and he did not look away. He ignored his dessert, a smile playing on his lips.

"Mrs. Baker," Mrs. Wilkins said. "Robert has told me on several occasions how grateful he is to your Miss Rutherford. She's such a steady friend to dear Hazel."

Grandmother seemed taken back that I would receive such a compliment. She bumbled for a reply, but Mrs. Wilkins spoke again. "I bought her a gift yesterday while we were at the dress shop. I hope you don't mind." Mrs. Wilkins popped another bite of dessert into her mouth.

Hazel chimed in. "She's going to look fabulous!"

Grandmother's hand froze, dangling her fork above her plate, and her head turned between the two women as if on a swivel. Then her gaze landed on me. "You ordered a dress?"

Mrs. Wilkins's laugh sliced through the tension. She placed a hand on her collarbone. "Heavens no. I ordered the dress. Miss Rutherford simply thought she was playing model for one of Hazel's new gowns."

"Hmm." Grandmother smiled, but it did not reach her eyes. "It sounds like Abigail to be unaware of such things. We could hardly afford such expense. Abigail should know as much."

In the middle of scooping a bite to her mouth, Hazel paused. She looked at Grandmother, then me. The delight I found in receiving a new gown faded. By not forcefully rejecting Mrs. Wilkins's offer the day before, I'd now been labeled naive.

"Do you not like surprises, Mrs. Baker?" Hazel asked. She lowered her fork and awaited Grandmother's response.

"Well, of course I do," Grandmother said.

"I believe that was my mother's intent. There is no fault to be had— rather, the simple enjoyment that comes from a new gown." Hazel smiled innocently.

Mr. Wilkins's gaze had not wavered. "From what I understand, women can fawn over a particular dress for a matter of weeks." We all laughed, and Mr. Wilkins winked at me.

"It is a lovely color. I can't wait for it to be finished," Hazel said. Then she resumed eating, but I could not take another bite. I had never enjoyed playing tug-of-war, especially when I was the one being tugged about.

Grandmother made no further mention of the gown. We retired to the drawing room, where Hazel played a new composition on the pianoforte. She enthralled us all, her talent obvious. Mrs. Wilkins sat on the sofa, beaming proudly. Grandmother and I occupied two nearby chairs, and Mr. Wilkins sat nearer to the piano; his eyes were closed, yet I knew he was not asleep, as his foot tapped in time with the rhythm. The song rolled and surged at all the right times, and my emotions ebbed with the tune.

Afterward Mrs. Wilkins asked for Grandmother's assistance in compiling a list of families to invite to the ball. Hazel and I played a silly duet. Once we finished, her mother called her over to ask a question about the fare.

I stood from the pianoforte, intending to be done.

"I hoped you might play another," Mr. Wilkins said. He'd moved to stand behind me.

His presence always affected me so. "I wasn't aware you were listening," I said.

"Always." Mr. Wilkins stepped nearer.

I retook my seat, lifted my shoulders, and placed my hands on the keys. I'd never been a virtuoso, but I'd taken the time to master a few songs. The notes flowed naturally from the innermost parts of my being out to my fingertips. Grandmother did not have a pianoforte, and I'd missed playing. Knowing Mr. Wilkins stood behind me altered the dynamics of the song. When I played the song from memory, each note ran through my mind. Normally I worked through each bar, counting measures and beats, but with Mr. Wilkins standing near, my rhythm changed. His breaths created the tempo, inhaling in and out, as my fingers played the keys. We moved together in a seductive sort of dance.

My fingers held the final note. And I held my breath. I hadn't played the pianoforte in almost a year, but I had played the piece perfectly.

"Amazing," Mr. Wilkins said on a whisper, and I finally drew a breath.

I slowly turned around on the bench to face him. When our eyes met, a shock ricocheted through me. It was a first breath, new sight, an awakening I'd never before experienced. With him I had the freedom to say the things I held back. Permission to smile and laugh and live. It was all there in the oasis of his eyes. The oasis that was him.

"Wherever did you learn to play like that?" he asked.

Each breath clung to my lungs, searing and warm, and I wanted only to keep breathing. "Plymouth" was all I said.

His eyes narrowed only a fraction, and his lips turned up the tiniest bit. But I noticed because I was aware of every part of him. The walls of the room disappeared. The candles supplied warmth and light, but from a place far away. The voices of the others floated around us in a lullaby. The trance was all-consuming. He was all-consuming. And I reveled in the fire lapping around me.

"Miss Rutherford?" Mrs. Wilkins's voice jolted me, reminding me we were not alone. "Might you come give us your opinion?"

Mr. Wilkins offered his hand, and my fingers shook as I placed them in his. I rose from the piano bench and noticed my breath remained synchronized with his.

"Thank you for the song," Mr. Wilkins said softly. My smile was free, and I willingly shared it with Mr. Wilkins. He inclined his head and escorted me to where his mother sat. He gave my fingers a gentle squeeze before letting go.

"We were just discussing whether we should have card tables at the ball." Mrs. Wilkins scooted to the side and patted the cushion next to her. I took a seat between Mr. Wilkins's mother and sister. He sat in the chair I had previously occupied, and I missed the feeling of his fingers holding mine.

"I fear the gentlemen will avoid the dancefloor and spend the evening in their games." Hazel placed a hand on my arm. "What good are new gowns if we are unable to dance in them?"

"Lady Marion liked a good game of cards herself. The gentlemen will expect the tables," Grandmother said.

"And there is our quandary," Mrs. Wilkins said with a sigh. "Is there an acceptable solution? What say you, Miss Rutherford?"

I imagined the Cattersley ballroom in my mind. It would be lovely to dance near the large windows overlooking the gardens. "Perhaps the tables could be arranged for cards before supper is served. Whilst the guests eat, the servants can dissemble the tables."

Hazel squeezed my arm. "All the guests will be on the dancefloor after supper."

Mrs. Wilkins clasped her hands in front of her. "What a brilliant idea, Miss Rutherford."

"I wish I had your cleverness," Hazel said. "It would come in handy during my Season."

"How do you mean?" Mr. Wilkins asked his sister.

She straightened her spine. "Well, if a gentleman I am not interested in asks me to dance, I'm bound to say yes because I will be so tongue-tied I will be unable to form an excuse." When we all laughed at Hazel's example, she provided another. "Or if I wish to partner in cards with a particular gentleman, it would be ideal to be clever. If Abigail were with me, I wouldn't worry about such things, for she could be clever on my behalf."

"Then, Miss Rutherford should come to Town with us," Mr. Wilkins said. All eyes turned to him, and any cleverness I possessed vanished.

Hazel stood. She walked to her brother, and I held my breath. "Do not trifle, Robert."

"I am quite serious." Mr. Wilkins motioned to the group. "We all agree Miss Rutherford has proven to be an ideal companion. Why should she not accompany you to London?"

"It is not possible." Grandmother's voice shook. "She does not have the funds or the ability to navigate London Society."

"I'd be delighted to sponsor Miss Rutherford for the Season," Mr. Wilkins said.

"And I will act as chaperone to both Hazel and Miss Rutherford." Mrs. Wilkins fairly beamed.

The freedom I'd felt moments before burgeoned into a multitude of possibilities. I looked at Grandmother clawing the lace at her throat. "You wish to take Abigail to London?" she asked.

Mrs. Wilkins turned a sweet smile to Grandmother. "She is of ideal age, and it would lighten my mind to know Hazel had a confidante and companion."

"She would require a new wardrobe," Grandmother said.

My heart pattered excitedly. "With a bit of twim, I can remake some of my older gowns." Grandmother was so befuddled she did not acknowledge my pronunciation error.

Instead she tsked her tongue. "You know nothing of fashion and will simply cause me embarrassment."

Hazel's pretty eyes narrowed. "Abigail was quite proficient yesterday. Why, she suggested a combination of sleeves and an overlay skirt that the modiste was absolutely taken with. I imagine it will be one of my favorite gowns, and I've little doubt the style will be duplicated before the Season concludes."

"My sponsorship would, of course, include a stipend to procure whatever additional items Miss Rutherford might require." Mr. Wilkins crossed his legs and pinned Grandmother with a stare.

"Mr. Wilkins." Grandmother offered a disingenuous smile. "It may seem a trivial thing to you, given your new position. However, Abigail comes from humble circumstances. To thrust her into the fray of Society, in lavish gowns, would be a disservice. I am afraid my conscience cannot allow it."

Mr. Wilkins's hands fisted at his side. Storm clouds rolled through his eyes, and while my heart plummeted with Grandmother's words, I'd found a champion in the man before me.

"Might I present an alternative, Mrs. Baker?" Mrs. Wilkins's confident tone allowed hope to once again flutter in my chest. "I shall have my maid rework several of Hazel's gowns. Miss Rutherford shall have the ball gown we ordered yesterday, and if you'll permit it, I'll order a pair of half boots that she may wear in the colder season. Then she may simply accompany us as Hazel's companion, and no further fuss will be made." Grandmother shifted in her seat, ready to deliver a counterargument, but Mrs. Wilkins held up her hand. "There is no need to rush to a decision this evening. Consider the proposal, and inform me at the ball if you are agreeable to the idea. I know the loss of your granddaughter will be a sacrifice. Assuming the roads are passible, you must come visit us in London as well." Mrs. Wilkins's dazzling smile convinced me she knew she had played a trump card, for Grandmother oft spoke of London.

"Well . . ." Grandmother fluttered. "I suppose I shall consider it."

Hazel and I exchanged a smile, and my heart started beating rapidly once again.

# Chapter Twenty-One

MR. ROBERT WILKINS

I WAS GRATEFUL MY ONLY part in the upcoming ball was to pay the bill. The women fretted and fussed over details I found trivial. Food and music—what more was needed?

The role I did need to fulfill was that of overseer of my land. The ball was still two weeks away, but the fruit trees in the orchard were ready to be harvested and preserved. Yesterday Mrs. Sommers had limited the duties of the household staff, and in the afternoon the maids, footmen, stable hands, and Monsieur Gastineau's small army helped pick the fruit we would store at Cattersley. I'd invited the tenants and some of the neighboring families to come on the morrow to gather all the fruit they could use. I was quite looking forward to the event. It would be the first tangible way I would witness the good Cattersley provided. And Abigail would be in attendance.

Hazel had sent the carriage for her almost every day, but Mrs. Baker allowed her granddaughter to come only with the understanding that she must be returned home by two o'clock. I never questioned the reason behind this odd request, at least aloud. But today after Abigail departed, Hazel stood at one of the tall windows of the Sky Room, watching the carriage pull away. "I don't know how Abigail stands it. Mr. Mead is dreadfully boring," she said.

"What does Mr. Mead have to do with anything?" I asked.

"He is the reason Abigail must return home. Her grandmother insists she receive Mr. Mead for his daily call."

"He continues to call every day?" I mindlessly scratched my chin. "I assumed he had only called daily after the picnic to ensure Abigail's—Miss Rutherford's—wellbeing."

Hazel turned from the window, crossed her arms, and shifted so one hip was higher than the other. She looked exactly as my mother did before reminding me of some obvious facet I had overlooked. "Truly, Robert?" I dropped my hand from my chin. Why was Hazel's face now filled with disappointment?

She shook her head with a sigh and walked to where I stood. Her eyebrows rose. "Why do you think he might call at Fern Cottage every day?" She pressed a finger to my chest. "And why do you think Mrs. Baker particularly wants Abigail there?"

The realization sank in, and my stomach tangled into knots. Abigail did not seem especially inclined toward Mead, and the way her eyes had lit when I suggested she join us in London did not lead me to believe she felt any sort of tendresse toward the man that would keep her from joining us. But her grandmother had been hesitant. And then there was the peculiar instance when Mead had happened upon us walking in the forest. He had obviously taken an interest in Abigail.

I determined to observe his behavior, especially as it pertained to Abigail. As he lived in the parish on Cattersley land, he'd naturally been included in the invitations to the harvest gathering. Horton had informed me Mead had accepted and would be present, along with his small household staff, so I would have ample opportunity to decipher his intentions toward Abigail.

But Hazel's words needled at me for the rest of the evening and hardly lent for a fit night's sleep. The moment it seemed reasonable to rise I began dressing in my riding attire. Graham walked into my chamber with a rumpled shirt, his hair matted like a rat's nest, and a giant yawn stretching across his face. "You're supposed to wake me, sir."

"I've dressed myself before, Graham. Go back to sleep."

He rubbed his eyes and then tucked in his shirttails. "Won't shirk my duty, Mr. Wilkins. Mr. Manning would have my hide."

"Very well. Fetch my brown jacket and boots." I decided to forgo a cravat. If Manning took issue with my appearance, he could take it up with me.

I skipped breakfast and saddled Barkley myself. Then I rode. Bent low over Barkley's neck, I dug my heels into her sides and urged her to go faster. The cool morning air combined with the orange and pink clouds of sunrise pushed the anxiety from my mind, replacing it with resolution. If there was to be a battle for Abigail's affection, I was ready to fight. Today would be spent scouting out my enemy, observing his movements and tactics to determine a strategy. Then I would form my own, for I believed this battle to be as dire as any I'd ever fought.

Abigail looked radiant. She wore no bonnet—only a sturdy brown dress and apron—as she came prepared to pick fruit for the residents of Fern Cottage. But oddly enough, against the plain color of the dress, her hair appeared to be highlighted with gold. The effulgent slivers suited her.

She had arrived early with Mrs. Baker and now stood on a small stool next to Hazel, plucking pears from the lower branches. Once she had filled her apron, she emptied the contents of her labor into a basket belonging to a widowed woman and her three children. It warmed my heart.

A little boy pulled my attention to the tree before me. "I can't reach that one." He pointed up to a dangling apple.

I lifted him up. "There you are." When I set him back down, he gave me a gap-toothed grin, then ran to show his sister his treasure.

Happy chatter wove through the orchard. Laughter and excitement from the children combined with instruction from Tucker and Felton. I tried to make myself useful. As the baskets filled, I carried them to the appointed cart, and I resituated ladders and stools so my guests could reach the unpicked fruit. And I spent far too much time staring in Abigail's direction.

I walked toward the section of orchard where she and Hazel worked. They'd moved from the pear trees to the apples, and I approached just as Hazel proclaimed her fear of heights. "I cannot climb up the ladder, Abigail." Hazel took a step backward.

"It is only a few feet, Hazel. Even if you fall, you'll not be seriously injured." Abigail stood with one hand on the side of a ladder propped against the tree trunk. "The height is no greater than that of the ladder I fell from that time in the library."

Hazel pressed her lips tightly together and folded her arms across her chest. "I simply must refuse."

Abigail sighed. Then she spied me standing near. "Mr. Wilkins, good day." A lovely smile touched her rosy cheeks. "Will you please assure Hazel that the ladder will not tip over? She refuses to climb up it."

"I thought you liked adventure, Hazel." I placed my hand on the opposite side of the ladder from Abigail.

Hazel turned her chin to the right. "I don't like breaking my neck."

I chuckled.

"Shall I go first?" Abigail shifted her skirt and squared herself in front of the ladder. "You'll keep the ladder still?" she asked me.

"Of course." I tightened my grip on the right post of the ladder and pressed the top of it against the tree trunk. "But mind you don't climb too high."

Abigail tipped her head up and then stepped onto the bottom rung.

"Oh, do be careful, Abigail!" Hazel covered her mouth with her hands.

"It is only a fruit tree." Abigail laughed and stepped higher on the ladder. "I am not scaling a castle wall."

She climbed just over halfway up the ladder, and then she gathered the hem of her apron. She held both the bottom of the apron and a rung on the ladder to secure herself. The apron folded over to form a sort of trough to hold the fruit. Abigail gathered the apples one at a time, twisting the stems from the branches and then placing the fruit into her apron.

"Do come down, Abigail," Hazel said. "You're making my heart frantic."

My heart was rather frantic as well, but not for the same reason as Hazel's was. Holding the ladder granted me close proximity. Despite Hazel's plea, my head was even with Abigail's shins. My hands held the ladder at the same level, and her skirt brushed against my arms. I had an odd desire to assist her. If she simply leaned backward, I could catch her in my arms. It would be an efficient way to descend.

"I think that is all I can manage," Abigail called down.

"Thank heavens," Hazel mumbled.

Abigail held her gathered apron in one hand and the ladder rung in the other. She lowered her right foot one step.

"Be careful. Oh, Robert, make certain she's stable." Hazel held her hands aloft as if she would catch her friend.

"Let me grab just this one more." Abigail stretched her right arm to pluck the fruit, but it was just out of reach. She shuffled her feet to the right side of the ladder, and with the shift in weight, the left side of the ladder began to lift off the ground. Abigail cried out in surprise.

I immediately turned to face the tree, grabbed the left ladder post with my left hand, and used my weight to offset Abigail's. At the same time she shifted her weight to accommodate for the shift in balance, and the ladder then tilted left. Again I adjusted my hold, compensating for the instability.

The movement stopped, and the ladder was once again secure. I looked upward to see Abigail smiling down at me.

She laughed lightly, still clutching the apples in her apron. "Thank you, Mr. Wilkins. I thought I might have to endure a lecture from Hazel if I fell."

Hazel harrumphed behind me. "While I am glad you did not tumble down, I still believe you should leave the climbing to the men."

"Then I'd miss all the fun." Abigail stepped down one rung, then another.

She had not been in any great danger, but my heart rate had sped when she'd cried out and I thought the ladder might tip. I determined to hold both hands on either post until her feet returned to solid ground.

I extended my arms and stepped back as far as I was able, but space was limited. I did not mind. In fact, my contentment grew as she descended. As Abigail neared the bottom rung, her shoulders brushed against my arms, and the load of apples in her apron pressed the warmth of her body into my chest. I inhaled. Savored.

"Thank you, Mr. Wilkins," she said on a breath.

"Please call me Robert." I watched the side of her face—the curve of her chin and her long dark lashes—as she gave a small nod. I did not move until a voice cleared behind me.

With a relenting sigh, I let go of the ladder and stepped away. Abigail turned around with a happy smile and a rosy blush.

Mead stood beside Hazel with his eyebrows pushed up to his hairline. "What do you think you are doing, Miss Rutherford?" he asked.

She laughed lightly and lifted the bundle in her apron. "Picking apples."

"Atop a ladder?" Mead motioned to where the ladder stood against the tree.

"As you see." Abigail tightened the grip on her apron. "It was the best way to reach the fruit." She then emptied the contents of her apron into a nearby wooden crate.

Mead turned to me. His chest rose and fell with a breath before he spoke. "I wonder that you would condone Miss Rutherford's behavior."

"We are at a harvest gathering, Mead. It is expected that the fruit be picked," I said. "Miss Rutherford wished to pick apples, and I assisted in that request." Hazel looked between Mead and me and pinched her lips tightly closed.

Mead narrowed his eyes. "As gentlemen, is it not our duty to correct the ladies when their judgment is askew? From what I just witnessed, it is obvious Miss Rutherford was not capable of negotiating the ladder. The ladies would do well to leave the more detailed work to the men."

"Are you saying you would like to make use of the ladder?" I motioned toward the object in question. "You are welcome to it."

Mead harrumphed at my suggestion. "I believe Miss Rutherford could use a reprieve." He stepped to her side and took her hand. Her eyes widened as Mead threaded her arm through his. "Let us get some refreshment, my dear. You look peaked."

Abigail offered Hazel a small smile, then stared at the ground as Mead led her away.

"I'm not sure what to make of that man," I said to my sister.

"It is obvious he is fond of Abigail," Hazel said.

Mead led Abigail toward the tables, where fruit, cheese, and drinks were laid out. Their pace was slow, and Mead leaned near Abigail and spoke. She nodded and then returned her gaze to the ground.

"Then, the question remains: is Miss Rutherford fond of the vicar?" I wasn't certain I'd spoken aloud until Hazel replied.

"How could she be, when you are near?"

I looked at my sister. She smiled with her happy eyes. Then she pointed to the crate of apples. "Come. Let's take these to Mrs. Baker's cart."

# Chapter Twenty-Two

MR. MEAD CHASTISED ME FOR a full ten minutes. I was a careless, featherbrained dolt. "Who would care for your grandmother if you were to tumble and brake a bone? And what would become of you if you marred your pretty features?" His mouth pinched in a frown. "It is a good thing I arrived and put an end to your folly."

He'd also put an end to my enjoyment of the day. The entire gathering had been festive and fun. Happy voices rang all around as the fruit was gathered and sampled. Children and adults alike joined in the tasks of picking and hauling, although it appeared Mr. Mead qualified himself to be the resident warden. Even as we walked, he chastised a little girl for trying to carry a bucket to the cart for her father. "That is a task for your brother," he said. He gave the girl a patronizing smile as we walked toward the far end of the orchard.

"If picking fwuit is not acceptable, what pursuits would you suggest I engage in?" I asked the question, curious about his answer but also convinced I would not agree with it. "Certainly you wouldn't have me sit around all day gazing out the window?" In my anger my letters did not fully form, but my temper made me indifferent.

Mr. Mead looked at my mouth and tsked. Then he patted my hand on his sleeve. "Not at all. You seem to enjoy the outdoors. You walk almost every day. Or, at least, you previously have."

Since Mr. Mead had begun his suit, I'd greatly minimized the time I spent out of doors. Was he speaking in generalities, or was he being more specific?

He waved to a member of the congregation and then continued. "Many of the fairer sex boast multiple talents. Music, art, embroidery—"

"Reading?" I interjected.

Again Mr. Mead offered a belittling smile. "I don't encourage worldly texts; however, the Bible is a blessing to all. But you need not worry, Miss Rutherford; it stands to reason that I should guide you on such things, given my position as both your clergyman and your intended." The word settled like lead in my chest, and my steps slowed. Mr. Mead noticed my hesitancy. He looked about. No one stood nearby, as he'd led us away from the main throng.

Again he placed his hand over mine, only this time he squeezed my fingers. "Abigail." My eyes jolted to his. I opened my mouth to protest, but he placed a finger over my lips. "Hush now, my dear. 'Tis not improper for us to address each other by our Christian names when soon we will be united in intimate matrimony." He stroked his thumb across my bottom lip, and I turned my head away. He placed his hand on my face and turned me back to him. "Please call me Daniel when we are alone."

I swallowed past the lump of distress in my throat. "We should not be alone, Mr. Mead. I have not agweed to be your wife."

He tsked his tongue again, this time in reprimand. "Daniel. And, might I remind you, this is not our first private tête-à-tête, Abigail. You do remember the picnic?" His eyes darkened.

"I am not feeling well. I think I shall weturn to my gwandmother." I cared not how my words sounded. I only wished to be away.

Mr. Mead frowned. "I knew you had overexerted yourself. Scampering up a ladder is not a woman's duty. Mr. Wilkins should know better."

I wanted to shout my disagreement at the top of my lungs. But I remained silent. Thankfully, Mr. Mead walked me to Grandmother, and once she was in view I granted him a small curtsy and hastily departed.

I was grateful for a quite evening at home. Grandmother was fatigued from her time in the sun and retired early. Mrs. Bearsly, too, had fallen asleep, although she did not make it to her bed. The woman sat snoring near the kitchen hearth.

I left Mrs. Bearsly in the kitchen and settled into the worn chair in the parlor. The notes of Hazel's latest composition funneled through my thoughts. I stared into the dying embers of the small fire, revisiting the happy parts of my day. When the ladder had tipped, I truly thought I would collide with the earth. Mr. Wilkins's—no, he'd asked me to call him Robert—swift reaction had saved me. Then to climb down the ladder and be encircled by his arms . . . it was like being embraced by the sun—warm and comfortable—and my heart raced with the memory.

But Mr. Mead, with his authoritarian posture and presumptuous expectations, had inserted himself and chased the sun away, demeaning me at every turn and then demanding I call him by his Christian name, as if I held some endearment toward him. Was condemning me synonymous with courting in his mind? In all the childhood dreams I'd had of being swept away in love, it was not with a patronizing lecture on my assumed inabilities.

But those were dreams I'd entertained before I understood the truth of my speech defect. My slurred words and sounds, despite my best efforts, made others presume a lack of intelligence. Mother had been embarrassed by my tongue, and so had even Louisa, on occasion. Grandmother continued where Mother had left off, ashamed to introduce me to friends or take me on social calls. At least she'd opened her home and provided a roof overhead. And she'd allowed Hazel to befriend me.

That was where Hazel, her mother, and Robert, were different. I had jumbled letters on various occasions in their presence, but they had never commented or even reacted. In fact, they seemed entirely indifferent.

I looked between the blackened ash and the coals still glowing orange and red—two opposite sides of the spectrum. Hazel and her family welcomed and befriended me. Mother and Grandmother belittled, and Mr. Mead assumed authority over my time, my pursuits, and my life.

How could I escape him? Perhaps if I spoke plainly with Grandmother. If I explained to her the truth of the picnic and Mr. Mead's ungentlemanly actions, would she release me from his pursuit? But if Mr. Mead chose to reveal the details of our encounter at the picnic and the resulting fire, it would be my word against his. He was an expert in his craft; speaking and declaring were strengths of his. His behavior led me to believe he would twist his words to gain his purpose. What chance did I have against such a man? It would be a far better future to remain at Fern Cottage than to become Mrs. Daniel Mead.

I determined to speak with Grandmother the next day. Unfortunately, due to my late-night musings, I did not rise until late morning. I greeted Mrs. Bearsly, who informed me that Mr. Mead was called away on business and would not be able to visit today. Pity. Craven had driven Grandmother to Henwick to purchase sundries, and she would be back for nuncheon—it would be the ideal time to discuss my concerns. Mrs. Bearsly and I chatted while I ate breakfast in the kitchen, and then I stepped outside, determined to enjoy a walk.

I had rarely walked since the day Mr. Mead had revealed he'd been watching me from afar. I would wander near the house only when Craven was chopping wood or helping Mrs. Bearsly in the gardens. And I had not been to visit Mr. Tucker for almost a month. I missed the solitude and security I'd once enjoyed. I knew better than to be caught alone with Mr. Mead. Knowing he was called away granted an opportunity to enjoy the fresh air and rustling leaves without apprehension.

Despite a few clouds overhead, the fresh air renewed my hope that somehow I might be able to extricate myself from Mr. Mead's designs. As long as I remained at Fern Cottage, Mr. Mead would continue his pursuit. I needed to get away, and thus far, two possible solutions had presented themselves. Acting as Hazel's companion in London would be an ideal situation. If Grandmother refused the invitation, I determined to locate Benjamin and request a place with him in the Americas. I walked through the trees and rehearsed what I would say to Grandmother. I paused on any words that might be challenging for my tongue and slowly sounded them out, over and over, until I felt confident I could present my argument without jumbling letters.

I stopped at the edge of the property and admired the prospect. Smoke curled from three of Cattersley's chimneys, and I wondered if Hazel was working on another composition. What was Robert doing? I ducked my head with a smile. I loved the sound of his name. Perhaps I would call at Cattersley on the morrow—to see Hazel, of course.

With determination I walked toward home. The clouds had thickened, and rain appeared imminent. I quickened my step until Fern Cottage came into view. The kitchen door opened, and Mr. Mead stepped out. My heart froze, and I ducked behind a tree. Unfortunately, the narrow trunk did not hide me.

"Abigail," Mr. Mead called. "There you are." He closed the distance between us quickly. "Odd. Mrs. Bearsly thought you were confined to your room with a headache."

I reached up and touched my temple. I had chosen not to wear a bonnet and fashioned my hair into a simple braided twist. "I thought fresh air might help, but alas, it has not. I shall retire to my room now." I bobbed a quick curtsy and meant to walk away, but he grabbed my arm.

"Come, now. There's no need to scamper off." Mr. Mead's words sat in direct contradiction to my feelings. He glanced up at the sky. "We should have a bit of time before the rain begins. Let us walk together."

"Mr. Mead, I really—"

"Daniel!" He snapped. His chest heaved as his eyes cooled. "Call me Daniel."

My trepidation swelled. With trembling lips I nodded agreement.

A ruthless smile consumed Mr. Mead's features. "That's better." He leaned close, his breath hot on my face. "Now, say it."

"Please . . ." How I wished to return home.

He tightened his grip on my upper arm. "Say it!" he spat.

I shuddered and did as he demanded. "Daniel."

He relaxed his hold a bit. "There now, that wasn't so hard." He leaned slightly away but still did not let me go. "Just a short stroll." Mr. Mead guided me back into the trees. His hand shifted from my arm to my back. Like a beetle caught in a sticky spiderweb, I wished to shake free of his grasp.

Mr. Mead sighed. "Tell me, Abigail, have I not been attentive to your needs? Have I not convinced you that I will make a good husband? That I will provide a good home for you?"

Mr. Mead led me farther into the woods. My chest ached with fear as his arm draped across my back and his hand moved to rest above my hip. "The Lord admonishes us each to find a companion; should we not fulfill his command?" he asked. When I did not answer, he pulled me closer still. The movement jerked me forward, and my feet caught, causing me to stumble. Mr. Mead stopped and wrapped both arms around me to keep me upright. Cold tendrils, like stiff, frozen icicles spread, causing my limbs to tremble. A tiny drop of rain splattered onto my cheek.

"Abigail, darling? Do you not agree?" He wiped the raindrop from my face.

"I-I-I only need mo' time," I said.

Mr. Mead chuckled at the dropped *r* and moved his hand again to my face. He ran his finger down the side of my cheek.

"We should weturn to Fern Cottage." I shook from cold and fear. My words shook as well.

Mr. Mead's hold on me tightened, and his dark eyes reflected a sense of control I no longer felt. Mr. Mead's voice dropped to a low growl. "Before we return, shall I convince you of my regard?"

The rain began to fall steadily. I moved my hands to his chest and tried to push away, but his hold was much too strong. "Mr. Mead, please, release me."

His smile fell. "Daniel! My name is Daniel! Say it!" He shook me, and my teeth knocked together. "Say it!"

"Daniel," I repeated on a sob. Tears streamed down my face as I cried with the heavens.

His upper lip curled. "Now, there's a good girl." He moved one hand to the back of my head and leaned down, intent to follow through with his scheme. His breath washed across my face as he drew closer. The pattering of the rain, the water seeping into my clothing, and the isolation surrounding us muted together, and I could think only on Mr. Thatcher, Father's drunk friend, from all those years ago. With all of my might I thrust my knee upward. Mr. Mead's hands fell away as he groaned and doubled over, falling to the ground. My arms, hands, my entire body shook as I stepped backward. I did not know how long Mr. Mead would remain curled on the ground. I turned and ran.

I wiped the rain from my face and looked back over my shoulder. Mr. Mead's angry eyes flashed up to meet mine. He tried to stand but winced in pain. My steps faltered, and I looked forward again, regaining my footing.

"Abigail!" he called. "Abigail! You *will* be my wife," he shouted.

I fled out of the trees. The rain fell harder in the open meadow. The downpour did not allow me to verify my course, but I refused to turn back. I lifted the hem of my skirt and pressed forward—anything to get away from that awful man.

A horse whinnied, but I could not tell from which direction the sound came. Was it possible Mr. Mead had returned to the house already and come to claim me? More tears fell, and my sobs echoed the drumming of the rain. And still I ran.

A flash of brown appeared to my right and then maneuvered into my path, forcing me to halt.

"Miss Rutherford?" Mr. Wilkins dismounted in one swift movement. He removed his coat and draped it over my shoulders.

What could I say? The truth condemned me to matrimony with Mr. Mead, but I could not lie. Not when Robert stood before me, rain dripping off his tall hat, his eyes yearning for the truth.

I quickly looked back over my shoulder. No words surfaced, but my tears continued to fall. I gave a slight shake of my head, and my body shuddered from the cold.

"I . . ." My lips trembled, and my heart shattered. "Please . . ."

"Dear girl," Robert said. Then he pulled me into his arms. "What has happened?"

I realized then that he was the first to ask the question. Grandmother always seemed to accept Mr. Mead's iteration of events. Truth proved to be a funny thing; it could be altered and manipulated to fit a scheme. Which version would Mr. Wilkins prefer? The thought touched my conscience, and I knew the answer. He would want the whole of it. But in revealing the events in their entirety, I risked the exact fate I hoped to avoid. Mr. Mead should not have imposed himself on me. I'd escaped before he could kiss me. But if it were found out that I'd been secluded with him, he would be forced to make it right. He could abandon me to the gossips or take me as his wife. Mr. Mead had made his desires known, and in doing so, he had ensured my compliance. Either way, I was bound to him. It seemed the only decision left to make was how much of a lie to tell the handsome man standing before me.

# Chapter Twenty-Three

MR. ROBERT WILKINS

How Abigail had come to be running through the meadow in the middle of a deluge she would not say. Neither could I coax the truth from her. She held to the tale that she'd been walking and was caught in the storm. But if that were true, why would she not return to Fern Cottage? Cattersley was a much greater distance. Beyond that, the look on her face when I'd intercepted her was not worry over having to re-pin her wet hair. It was pure, undiluted fear. I'd seen that look in the eyes of too many soldiers on their first day of battle. From what battle had Abigail fled?

I considered that perhaps her grandmother had upset her, or maybe something in the forest had frightened her. While I would continue to wonder at the cause of her flight, I found great relief in knowing her path had intersected with mine. She shivered from cold and fright, and I could not help but pull her into my arms.

Upon our return to Cattersley, Mrs. Sommers had ordered the fire in the west library to be stoked before she called for Hazel, Mother, and a fresh pot of tea, as well as blankets and dry clothing for Abigail, whom I left to the care of my mother and Hazel. I returned to my chamber, where Graham assisted in pulling off my wet boots. I quickly changed into dry clothing before returning to the library.

Abigail now sat near the fire, swaddled in blankets. With her cup in hand, she tried to affect a convincing smile. "See? All is well. I was simply chilled and not in my right mind." She took another sip of her tea.

I was not convinced.

"Shall I get you another blanket?" Hazel asked.

Abigail forced a laugh. "You have proven more than hospitable." Her eyes flashed to mine. "All of you." She inhaled and turned toward the fire. "It is far better than I deserve."

"Nonsense," Hazel said and moved to sit beside her. "You are a dear friend. I am grateful Robert found you and brought you here."

Abigail set her teacup aside. "Yes. Thank you, Mr. Wilkins." I raised my eyebrows, and she gave a small smile. "Robert," she said before ducking her head.

"Tell me again how you came to be in the meadow," Hazel said as she pulled Abigail's hand into her own. I once again envied my sister.

Abigail pressed her eyes closed. It was only a moment before she opened them again, but when she answered, her words did not contain her usual contentment. "I have not been able to call on Mr. Tucker for quite some time and hoped to do so. I did not realize the clouds threatened such a lashing, or I would never have ventured out."

Her account did not explain her tears. And I could not dismiss them.

"Why not return to Fern Cottage?" Mother let the question dangle.

"I thought I could outrun the storm." Abigail pushed a wet piece of hair behind her ear. "I suppose I am foolish for thinking so."

Manning stepped into the room. "There's a young man here asking after Miss Rutherford."

I looked at Abigail. She pulled her hand from Hazel's and pressed her fists into her lap.

"His name is Craven, sir," Manning said. "He's been sent from Fern Cottage to inquire after her."

Abigail's eyes lit with recognition at the mention of the young man's name.

"Please have him join us," I said. "Thank you, Manning."

Abigail pulled the quilt from her lap. "Grandmother must be furious," she said softly and moved to stand.

"Please sit down, Miss Rutherford." My stern words halted her movement. "You must remain here until the storm has passed. Craven may tell Mrs. Baker you are well, or he may remain with you and I shall send one of the stable hands to inform your grandmother of your whereabouts."

"I can't—"

"Nonsense." Hazel placed her hand again over Abigail's. "Robert is right. The storm has gotten worse. You cannot travel even so short a distance, until the skies have cleared."

Manning cleared his throat, and I turned to see a healthy lad standing in the doorway. He clutched his hat in his hands. "Hello, sir." He bobbed his head several times. "I'm James Craven."

"Hello, Craven. Mrs. Baker sent you?" He nodded at my question. "Please come warm yourself by the fire." I motioned to a place next to the hearth.

The boy glanced around the room, but he made no attempt to move until Abigail addressed him. "You are soaking, Craven. I'm sorry to make you come out in the storm." This time Hazel did not stop Abigail when she stood and coaxed the young man to the fire. "Let me take your jacket." She pulled it from his shoulders.

"'Tis only a little water, miss." Craven let her remove his coat, and Abigail arranged it near the crackling flame to dry.

"Is Grandmother very upset?" she asked quietly.

Craven shrugged. "She returned home just as the storm hit. Mrs. Bearsly assured her you would return soon, and she seemed appeased until Mr. Mead came—"

"Oh yes. His daily call." Abigail waved a dismissive hand and tried to appear unaffected, but her lips pinched in a forced smile.

Craven's eyes narrowed. "But he'd come by earlier, miss. Mrs. Bearsly sent him away, so she was rather surprised when he returned. He insisted upon seeing Mrs. Baker and was ranting something about you—"

"That's quite enough," Abigail snapped. She bent low and rearranged the sleeves on Craven's coat.

Craven tucked his head low and stepped back against the wall without uttering another peep. Hazel, Mother, and I subtly exchanged questioning glances.

Abigail stood from her task. "Naturally, I came to Cattersley and have been welcomed warmly. Grandmother should not make such a fuss." She inhaled a heavy breath. When her shoulders fell and she turned around, she produced an almost believable smile. Her eyes betrayed her, for they were still lined in red from the tears she'd shed. I determined I would figure out the remainder of the tale.

I'd observed her far too often not to notice something was amiss. Through her difficulties, Abigail had shone with determination. She knew her mind. She possessed a sharp intellect. She was beautiful, and nothing could compromise that. Yet it could not be denied that something, or someone, had stolen her brightness, and I had every intention to discover the root of her gloomy spirits.

Craven and Abigail returned to Fern Cottage once the rain lightened. They refused my offer to escort them; however, they did agree to take my carriage. After their departure, Mother and Hazel spoke of Abigail's odd behavior and the curious circumstances surrounding her appearance in the meadow. I listened mostly in silence, only speaking to confirm my part in her rescue.

The next morning I asked Hazel to pay call with me to Fern Cottage. She was happy to do so, and we arrived to find Abigail recovered from the previous day's events, though the heaviness shrouding her light still hung aloft. Mrs. Baker thanked me for my attentions and scolded Abigail for her recklessness.

"The poor vicar was beside himself when he could not discover you in the woods." Mrs. Baker shook a finger at Abigail. "He searched for nearly an hour and was soaked through." The older woman tsked. "Running to Cattersley rather than returning home. It is no wonder he could not discover you."

"Please, Grandmother. Everything turned out. Let's discuss it no further," Abigail said.

"I suppose you are correct." Mrs. Baker rang a bell and asked Mrs. Bearsly to bring some refreshment.

"Is Craven present?" I asked. "I'd like to thank him again for escorting Miss Rutherford home.

Mrs. Baker smiled at the mention of the man's name. "Young Craven is a fine lad indeed. Always reliable, that one is, and quick to do as he's told. Thorough too. He comes to Fern Cottage twice a week. Works for Mr. Hart the remaining days. He'll return tomorrow. I'd be pleased to pass on your gratitude."

"Thank you," I said. I was disappointed I could not speak with Craven immediately but grateful I knew where to find him. I did want to thank him, but I also hoped to unveil a bit more of the circumstances of the day prior.

We discussed everything mundane until Hazel and I took our leave. I returned my sister to Cattersley and rode to Mr. Hart's home, hoping to speak to Craven. Unfortunately, Craven had left on an errand for the man. Hart and I visited briefly, and I returned home discouraged.

Estate business did not allow me to return to Fern Cottage to question Craven, thus it wasn't until church the following Sunday that I learned more of the situation. Hazel remained home with a headache. Mother and I claimed our regular pew and listened to Mr. Mead's lecture on honesty.

The vicar's impassioned sermon elicited head nods of agreement throughout the congregation. Mr. Mead spoke well on the subject, and I agreed with his admonition as he began with the commandment listed in Exodus and quoted numerous other scriptures on the subject.

After the benediction Mother visited with Mr. Poppy and Mrs. Christiansen. As I waited for my mother, I saw Abigail. She sat in her pew, her posture and pallor resembling a statue. Her eyes focused forward, and her knuckles, clasped in her lap, were as white as the near-translucent skipping stones I had collected as a lad.

I leaned close to Mother. "I shall meet you outside." She looked at me for a moment, then gave a small nod before continuing in conversation with her friends.

"Miss Rutherford." I maneuvered over to her bench. "I hope the remainder of your week has been pleasant."

She turned cautious eyes to me. "Mr. Wilkins," she said simply.

"May I?" I indicated the empty space on the bench next to her. She glanced around the parish. Mrs. Baker stood near the door visiting with Mr. and Mrs. Lane. "Do you need to join your grandmother?" I asked.

She shook her head and blinked her eyes clear. "Is Miss Wilkins unwell?"

"Not to worry. Hazel only suffers from a headache. I anticipate a day of rest will cure her ailment." Although I hadn't received permission, I sat on the bench.

"I am glad to hear it. Will you pass along my sympathies?" Abigail's eyes met my own for a moment.

"Of course." Surrounding conversation blended with the air wafting through the open door. Abigail's breathing evened, and her shoulders relaxed, if only slightly. "Might you tell me more about your siblings?" I asked. I wished to prolong our time together, and this seemed a safe topic.

"Louisa is happy in her employment. I do long to see her, but I am grateful Mother found her a respectable position." Abigail smoothed her hands over her skirts.

"And your brother?" I asked.

"Benjamin?" The simple mention of his name brought a smile to her lips.

"You miss him."

"Very much. I know there are many opportunities for him in America. He's a hard worker, and I've no doubt he will find success. I only wish I could know of his adventures. Perhaps even join him."

Her words crashed into me like an anchor. She wanted to go to America? I tried to mask my disappointment. "You still have no word from him?"

Abigail nodded. "I only know that he sailed on a ship named *Guinevere's Hope*, but beyond that I know not how to find him. Louisa and I write to one another. She, too, has tried to locate Benjamin, but neither of us has met with success." Abigail gave me a sad smile.

Here was something I could do. I would fight, and beg if necessary, for Abigail to remain in England, but I might at least provide a means for her to communicate with her brother. "Would you like me to make some inquiries? I have several contacts who might be able to locate him."

Her eyes lit, as if touched with the new rays of dawn. "Truly?"

"It would be my pleasure." I hoped I was not raising false hopes. "I will reach out to some acquaintances."

Abigail moved her hand to my arm. "Thank you, Robert."

My heart warmed at her touch and the joy now flooding her face. We both stood. "May I escort you home?" I asked.

Her excitement evaporated as easily as it had appeared. "I . . . I thank you, but no." She glanced again around the room. "Mr. Mead will be seeing Grandmother and me home today."

"Mead?" I asked.

She dipped her head. "Please excuse me, Mr. Wilkins." I missed her calling me Robert, but I stepped aside. "And do give Hazel my love," Abigail said as she moved past me.

I stood in a haze as she hurried to where her grandmother stood. Mead joined them shortly thereafter. The trio exited the building, and understanding nagged at my gut. The vicar was a pivotal piece of the puzzle I hoped to solve, for every time a concern arose, his name was involved.

# Chapter Twenty-Four

### MISS ABIGAIL RUTHERFORD

I LISTENED HALFHEARTEDLY TO MR. Mead's ceaseless blather. Robert had promised to try to locate Benjamin. The hope his promise gave me took root, and my thoughts swirled around possibilities. Life in Henwick had been decent. Until recently. Grandmother had allowed me to wander through the country. I'd found a true friend in Miss Wilkins, and Grandmother's belittling had merely mirrored Mother's. I had become accustomed to the corrections and scolding, but if I could locate Benjamin, perhaps I could join him in his new life and escape a future with Mr. Mead.

Grandmother persisted in pushing the vicar and me together. Mr. Mead continued to call every day. He mentioned nothing of what had happened in the woods, but he did not need to. He meant to claim me as his. I waited in petrified fear, not knowing how to extricate myself from his schemes. Grandmother remained oblivious to it all. Mr. Mead easily fooled her with his false flattery, his pretended concern for my wellbeing, and his patronizing looks of sympathy shared with Grandmother every time my tongue tangled.

Grandmother believed he would fix me. If the vicar could accept me as a wife, then Society would accept Mrs. Josephine Baker despite her dumb granddaughter. I had wanted to speak to Grandmother the day I'd been caught in the storm. Instead she'd scolded me upon my return home, and I had not gathered the courage to broach the subject. Yet I knew it must be done, for it was the only way to convince her of Mr. Mead's true nature. Watching her rapture with the man as he prattled on about the blessings of paying a plentiful tithe, I doubted I could break the spell Mr. Mead had cast. He never misbehaved in Grandmother's presence. Her near-constant company was my saving grace.

We neared Fern Cottage, and the topic turned to the upcoming ball at Cattersley. "I received my invitation yesterday," Mr. Mead said. Then he turned to me. "Might I speak with Miss Rutherford alone, Mrs. Baker?"

Grandmother beamed in excitement. "Certainly."

My stomach plunged to my toes.

"I'll be just inside." Grandmother pointed to the door. She looked back over her shoulder no fewer than three times as she made her way across the threshold.

I clasped my hands together and prayed for strength.

"Abigail," Mr. Mead began. I flinched but said nothing. Mr. Mead's usually flowing tongue paused as if he carefully considered his words. "I wish to discuss the upcoming ball with you. It would be my honor to escort you to Cattersley. Mrs. Baker has agreed, and of course, she will join us."

"Is that all, Mr. Mead?" I longed to join Grandmother inside.

"On the contrary. I wish you to know so you might be prepared to dance the first set with me."

I had no desire to be near Mr. Mead. I looked him directly in the eye and spoke with perfect conciseness. "Are you asking me, sir, or informing me?"

His lips twisted, and he gave a mirthless chuckle. "You are a willful little minx." He reached forward, but I stepped back. His expression soured, and his hand fell to his side. "Your grandmother has given her permission, Abigail. There is no use fighting our union. I shall expect your hand in the first dance, and I shall expect your acceptance of my offer at the ball as well."

He leaned near. "Do not think I've forgotten your antics from the other day. Running away to Cattersley. You cannot trust the Wilkinses. Why, Wilkins himself has designs on you, but he will not give you marriage. Not as I am offering you, Abigail. Wilkins would never desire a wife such as you. He sees your pretty face and only wishes for a night or two of pleasure. His wealth, his grand estate, are tempting. I can forgive you for your covetous nature, but make no mistake; he will ruin you." Mr. Mead grabbed my hand, and I swallowed past the lump in my throat. "Be warned, Abigail. Do not cross me again."

The warning trickled through me—a slow burn, like a creeping fog.

Mr. Mead pulled my hand to his lips. "'Til tomorrow, my dearest."

He released me, and I could not retreat to the house quickly enough.

Grandmother did not cease talking for the duration of our evening meal. How she cleared the food from her plate I had no idea. She spoke of my union with Mr. Mead as if it were already decided and would be the most glorious occasion conceivable.

The ball was only five days away. Mr. Mead had made clear his intention to continue to call every day, and I did not trust him to remain a gentleman. He meant to secure my agreement to our marriage by whatever means necessary. Even if Robert located Benjamin, there would not be adequate time to correspond and secure my brother's agreement for me to join him. The only option left was to apply to the sympathy of my grandmother.

We moved to the sitting room after supper. "You did not have Craven move the sofa this week," I said.

Grandmother smiled. "As Mr. Wilkins said, this arrangement provides optimal light."

Maybe there was hope. "Grandmother, did you love Grandfather?" I'd never met the man, and Mother had rarely spoken of her parents.

Grandmother's smile slipped. "What are you about?"

"I am only thinking on my future. I hope to marry a man who returns my regard."

She sighed and pressed her hand to her chest. "You are very fortunate to have caught the vicar's notice."

Oh dear. "But I do not care for him. And certainly not in the way I should think one would care for a spouse."

Grandmother waved away my concern. "Those books you borrow from Miss Wilkins have addled your mind."

"You did not love Grandfather, then?" I hung my head.

"On the contrary; he was rather charming." I looked up to see Grand-mother smiling. "He was handsome, to be sure, and flirted with me often. He quite won my heart." Grandmother stared at nothing in particular. "But things change." She looked at me. "Love is a fickle thing, existing where it ought not to exist and disappearing in a fleeting manner."

"I do not love Mr. Mead," I said.

Grandmother scoffed. "Really, Abigail. Is that what concerns you?"

"Should it not?"

"The vicar is a fine man. His living will provide well enough for the both of you." Grandmother picked up her needlework.

I spoke concisely. "I do not trust him." Every word formed correctly.

My pronouncement did not produce the response I'd hoped for. Grandmother chuckled. "You don't trust the vicar?"

My opportunity to sway her sat before me. "He's tried things. When we are alone."

Grandmother pulled her thread through the fabric, then set it in her lap. "He's anxious to be wed is all. It's not uncommon for one's intended to sneak a kiss or two. Your naivety is truly amusing." She began her work again.

I ducked my head. "He makes me extwemely uncomfortable."

"Ha." Grandmother shook her head and again set her embroidery aside. She reached forward and rested her hand over mine. "The vicar is a wonderful man, and you are very lucky to have gained his notice." She gave me a stern look. "I realize you are not used to having the attention of a respectable man. Thankfully, Mr. Mead acknowledges your beauty and is willing to overlook your frailties. This may be your only opportunity. Do not mess it up." Grandmother pulled her hand away and retook her embroidery once again.

"What of Hazel's invitation to join her in London?" I asked.

"I've considered this quandary, and I believe Mr. Mead will support the idea. The banns need to be read and preparations made. You could be wed upon your return in the spring." Grandmother smiled and then turned to her task.

I retired to my room with a leaden heart. Grandmother's sympathies lay with my stuttering tongue, and I would not be able to convince her of Mr. Mead's nefarious advances. But what option did I have? Confiding in Hazel or Louisa would not alter the situation. Perhaps time in London would provide a solution. As with so many aspects of my life, it seemed the choice of my husband, too, was out of my control.

# Chapter Twenty-Five

## MR. ROBERT WILKINS

PREPARING FOR A BALL TOO closely resembled preparing for battle. Energy pulsed through Cattersley, both excitement and anxiety. Servants flurried about like foot soldiers, carrying out orders. Monsieur Gastineau directed the kitchen staff as succinctly as any officer in the field would command his troops. Despite the enormity of Cattersley, I could not escape the chaos.

Thankfully, Mother had tasked me with an errand in Henwick. While I'd wanted to bring Barkley, Mother had insisted I personally retrieve Abigail's and Hazel's gowns, and I would need an equipage to transport the parcels. I had yet to drive the gig and asked Pratt to harness the black stallion Mr. Kane had previously specified was stabled for that precise purpose.

The light carriage was well sprung, and for once I felt the part of a gentleman as I drove through Henwick. First, I stopped at the inn to post three letters I'd written—one to my former commander, another to a friend from university who worked at the foreign office, and a third to John's brother-in-law, who worked as a barrister—all in the hopes of locating Benjamin Rutherford. Then I visited the modiste's shop. The dresses were ready as promised, and I was anxious to deliver Abigail's so that I might see her face light up.

I lifted the packages into the gig and prepared to climb in.

"Excuse me, sir." A masculine voice halted my movement. I held the reins and acknowledged the older man before me. He turned the brim of his hat in his hands. "Are you Captain Wilkins, nephew to the late Lady Marion Brown?" he asked.

I eyed the man. His coat was worn but clean. "It's Mr. Wilkins now. May I be of assistance?"

"Well, I'll be . . ." The man smiled and rubbed a hand over his face. "I see the resemblance. You've Lady Marion's eyes. Nothing got past her."

"And how were you acquainted with my aunt?" I asked.

The man grinned again. "Served at Cattersley for thirty-eight years."

"What did you say your name was?" I retied the stallion.

He gave a small bow. "Name's Jacob Mathison. Me son served under your command. Kilroy Mathison."

I remembered the lad. He had fought hard and sustained severe injuries. In the end, his leg had had to be amputated. "Your son was a brave soldier. It was an honor to serve beside him."

"He says the same about you. His mother and I was devastated to learn about his leg, but he would have lost his life if you hadn't risked yer own to save him."

Flashes of gunfire and smoke shook my memory. My commander had relayed our orders. We were to attack the enemy's western flank as they marched toward the crossroads at Quatre Bras, but due to faulty intelligence, we were unaware of the cannons awaiting us. The fog had been heavy that morning. We had charged directly into their path. When the cannons began to fire, my troops had been mowed down. I'd ordered a retreat, and men had scattered every direction. Kilroy had stopped to aid an injured comrade. He'd hefted his friend over his shoulder and staggered back toward our line. Then another cannon blast had sounded, and the round shot had struck Kilroy and his companion down. I'd seen Kilroy's face as he was hit. I could not leave him on the battlefield.

"Lady Marion asked about him every Monday afternoon. She was a creature of habit, and that was her library day. I'd carry the firewood into her library and fill the woodbox. She wouldn't say a word as I carried in the first two loads, but after the third I'd stand up to leave, and she'd say, 'Mr. Mathison, how does young Kilroy fare?'" Mr. Mathison chuckled at the memory. "She asked me every week from the time he was four years old—that's when I came to work at Cattersley." He shifted his feet. "Always wanted me to tell her a story about Kilroy's adventures. Nothing changed when he was drafted into His Majesty's army.

"After he was assigned to yer unit, she nearly beamed. 'That young lieutenant is my nephew,' she told me. And she reminded me every week after that."

"And then the battle of Quatre Bras," I said. Dragging Kilroy and our comrade Heath away from the enemy line had been the only success I could claim that day. Many men had lost their lives.

"Yes, sir." Mr. Mathison reached forward and rubbed a hand over the stallion's face. "When she heard what you'd done for Kilroy, she asked me if you'd received commendation. O' course, I didn't know. And Kilroy had been sent to the Royal Hospital in Chelsea to recover. And then his mother and I left to look after him. About a year later yer aunt saw me here in Henwick." He looked across the square and pointed to the apothecary shop. "Right over there. I'd come home for me mum's funeral. Lady Marion asked after Kilroy. By that time he was engaged to be married." Mr. Mathison smiled. "I told her again how grateful we was to you, Captain Wilkins. I asked her if you ever got yer commendation, and she said not to worry. You'd been promoted to captain for yer actions that day, and she'd found a way to reward you herself." He chuckled and motioned to my person. "Now here you are—master of Cattersley. Don't surprise me one bit."

Unlike Mr. Mathison, I was surprised. Utterly dumbfounded. Had Lady Marion named me heir because of my service to the crown? Because I'd saved the life of a comrade in battle?

I gripped Mr. Mathison's arm in a firm hold. "Thank you, Mr. Mathison. I am pleased to know Kilroy is well settled. Please give him my regards." We bade each other farewell.

I climbed into the gig in a daze. I hadn't given a second thought to jumping into the line to save Kilroy and Heath. We'd been among the lucky ones that day. The Battle of Waterloo followed only two days after the events at Quatre Bras. Some horrors could not entirely be erased from memory.

Despite my desire to see Abigail, I did not deliver her dress that afternoon. I returned home, making every effort to push aside the sound of cannon fire and the metallic smell of blood. I asked for my dinner to be brought to my chamber.

War always left scars. Horrible, deep scars. I'd heard men talk of recurring nightmares and fits of panic. I was fortunate in my circumstances and found that when I kept busy, the memories remained at bay. I was pleased to know Kilroy had found happiness. So many others had not.

Loss was always the hardest part of being a commander. Leading a charge with a brave face despite the fear that had clawed at my chest had been difficult, to say the least. I'd suffered cold and hunger and witnessed death. And it seemed Lady Marion had felt that had qualified me to be named as her heir.

Hazel rode with me to deliver the dress the following day. Mrs. Baker greeted us and led us to the parlor, where she sat on the sofa. I set the dress box on the table by the stairs.

"For you, Miss Rutherford," I said and stepped back.

Hazel clapped her hands together and held them to her chin while Abigail slowly lifted the lid. A small gasp of elation fell from Abigail's lips, and she pulled the dress from the box as if it were a delicate butterfly.

Abigail's gaze remained fixed on the garment. She held it aloft, and her smile did not disappoint. "It is exquisite!"

In that moment I silently praised my dear aunt. Her gift to me had allowed me to shower Abigail with a small fraction of the happiness she deserved. I knew pure joy because Abigail was happy.

"Well, turn around and let me see it," Mrs. Baker said. Abigail turned with the dress held to her shoulders.

"Oh, Abigail," Hazel said. "You shall outshine us all." Hazel's eyes flicked to mine, and a mischievous smile tugged at her lips. "What say you, Robert? Won't Abigail be the belle of the ball?"

"There's no doubt," I said. Abigail's cheeks colored to match the fabric of the dress.

"Abigail," Mrs. Baker said. "Tell Mr. Wilkins how grateful you are." Mrs. Baker fluttered her hand in my direction.

Abigail laid the dress back in the box and ran her hand over the silky fabric. "It is the finest gift I have ever received. Thank you, Mr. Wilkins." Her eyes met mine, and although she did not call me by my Christian name, my heart swelled that I could be the one to give her something worthy of . . . her.

As we rode away, Hazel grinned at me. "Abigail's fond of you."

"What has made you so certain?" I asked.

"The blush that stains her cheeks every time you are present."

Hazel spoke true. I found Abigail's blush delightful. Her blush, her bashful smile, even the way her tongue tangled on letters when she spoke excitedly about something. They were all parts of the unique and fascinating woman who had stolen my heart. Perhaps if she felt the same tendresse toward me, she might remain in England rather than join her brother in America. If I could convince her of my regard, would it be enough?

Hazel's mischievous look returned. "And I daresay you are fond of her too," she said. My sister had hit the mark directly. I *was* fond of Abigail. Very much so, and I wanted to grant her the opportunity to smile every day.

I considered that perhaps this was the purpose of my great-aunt bequeathing her inheritance to me—I could bring joy to others. Through the means Cattersley provided, I could spread smiles and comfort, and I considered the immense blessing of such an opportunity, for helping others also benefited me. I cared little for the money spent on Abigail's dress, but the gratitude in her smile would warm my soul for a very long time.

# *Chapter Twenty-Six*

### MISS ABIGAIL RUTHERFORD

WHILE GRANDMOTHER ADMONISHED ME NOT to wear the gown until the ball arrived, it could not be helped. The morning after Robert delivered the dress, I woke and slipped it on. The smooth fabric draped over my skin like the caress of a warm bath. The rich jeweled shade of maroon pronounced the rosiness in my cheeks and lips. I turned in front of the mirror and could find no flaw in the dress, no place where it hung awkwardly. It was divine.

I configured my hair in a variety of styles and determined a braided twist would suit me best. All that was left was for the ball to arrive. After changing into my pale-lavender gown, I grabbed my straw hat with the matching lavender adornments and received Grandmother's permission to walk to Cattersley to visit Mrs. Wilkins and offer my express gratitude for her gift. Grandmother made me promise I would return prior to Mr. Mead's daily call. I had not walked since the incident with Mr. Mead in the rainstorm, but this morning when I'd heard Craven chopping wood behind the cottage, I'd determined to request his escort to the meadow on Cattersley land. Hopefully, Mr. Mead would not trespass there and I could enjoy a walk without fear of him appearing.

Craven was agreeable to the idea, and if he found my request curious, he did not say so. We chatted easily about his family and the duties that were expected of him from Mr. Hart. Grandmother had pointed the Hart family out at church one Sunday, but I had no further knowledge of them. Craven talked about how kind Mrs. Hart was to him and how their fourteen-year-old daughter, Jane, made the best apple pie. His eyes lit as he told me about the girl and listed her numerous redeeming attributes. It seemed he was quite smitten with young Jane Hart.

We had walked halfway across the meadow when Craven came to an abrupt halt. "Forgive me, Miss Rutherford. I've been blabbering and kept you from your errand."

"Not at all." I smiled. "The walk has been refreshing, and I thank you for your company. You'd better return to Fern Cottage before Grandmother takes issue with your absence."

Craven gave a hasty goodbye, then sprinted back toward home. I continued to Cattersley and meant to say only a quick hello to Mr. Tucker before seeking out Mrs. Wilkins, but relieving Mr. Tucker's worry over my extended absence took longer than I had planned.

"I wanted to show you the new blooms on Irene's bush, but there are only a few left," Mr. Tucker said.

"I am sorry to have missed it. Grandmother has required my pwesence at home, and I have been unable to get away." My letters slipped a bit, but I did not mind so much in Tucker's company. He always treated me as his equal. I fingered the fuzzy leaf of the plant Mr. Tucker pruned.

He finished his task and tucked his shears into his pocket. "Come. Let me show you what remains."

I followed him to the roses, and he knelt by the pot he had so lovingly nurtured. Two beautiful peach-colored flowers with pink-tipped petals opened wide, and one small bud stood like a lone kiss on the bush. "Mrs. Tucker would be very pleased," I said.

Without a word Mr. Tucker pulled his shears from his pocket, clipped one of the roses, and held it out to me.

"There are so few left; you should keep it," I said, refusing to take the flower from him.

Mr. Tucker lifted my hand from my side and pressed the rose into my palm. "Irene would say such beauty needs to be shared. She would want you to have it." I accepted the gift and lifted the flower to my nose.

"It is perfect. Thank you," I said.

Mr. Tucker's cheeks reddened, and he shrugged. "More will bloom next year." His gaze suddenly darted to something behind me, and he ducked his head. "Hello, Mr. Wilkins."

Excitement jolted through me, and I turned around. "Good day, Mr. Wilkins." I curtsied. Mr. Wilkins's eyebrows rose, and he shook his head with a playful frown. I laughed. "Very well. Good day, Robert." I had been practicing how to say his name, in particular, and I annunciated perfectly. Mr. Tucker smiled beside me.

"And to you, Miss Rutherford. I am glad to find you here."

"Oh?"

"Would you care to walk with me?" Robert asked.

I looked to Mr. Tucker, who nodded and shooed me away. "Go on."

"I've a perfect place for this." Robert stepped forward and took the rose from my fingers. With his free hand he slowly . . . gently . . . pushed aside the brim of my hat, brushed aside the wisp of hair near my ear, and tucked the stem of the rose into the braid on the right side of my head. He stood so very near. I watched the rise and fall of his chest. His fingers lingered in my hair, and I felt as if I stood in a shower of sunshine.

Movement caught my eye, and I looked away from Robert to see Mr. Tucker disappearing into the gardens. My gaze darted back to the man before me. I tipped my chin upward to meet his eyes, and his hand fell away.

A soft smile touched his lips. "You are very lovely, Miss Rutherford."

I stopped breathing then, for I wanted only to feel the emotion of his words, the warmth of his touch, and the nearness of him. Absolute comfort was a rarity for me. Peace and solace were descriptors meant for others; they were words in poems and literature, belonging to an imaginary place I had no right to claim.

Robert lifted my hand to his lips. I had not worn gloves, and he pressed his lips to my skin for several serene heartbeats. Without releasing his grasp, he guided my arm to rest on his. He pulled me close and began to walk. Only then did I begin to breathe again.

"I've come to thank your mother for the beautiful gift," I said.

"Then I shall take you to her." Robert led me toward the house.

In a matter of minutes Robert had me laughing at the expense of his poor valet. It seemed that while Graham was in the process of ironing his master's pantaloons, Mrs. Sommers had called him away for a quick errand. When the valet returned, he realized he'd left the iron sitting atop Robert's clothing. The iron had burned directly through the seat of the pantaloons. Mr. Manning had been so irate he'd insisted Robert discipline the young valet. Thus, Robert had decreed that Graham would be required to wear the damaged garment for a period of four hours.

"He turned as red as a turnip at my chosen punishment," Robert said. "But once Manning departed, I suggested Graham fulfill his required penance while he slept. The relief on his face was palpable."

Robert guided me through the garden paths with ease. My heart sighed in contentment. Conversation came easily. I felt no need to tether my words. Not all of my letters formed to perfection, but I wanted to speak, to share my thoughts with Robert, and I knew he would not condemn me should I falter. It felt important that he understand my view of the situation. "Well done, Robert. Graham made a mistake, and Mr. Manning wanted to teach a lesson. You pacified both parties with your solution. I imagine you utilized similar reasoning while commanding your regiment."

"Discipline was a difficult but necessary part of my responsibilities. I tried to be fair," Robert said. We reached the house, and he led me inside.

"A soldier can ask no more from his commander," I said.

Robert settled his hand over my own. "Many times I wished I had more to give."

Warmth pulsed through my fingers and into my smile. "Your courage will not be forgotten. Your men were indeed fortunate."

"La!" Hazel said as she came upon us. "I am so happy to see you, Abigail!"

Robert released my hand, and while I immediately missed the contact, I smiled at my friend. "I've come to thank your mother for the gown," I said.

"I can hardly wait to see you wear it." Hazel looped her arm through mine. "Come. Mother's in the Sky Room."

"Horton is expecting me. I shall leave you ladies to your visit," Robert said.

We began to walk away, leaving Robert standing alone in the corridor. I looked back over my shoulder to see him smiling. He raised his right hand and gave me a small salute, and I knew he had captured my heart.

# Chapter Twenty-Seven

## MR. ROBERT WILKINS

I ENJOYED DANCING AND LOOKED forward to the feast Monsieur Gastineau prepared, but tonight Mrs. Baker would either grant or deny her permission for Abigail to join us in London. If it was agreed she could come, it meant she was not sailing off to America. The anticipation of Mrs. Baker's decision consumed me. I hoped Mother's invitation for the woman to visit had provided adequate enticement.

Graham took extra care in my preparations. It was the first occasion I'd had to wear the formal black tailcoat and breeches. In truth, it was the first ball I'd attended where I would not wear my officer's uniform.

After Graham tossed aside the third cravat, I suggested he allow me to tie the neckcloth myself. "Sorry, sir." Graham handed me the pressed cloth and took a step backward. "I know it's a big night. Wanted it to be perfect, and it seems I am more nervous than you are."

I looped the neckcloth over and around itself and then adjusted the ends. I looked in the mirror to verify the knot sat squarely centered. "What have you to be nervous about?"

Graham held my superfine black jacket, and I slipped my arms into the sleeves. "I suppose whatever Mrs. Baker decides, you'll at least secure a dance or two with Miss Rutherford," he said.

I straightened my cuffs and turned to face Graham. "You're worried about my dance partners?"

"Just the one." Graham stepped behind me and brushed the shoulders of my jacket. "You'd best impress her. Avoid stepping on her toes."

"Cheeky."

Graham simply smiled.

I walked away from his ministrations and picked up my gloves. "Enjoy your evening, Graham. I expect it will be a late night."

"Enjoy your dance, sir." Graham gave a mocking bow, but I liked him too much to be angry. Instead I laughed and went in search of Mother.

I walked into her sitting room as her maid secured a jeweled necklace around her throat. It had been a gift from my father.

"Hello, Robert." She looked me over. "You cut a fine figure."

"And you look lovely, Mother." I kissed her cheek. "Shall we prepare to greet our guests?"

Hazel joined Mother and me, and with Mother standing between us, we began to welcome the first arrivals. Mr. Poppy and Mrs. Christiansen were gracious as always, and Mr. Poppy presented a new riddle to Mother before greeting me. Any time we had a lapse in the line, Mother would attempt to reason through the puzzle, asking Hazel and me to assist. "I have yet to solve one of Mr. Poppy's riddles, and I am determined to do so," she said.

Guests continued to arrive, but the one person I longed to see had yet to appear. I'd offered to send our carriage to retrieve Abigail and Mrs. Baker but was told they would be accompanied by Mr. Mead. I knew I should feel relief that someone else was aware of the occupants of Fern Cottage, but Mead's constant presence ruffled me.

I made the acquaintance of Mr. Jenkins, a prior army commander who lived on the outskirts of Henwick. I looked forward to furthering my association with the man and was commenting as much to Mother when I first noticed Abigail. My words died on my lips, for her beauty stole all thought.

The dress she wore punctuated the grace of her figure. The dark-red gown fit her to perfection, and the color dismissed all pallor from her cheeks. She wore no jewelry, and her hair was pinned up in an arrangement of knots and braids. Her look was simple. Refined. She was perfection. And I realized how desperately I wanted Mrs. Baker to allow her granddaughter to accompany Hazel to London, for then I might spend time with her. Court her. And convince her I would cherish her always.

When she stood before me and placed her hand in mine, I felt every bit of the thrill I had anticipated. I pressed a kiss to the back of her gloved hand.

"Good evening, Mr. Wilkins," she said.

I reluctantly let her fingers slip away from mine. "Please permit me to tell you how lovely you look, Miss Rutherford."

Her cheeks colored. "I have not had occasion to dress in such a fine gown." She turned to face Mother. "Thank you again, Mrs. Wilkins, for the generous gift."

"I hope we may provide many more such occasions for you to wear it," Mother said. "Has your grandmother made a decision?"

Abigail looked to where Mrs. Baker and Mead stood conversing with Hazel a few feet away. "I cannot say," she said on a whisper.

Mother laid a hand on her arm. "Not to worry. I shall speak with her."

Mead stepped forward then and offered his platitudes. Abigail curtsied again, and before she walked away, I leaned near and whispered, "May I have the honor of the first dance?"

She startled, and I stepped back to find Mead's hand upon her back. "Shall we, my dear?" he asked, motioning toward the ballroom.

Abigail's lips turned down. She stood stiffly, as if paralyzed. Gone was the happy color that had touched her cheeks moments before.

Mead faced me again, his hand not wavering from Abigail's back. "I've been looking forward to this evening for quite some time," he said. "I anticipate good things will come from this night." Mead looked at Abigail with a smile that was too broad and too cheery, given her current state of distress. It made my skin crawl. "Come, Miss Rutherford, I believe the first dance is mine." He raised a single brow, as if to dare me to contradict the claim.

I clenched my fists at my side and offered a small bow. "Until later, Miss Rutherford." She said nothing further as he led her away, and I stood feeling as if I'd been kicked off a horse.

An hour passed before Mother, Hazel, and I could relieve ourselves of our duties. Despite my desperate attempts to locate Abigail among the throng, I had not seen her again. I escorted Mother to the edge of the dancefloor and procured her a cup of punch. Mrs. Christiansen and Mr. Poppy joined us, and once they were engaged in conversation with Mother, I excused myself. I knew not what Mead's actions meant, but I would search out Abigail and use whatever means necessary to secure a dance with her.

I walked around the ballroom and discovered Abigail standing beside Mead, who spoke to Jenkins near the musicians. It was time for battle. I moved quickly and joined them.

"May I have the next dance, Miss Rutherford?" I asked so only she could hear.

She glanced at Mr. Mead.

"Are you spoken for?" Trepidation tripped through my heart.

Abigail shook her head the slightest bit, and her gaze kept darting toward the vicar. He continued conversing with Jenkins, but his eyes narrowed in warning. Mead should know he was no match for a battle-worn soldier.

I pulled Abigail's arm through mine and cleared my throat. "Miss Rutherford, Hazel asked that I find you." I turned to Mead. "I'll ensure Miss Rutherford is returned to her grandmother." Without waiting for a reply, I led the lady away.

"Thank you," Abigail said. Her chin remained high and her posture perfect, but her fingers shook where they lay on my sleeve.

I covered them with my free hand. "Shall we walk in the gardens?"

She nodded. Tucker and Felton had lit lanterns throughout the grounds. In the dwindling light the dancing flames cast a soft glow across the stones. I wanted to ask Abigail what unsettled her, but contentment that she was near my side granted me patience.

I led her on the familiar paths, staying within view of the general crush. We walked in silence until Abigail swept a tear from her cheek. I had not realized she was crying. A squat oak tree, with its leaves turning the first stages of orange, provided a bit of privacy.

"There, now." I handed her my handkerchief. "What has upset you?"

She shook her head as she took the linen and dabbed her eyes. "I am in a beautiful dress, at a beautiful estate, prepared to dance the night away. What right do I have to be sad on such a special occasion?"

"My brave girl." I touched a finger to her chin and drew her eyes to mine. "Allow me to help. Tell me how to bring a smile to your lips."

She looked toward the Cattersley ballroom. "You did mention a dance."

"Indeed I did." I bent over in an exaggerated bow. "Miss Rutherford, would you do me the honor of dancing with me?" I extended my hand.

She blinked her tears away and laughed lightly, placing her fingers in mine. "It would be my pleasure."

Abigail returned my handkerchief, and we walked back to the edge of the dancefloor, waiting for only a moment until the next set was called. Hazel stood up with Mr. Edwards a few formations away. The quadrille began, and Abigail seemed hesitant in her steps. When we partnered for a combination, I took extra care to guide her movements with gentle pressure on her fingers, a hand on her elbow, or a light touch on her back. With every contact my heart sped more.

We danced through the forms and met for a series of joined steps. I placed a firm hand on her back and narrowed the gap between us. Abigail gasped, and I followed her gaze to where Mead stood watching us. His face was a mask of indifference, but his eyes betrayed his duplicity.

"What does he want?" I whispered low.

"My freedom." Abigail said nothing more. She didn't need to. I scooped her hand in mine and wove through the crowd to pull her quickly from the room. I led her directly to the west library.

Her breaths came quickly, as did mine. I left the door ajar, but only slightly so. Candlelight frolicked on the spines of the books, but I could not take my eyes off the lady before me.

"Do you have an understanding with the vicar?" I asked. I awaited her answer as I had awaited calls to charge. My chest tightened with every second that ticked by.

"No." The simple word, spoken so softly, drew a smile from my soul. Hope pressed around my heart.

I stepped near, closing the distance between us. "I am extremely fond of you, Miss Rutherford."

"Abigail," she said.

I cupped her cheek in my hand. "Abigail."

She shuddered, and I pulled her into my arms. Her form fit so perfectly with mine. I inhaled the warmth of her hair, felt her body near, and closed my eyes in contentment.

Her hands lay flat against my chest, and with the smallest bit of pressure, she pushed away. "There is something you need to know."

I opened my eyes and reluctantly pulled back. Abigail swallowed, and tears once again sprang to her eyes. "The fire at the picnic—"

I ran my hands down her arms. "Is forgotten."

She blinked quickly and shook her head. "Mr. Wilkins—"

"Robert." I smiled and began to play with a strand of her hair near her left ear. She blushed and turned her face away.

"Please let me finish."

Guilt threaded through me for pushing her so. My arms fell to my side, and I leaned away, for if I did not put some distance between us, I would scoop her into my arms again. I nodded for her to continue.

"I was not alone when the fire erupted," she said, and for a delayed moment her words did not register. "Mr. Mead discovered me, but he did not call out."

Dread, like the pounding pulse of a battle drum, knotted in my stomach.

"He—" Abigail shuddered again and looked at her feet.

"What did he do?" I fought to keep my voice steady. "Abigail." I reached forward and tilted her face up to meet mine. "I need to know what happened." Perhaps it was the part of me that demanded justice, the soldier who hoped for a better world and was willing to fight to achieve it. Drawing breath became difficult.

"And when you found me in the rainstorm . . ." Abigail covered her lips with her fingers.

Footsteps sounded from the corridor, followed by Mrs. Baker's voice. "Did she claim to be ill?"

Urgency gripped me. "Did he harm you?" I asked.

Tears crested in Abigail's brown eyes. "No," she said on a breath. "Both times, I found you."

"Her behavior is most unbecoming. Let us search the library." I recognized Mead's voice.

"Abigail," I whispered. "Do you care for him?"

"Not in the least." Her eyes whispered a disquieted prayer, a plea for help.

I wrapped my right arm around her waist, and my left hand cupped her cheek. I pulled her body flush with mine and pressed my lips to her mouth in the same moment the door swung open. Delicious fireworks erupted between us as chaos ensued.

# Chapter Twenty-Eight

## MISS ABIGAIL RUTHERFORD

ROBERT. KISSED. ME!

No matter that Grandmother had melted into a puddle of hysteria or that Mr. Mead had condemned me to hell. I had been properly kissed by a proper gentleman. And what's more, his name was Robert Wilkins.

It did not matter that he owned the grandest estate in Herefordshire. Nor did it matter that I, in no way, deserved his notice. When his lips touched mine, all rational thought fled. Concerns over Mr. Mead's intentions, his threats upon our arrival to the ball, and what my future held vanished. Every particle of reason was replaced with the sensation of Robert's arms wrapped around me and the warmth of his mouth moving against my own. I was wholly consumed. And so, while Grandmother ranted about my stupidity, I savored the tingling sensation that ricocheted from my lips to my core.

As Robert pulled away, I wondered, for only a moment, if he realized what he had done. He stood regal and undaunted as Grandmother and Mr. Mead took turns stating their blatant outrage.

Cattersley's butler appeared in the doorway. He turned only to his master, and with a booming voice he cut off Mr. Mead's diatribe. "Might I be of assistance, sir?"

A smile danced on Robert's lips, the lips that had so recently waltzed with my own. "Yes, Manning. Will you please ask Mrs. Wilkins to join us?" Robert asked.

"Of course, sir." Mr. Manning disappeared.

"I ought to call you out." Mr. Mead's reddened cheeks shook with fury.

"Please do," Mr. Wilkins said. He naturally stood taller than Mr. Mead, and with his military bearing, he loomed over the vicar. "I'd wager I am far better with a sword and a pistol. You might get in a facer or two in a bout of fisticuffs, but it would hardly be a fair fight."

To think that two men would consider dueling on my behalf! I knew whom I would choose as champion and felt only a moment's guilt at wishing to see the vicar with a bloodied nose.

"Robert?" Mrs. Wilkins entered the room, followed by Hazel. "What is going on?" Mrs. Wilkins moved to stand between Grandmother and myself. Mr. Manning resumed his post in the doorway, and Hazel stood behind her brother.

"Your son has compromised my granddaughter!" Grandmother pointed a shaky finger at where I stood near the fireplace.

Hazel crossed the room and took my hands. She searched my face. I felt only joyous bewilderment, and Hazel was obviously confused by my heated cheeks and startled eyes.

"Is this true?" Mrs. Wilkins asked, looking between Robert and myself.

"Yes. I kissed Miss Rutherford," Robert said. "It was delightful."

Hazel's eyes shot wide, and she covered her mouth with one hand to stifle a giggle.

"The late Lady Marion would be ashamed." Mr. Mead puffed out his chest like a preening fowl. "To so desecrate the hallowed walls of Cattersley—you have disgraced your aunt's good name."

Robert turned to the vicar—his back taut and shoulders tall—all handsome magnificence. "Are you telling me, Mead, that you did not set your own designs on Miss Rutherford?" Mr. Wilkins asked.

The vicar sputtered. "I've no idea what you mean. Miss Rutherford is my intended."

Hazel gasped beside me, and Mrs. Wilkins's eyes widened. Grandmother's chin notched up a bit, but Robert did not falter. He stood as a man prepared for war.

"The fire at the picnic was not Miss Rutherford's fault. You cornered her that afternoon, and she struggled to break free." Robert's eyes brightened as realization dawned. "That is why you offered to pay for the damage. To secure Miss Rutherford's silence. Do you deny it?"

Grandmother fell into a nearby chair. Mrs. Wilkins sat near her, opened her fan, and waved it near Grandmother's face.

"And again in the forest, you tried to force your suit. Your claim to her hand is based on blackmail and lies. She deserves better than the likes of you." Robert's voice never wavered, and my chest squeezed with the realization that he meant every word he spoke. He believed me without question. I hadn't even needed to say the words. Robert understood what Mr. Mead had done. And even more wonderful, he believed I was entitled to happiness.

Mr. Mead clenched his jaw, and spots of red speckled his face. "And what of your design on Miss Rutherford? You can offer no proof of your claim, yet Mrs. Baker and myself witnessed your indiscretion." His lips twisted in a sneer. "You cannot condemn me with only the word of a stupid girl."

In one swift movement Robert crossed the room, and his fist crunched against Mr. Mead's nose. "Get out of my house!" Robert roared. "And if you ever speak Miss Rutherford's name again, I will ensure they are the last words you ever utter." Robert took a breath, and when he spoke next, his voice was eerily calm. "You are no longer welcome here. Remove yourself from Mayview Cottage by week's end."

Mr. Mead shook with fury, but it was obvious to all that he was no match for Robert Wilkins. With a huff Mr. Mead turned on his heel and marched from the room.

"Ensure he is entirely removed," Robert said to his butler.

"It will be my pleasure, sir." Mr. Manning bowed, then left.

Hazel tugged on my hands, pulling my attention to her. "Is it true, Abigail? About the fire at the picnic?"

I nodded.

"And when I came upon her in the storm," Robert added.

Hazel's eyes scrunched in confusion. "Why did you not say something sooner?"

"She tried," Grandmother cried out, then patted her hand against her chest as tears sprang to her eyes. "I didn't listen." She held her hand out to me. I walked to the chair where she sat, and knelt beside her. "I am so sorry, Abigail. I forced his suit upon you. You tried to explain, and I dismissed your concerns." Tears trailed down her cheeks, and my heart opened as my grandmother grasped my hand in her own.

"He was courting you?" Hazel looked between her brother and myself.

"I never encouwaged him," I said, ignoring the fact that my letters didn't form. I cared only that my position be understood.

"Good heavens," Mrs. Wilkins said. She closed her fan and stood. "Robert, you are party in this. What have you to say?"

Robert inhaled deeply, and his shoulders relaxed. His fingers clenched, then opened as his anger visibly receded. "I stand by every word I said. I wish to court Miss Rutherford myself."

Delight pinched my cheeks. Robert stared at me, and I recalled the day we met. It was the only other time I'd seen a trace of doubt slip through his confident facade.

How could he doubt? How could he not know? He was my champion.

I slipped my hand from Grandmother's and stood. "May we finish our dance now, Mr. Wilkins?" I asked.

His smile banished any unpleasant reminder of Mr. Mead. My heart beat a steady, solid thrumming rhythm as he answered, "It would be my honor."

# Chapter Twenty-Nine

MR. ROBERT WILKINS

I CARED NOT THAT A stupid grin filled my face. Abigail's smile matched my own, and a pretty blush crept into her cheeks.

My mother laughed and shook her head. "You are setting a precedent, Robert."

I did not look away from Abigail. "Whatever do you mean?"

Mother stood. "Every event you've hosted since your arrival at Cattersley has provided enough fodder to satisfy the gossips for weeks."

Hazel giggled. "Oh, but this"—she waved her hand between Abigail and me—"is far better than a boring old fire."

I walked to where Abigail stood and gave an exaggerated bow like the one I'd offered earlier. "My dear." I extended my hand. Abigail slipped her fingers into mine, and I gave a gentle squeeze.

Mrs. Baker, Mother, and Hazel followed us back to the ballroom. Open stares and flapping tongues could not hinder the joy I felt. I proudly stood on the edge of the dancefloor, keeping hold of Abigail's arm, while we waited for the current set to finish.

"Thank you, Robert," she said. "For ridding me of Mr. Mead."

"My motives were entirely selfish." I nodded in greeting to Edwards as he walked past. "Although, had I known the truth of it . . ." My entire body tensed.

Abigail slipped her fingers down my arm toward my hand. Warmth from her touch infused peace through my soul. I realized then that I did not want her to come to London as Hazel's companion. I wanted her to join us as my wife, and I began to execute a plan to make my wish a reality.

Whether a battle was won or lost depended on many factors: the number of troops on each side, the weather, the objective, the enemy's position, and stratagem. Thankfully, time represented my only enemy. I knew I wanted to marry Abigail. And I knew I wanted it to happen as soon as possible.

The set ended, and I continued to plan. "Shall we?" I flipped my hand around to escort Abigail onto the floor.

It was to be a country dance. As we moved forward, the guests stepped aside so that I, as host, might take the lead position. I guided Abigail into place and regretfully released her hand. The music began, and we moved toward each other. Every part of me was drawn to her. Moving together, being together—it was where I longed to remain. Alas, the steps required us to part, and I stood, waiting for a chance to reach for her again. Blood pulsed through me, and every sense was alert, poised for the call to charge forward and take her hand, to touch, to connect with her in some way.

The dance was simultaneously exultant and mocking. Each contact was a high, each separation a cold abyss. The minutes ticked by. Abigail smiled. She moved with grace. Her eyes fixed on my own. And I knew I could not continue twirling in this never-ending circle of steps and curtsies and figures.

The music swelled. We stepped forward, and Abigail turned her back to nestle into the crook of my right arm. The fingers of our right hands entwined in a promenade hold while I led her through the paces. The dance required her to return to the line, but I refused to release her.

I kept her hand in mine and whispered near her ear. "Come."

Shocked cries rang from behind as we fled our position. But I'd learned from experience not to look back. I pulled Abigail out the grand doors that led to the gardens. We stood at the top of the stairway, the lighted gardens before us and the ballroom, with its tall, looming windows, at our backs.

"Abigail." Her name felt like a prayer on my lips. "I did not release you from one courtship only to bind you to another. You have become very precious to me, and I want only your happiness. Is it possible you would choose me? Can I provide that happiness for you?"

Her lips spread in a slow, seductive smile, and it took every ounce of gentlemanly bearing I could muster to refrain from pulling her into my arms. "Robert, there has only ever been you."

"Then we must find your grandmother." I again held her hand and led her back through the murmuring crowd.

"Robert." Abigail giggled beside me. "What are you about?"

"There." I pointed to Mrs. Baker, who stood talking with Hazel and my mother.

At our approach, Hazel grinned like a cat. "Pardon my interruption," I said.

"Is the set over so soon?" Mother asked.

"Something quite urgent arose." I tried to affect a serious tone, but Hazel's laugh signaled I had failed.

Mrs. Baker's eyebrows pulled together, and her face paled. "Has the vicar returned?"

"Nothing of the sort, madam." I reluctantly released my hold on Abigail and knelt before her grandmother. "It occurred to me that you were due to either grant or deny your permission for Abigail to join Hazel in London."

Mrs. Baker's hand pressed against her breast. "That is true. But with everything that has happened . . . well, it takes one time to process it all."

"Would you, then, allow me to alter my invitation?" I stood and looked at the radiant woman beside me. "I would like Abigail to accompany us to London not as Hazel's companion but as my wife."

Mrs. Baker's mouth hung open, and she remained silent for an entire minute. "Are you in earnest?"

"Absolutely. I adore your granddaughter, and I do not wish to be separated from her." I retook Abigail's hand.

Mrs. Baker sat in silence. Her hands fluttered near her neck. "Abigail," she finally said. "The choice is yours—as it should have been from the beginning."

My heart hummed happily as Abigail turned to face me. Her answer altered my life forever. "Then it is quite simple. I choose Robert."

# Chapter Thirty

## MISS ABIGAIL RUTHERFORD

In the week before the wedding, Robert personally selected the new vicar. Mr. Lansing was a recent widower looking for a change of scenery. He was also sixty-one years old. He let Mayview Cottage and settled in well. Grandmother seemed quite taken with Mr. Lansing, and I praised my fiancé for his choice of a clergyman.

Anytime Robert gazed upon me, the air between us stirred. Every moment together added to my store of happiness and hope. We planned to wed the day after he procured a special license. The prestige associated with his inheritance allowed for some acceptable favors.

Little did I know Robert's rank as a captain also granted partiality with men of high esteem and lofty connections. Two nights before the wedding, Grandmother and I were invited to dine at Cattersley with Mr. Poppy, Mrs. Christiansen, and Robert's brother, John, who had come for the ceremony.

Mr. Manning introduced us, and we entered the Sky Room to find Mr. Poppy rehearsing another of his riddles. "You hear me only when I call. You feel me only when I run. And when I am still, I am nowhere to be found."

Mrs. Wilkins's face lit. "I believe I know this one. Is it the wind?"

"Quite right, Mrs. Wilkins. Well done." Mr. Poppy bowed, and I joined the others in applauding Mrs. Wilkins's success.

I walked to Robert's side. "Where is Hazel?" I quietly asked.

"She should arrive any moment." His eyes glanced toward the door, and he gave a nod so slight that if I had not been watching, I would have missed it.

A moment later Mr. Manning stood in the threshold. He pressed up on his toes, cleared his throat, and said, "Miss Hazel Wilkins and Miss Louisa Rutherford."

Then my sister walked in, followed by a beaming Hazel. I had written to Louisa about the wedding, but her duties would not allow her to attend. Or so I'd been told. I grabbed Robert's arm. "Did you do this?"

His blue eyes danced brightly. "I wanted to surprise you."

"It is the very best of surprises." I ran to my sister and embraced her. Joy consumed me.

"I am so very happy for you, Abigail." Louisa looked radiant. She wore an umber-colored gown trimmed in yellow. "Your husband to be is—"

"Everything!" I cut her off.

"That's laying it on a bit thick, don't you think?" Mr. John Wilkins said from where he stood conversing with Mr. Poppy near the mantel. Mr. Poppy laughed.

"Hush, boys," Mrs. Wilkins chided.

"You are very fortunate, Sister." Louisa hugged me again as Robert walked near.

"I have something else for the both of you." Robert reached into his pocket and pulled out a letter and handed it to me.

Curious excitement riffled through me as I broke the seal on the letter. I unfolded the note, and my eyes skimmed to the signature at the bottom.

"You located my bwother?" I took no thought for how to sound the letters for the fierceness of my emotions. But no one commented. Not one person snickered. Instead, happy, joyful, friendly faces matched my exuberant grin.

Louisa grabbed my arm. "What does Benjamin say?"

"*My Dear Sisters*," I read aloud. "*Life in America has proven very different from my expectations. Uncle received me warmly, but circumstances did not allow me to remain with his family. I have taken a position as an apprentice at the newly formed Suffolk Bank in Boston. Upon completion of my required tenure, I have decided to accept Mr. Wilkins's offer of employment and return to England. I miss you both greatly and look forward to our future reunion. Yours, Benjamin Rutherford.*"

"Employment?" I asked Robert.

He shrugged, looking all too pleased with himself. "Horton and I have been discussing hiring additional help. He could use an assistant. Why not your brother?"

"Robert, you have outdone yourself!" Hazel clapped her hands together.

"Benjamin is coming home." Louisa grinned.

I pushed up on my toes and pressed a kiss to Robert's cheek. "I am to be married to the best of men."

John coughed loudly, but I ignored his jest and stared at the man before me. Robert was my champion.

Thankfully, other than the wedding itself, nothing gossip-worthy occurred. Mr. Lansing performed a beautiful ceremony to unite us as husband and wife. Hazel honored us with a composition she wrote for the event. And my sister stood beside my grandmother to celebrate the day. Even John behaved himself.

A week after the ceremony the guests returned home, and I walked with my new husband in our gardens. Thick clouds covered the sun, and Robert pulled me nearer to his side as a brisk wind blew.

"Come. There's something I want to share with you." Robert ducked into an alcove surrounded by a high hedge that blocked the cold air. He took my hands in his and pressed a kiss to my knuckles.

"Do you know a Mr. Mathison?" he asked.

I shook my head.

"I met him several weeks ago in the village. His son served under my command. Kilroy was his name."

*Was?* I squeezed my fingers against his, and his thumb brushed over my skin. Emotion erupted, fiery and sweet, aching and fierce. Nothing existed beyond this moment, listening to Robert, touching him, feeling his soul through his words.

"Kilroy lost his leg, and two of his comrades were among the dead." Robert spoke to me, but his words floated on the breeze. The memory whisked away, then returned in a breath.

I pressed his fingers between mine. He hurt. The memory hurt. I wanted only to comfort, to console him in some small way.

Robert looked down at our hands, then into my eyes, his own a solid shade of blue. "Kilroy's father knew my aunt."

"Lady Marion?" I asked on a whisper.

Robert nodded. "Mr. Mathison worked at Cattersley. He told me Lady Marion asked every week about Kilroy and was delighted when he was assigned to my regiment. It seems she followed my career."

The idea warmed my heart.

"I never realized," Robert said. "I did not know my aunt. But I suppose, through Mathison, she knew me." Robert's eyes grew distant. I recognized his need for a quiet moment and so stood silently. Mr. Mathison had given him a connection to his aunt. To Cattersley.

After several breaths, Robert spoke again. "I didn't think on my actions that day. I have hardly thought on them since. Pulling Kilroy and his comrade from the battle was instinct. When surrounded by such things . . . one clings to the living, to the hope that there is a reason to live, a reason to press forward, to keep fighting." Robert turned to me again. The deep, frothy blue of his eyes seemed to churn with the entirety of the sea and the sky. His hope pulsed from him as even as his heartbeat.

A solemn reverence fell over us, a shroud of understanding. "You saved him that day," I said. It wasn't a question, because I knew the answer. I lifted my fingers to his cheek, hoping to convey all that I felt.

"Kilroy survived the battle, yes." Robert turned his head and kissed my palm. Then he pulled my hand from his face and began to play with my fingers. "Mr. Mathison said he is happily married and expecting his third child."

I smiled. "Hope is a blessing. It provides strength in the darkest of times." I knew this truth as certainly as I knew I breathed.

Robert's fingers stilled. "But Lady Marion believed me to be a hero."

The brightness in his eyes began to fade. I grabbed both of his hands in mine. "And Mr. Mathison, Kilroy, his wife and children—they believe it too. Your actions gave them all a future together."

Robert shook his head. "Abigail, I am not a hero."

A warm smile spread across my face, and I returned my hand to Robert's cheek. "That you would say so is the precise reason you are." Robert covered my hand with his own. "Everything I've learned of Lady Marion is that she was not a fool. She knew of your hope. Your courage. And she chose a hero to be her heir. She chose you."

I moved my arms around his neck and stepped closer. "I chose you too." I pressed up on my toes, and his mouth met mine. Delicious warmth erupted down my spine as Robert's arms tightened around me. He held me close and deepened the kiss. His hands tangled in my hair, and he trailed kisses down my neck.

Slowly he pulled back, holding my face in his hands. "When Lady Marion named me as heir to Cattersley, she brought me here, to you. And for that I shall thank her every day."

"As shall I."

Robert dropped one arm to surround my waist. With the other hand he pulled my face toward him and met my lips again with his own. His kiss swirled delightful raptures with bold perfection. His kiss was home. And I was content to remain for a very, very long time.

# ABOUT THE AUTHOR

CHALON LINTON WAS FIRST INTRODUCED to the Regency era by a dear friend, and now she can't get enough of handsome men in tailcoats. Chalon's interest in the genre stems from a nostalgic longing for manners, wit, and true love.

Fortunately, she found her dashing gentleman, married him, and now lives happily ever after in Southern California.

You can learn more about Chalon's books at chalonlinton.com.

Twitter: @LizzyLint26

Instagram: lintonloveslife

Facebook: Author Chalon Linton